DOWN WITH LOVE

LAWS OF ATTRACTION

KATE MEADER

CHAPTER 1

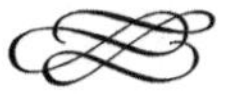

"Love, the quest; marriage, the conquest; divorce, the inquest."

— HELEN ROWLAND

Max

"Ramen. Freakin'. Noodles."

In case the word choice doesn't quite convey my point, I infuse into that statement as much disdain as possible. My brother, James, is already chortling.

"Hold on, Max. I'm gonna need the top-shelf shit for this." He flags down a server at the Gilt Bar on Kinzie, where we've been meeting every Thursday night for the last six years, snowpocalypse or heat wave.

The blond server is one I haven't seen before, and she simpers over James's coal-black hair and cool blue eyes, features we both inherited from our dad. Baby bro gets hit on constantly because he's the Grinner-in-Chief, and that smile guarantees him more action than a boy bunny rabbit in

1

a den full of girl bunny rabbits. But he doesn't follow up anymore because he's currently off the market.

I, on the other hand, also receive my fair share of female attention, and—you've guessed it—have no problem following up. I'm a more seasoned, rugged version of James (we argue about this but I'm older and a lawyer so I win). I know I'll have no problem snagging the focus of our server and yep, there it is. She blinks because I've brought out the grande gun—a bigger, brighter, better-for-its-rarity grin— and she realizes she's wasted fifteen seconds of her life on a pale imitation.

As it's my turn to pay, James orders a Glenlivet 18 Year Old, though he doesn't have a clue about scotch. I order a Laphroaig Quarter Cask because I do.

"Okay," our server says, not sounding okay at all. But I get it. I'm wearing a Ted Baker suit, and I scream wealth, confidence, and the promise of a good time. She stumbles off in a daze.

"Fucker," James mutters at me, making me laugh. "So. Noodles."

"Ramen noodles," I clarify because that's the point of the story. "Three months I've been going around in circles with these two and finally he produces the statement of property."

"Statement of property?"

"Yeah, if they can't agree on the big stuff or well, anything, we have them do an inventory of the assets in their homes. Who wants what, that kind of thing. And this asshole"—not my client, thankyouverymuch—"lists ramen noodles on the statement. And you know what else?"

James is starting to lose it, not because of the ramen noodles but because of my delivery. As a divorce attorney, I have witnessed pretty much every shitty stunt there is, so when I devote the first part of our weekly meet-up to an office story, he knows it's going to be good.

"What else?"

"Right beside it in the estimated value column, he puts nineteen cents. Nineteen fucking cents! There's only one package of ramen on the list, and one of the staff must have left it in the pantry for shits and giggles because these people are not eating instant ramen." I can't reveal their identities, but these people are two of the wealthiest philanthropists in Chicago. Two years ago, they married in a glitzy society wedding, the cost of which could have inoculated the entire West African population against yellow fever. Charity is supposed to start at home, but tell that to the asshole listing out a package of ramen noodles as an asset.

James is holding his side, practically doubled over in the booth. "How do you do it, man?"

It's not the first time he's asked, and despite the laughter, I hear it. The thread of worry that witnessing the disintegration of love has somehow changed me. It hasn't. I've always been the guy who doesn't see the glass as half-empty or half-full. Instead I ask if there's enough liquid to quench my thirst. Of the two of us, I'm the realist.

My people (as in my legal brethren, not my British-German-Swedish ancestors) have a saying: in criminal law, people are on their best behavior. In family law, they're on their worst. I've had clients who once claimed undying love spit and claw at each other across a conference room table. One guy served his wife with divorce papers while she was on her hospital deathbed with cancer. Another wanted the judge to order his wife's dog be cremated so they could split the ashes fifty-fifty. I told him His Honor was an animal lover, so he needed to figure out another way to stick it to his former lady love.

By all accounts, these were once normal, productive, *sane* citizens. To say people change when they get married is an understatement.

"Everyone deserves a fair shake," I say, my stock answer. In truth, I enjoy it. I enjoy winning, especially when it's a wife who's been screwed over by her ex. With an eighty percent female client list, my specialty is the empty-nester demographic, women who've just sent their kids to college and got divorce papers as their reward. These loyal wives changed stinky diapers, hosted sparkling dinner parties, and ran the hub's life like clockwork only to discover he had been planning his exit strategy since Kid One hit puberty.

Where the exit strategy involves a twenty-two-year-old personal trainer and an account in the Caymans.

The first thing I tell them is this is not the end, it's their new beginning, and then I get to work ensuring they receive every last penny coming their way.

The server returns with our drinks. "Let me know if I can get you boys anything else," she says, all come-hither, where "anything else" is open to interpretation.

As she walks away, my gaze tracks her because I don't want to be rude. She's made the effort so it's incumbent on me to return the favor. The servers here dress in black, and she's wearing a tight skirt that makes her ass look like a couple of cantaloupes fighting for supremacy. Nice hip swivel, good legs tapering to heels that must kill her arches while she's running around all night. I'd be happy to help put her feet up later—over my shoulders.

I'm about to tear my gaze away when she walks by the end of the cherry-wood bar, her slender frame a sliver of black contrasting against a riot of bright pink in the background. Like someone slashed a knife through an oil painting. For a moment, I'm blinded, not by the pink, though that's plenty for my eyeballs to adjust to, but by who's wearing it: a woman.

Astounding deduction, Henderson. But . . . this woman is simply stunning.

She's sitting at the bar, one leg crossed over the other, a black high heel locked on the foot rail of the barstool. Average height, I think, but that's where the average ends. Honey-gold skin gleams in the semi-dusk of the bar where the daylight can't penetrate. It's late April, baseball season has started, and Chicago is in fine fettle, along with its female denizens. Ladies are digging out their summer wardrobes and unleashing sexy arms and killer legs on a male populace that hasn't seen skin in months. The woman's dress has a flirty ruffle at the hem, and it probably falls to knee-length when she's standing, but sitting, there's a decent flash of thigh.

Indecent, really.

I'm working my way up when I hear a cough. Sighing, I return to *dickus interruptus*—my brother. "Yes?"

"Jesus, Max, get the server's number, then please grace me with your undivided attention."

As I moved on from the server within ten seconds, following up is probably a little low class. My skin prickles with awareness because I'm dying, *dying,* to turn back to the bar and the woman in pink.

"So how's Gina?" I ask instead. James falls in lust every other month but he's stuck with Gina Torres for the last three. I like her because she's one of the guys. She goes to Blackhawks games with us and knocks back beer like she doesn't have a job teaching kids in a fancy prep school in Lincoln Park. Come to think of it, this is possibly why she drinks on school nights.

Another thing I like about Gina? She's not in a hurry to tie my brother down. By now, most women would be clamoring for a spare key to the condo, a move-in date, and the dreaded "where is this going?" conversation. My brother's still only twenty-eight, two years younger than me, and I want him to enjoy the hell out of his life before he thinks about all that.

Better he not think about it at all, my divorce lawyer brain chimes in.

A dreamy smile creases James's face, which could be the scotch warming his belly but is more likely down to the mention of his girl. If I ever look like that when a woman's name enters the conversation, load up the freakin' gun.

"She's awesome." He twitches his lips and picks up the scotch. I'm about to press him on this odd little quirk when a movement at the bar draws my gaze.

A new player has entered the game, a guy in a Brooks Brothers suit now leaning in to kiss the goddess in pink. On the cheek, but still. I know it's rude—both to ignore my brother when he has mouth-twitching that needs examining and to stare at this woman—but I'm compelled to finish that inventory I started earlier. She's a Hitchcockian blonde, all Tippi Hedren cool with upswept hair and a flawless profile. Perfect slope of nose, perfect cut of cheekbone, perfect sweep of jaw. I can't see her eyes but given her coloring, they are probably blue.

I should look away because once she turns, she'll move into Casa Reality, and I prefer where she resides now: strictly in my fantasy. I don't like to muscle in on another guy's action, so it's better I don't know what I'm missing. My eyes and brain duke this out for a good three seconds.

Feeling oddly agitated and strangely competitive, I switch to the guy. I only want her profile but I sure as hell don't want him to have the rest of her. (The eyes are winning, but the id is making a late charge, apparently.) He looks like an investment banker or a Board of Trade broker or the shit-head with my perfect-in-profile woman.

Blinking away that slice of crazy, I redirect to James, who's looking at me curiously.

"That's a lot of action going on over there, Max."

I shake my head, a tad embarrassed at my runaway thoughts, which must be playing like a movie on my face. "Got hijacked for a second."

"By our server?" He looks around just as I say, "The woman in pink." I may as well own it. It's not as if anything's going to happen as she's clearly on a date.

James's eyebrows rise and something like amusement flashes over his face. "Well, well, well."

"Well, well, what?"

He waves a hand in front of my face. "She's not the droidette you're looking for."

Alert to his tone, I snap to attention. Not because he's referencing the Jedi Mind Trick, though props for changing it up there with the droidette variation, but because he's actually trying to put me off. There's only one reason he'd do that.

"You know her?"

"I do." Again, with that glint of glee. "And she's not your type."

My curiosity rears up like a punch. If it looks like her, it's my type.

"She's a friend of Gina's?"

He shrugs a negative.

"She's married?" Evidently the fact she might be on a date is no longer an obstacle.

He throws a glance over his shoulder, taking in the scene before him. Brooks Brothers is leaning close, but her body language is different to his. She's not recoiling exactly, but she's not imagining going home with him, either. She's not imagining how he would lift that skirt up past those lovely golden thighs to curl a finger in her thong. A black silky thong that would be soaked by the time I got there.

James faces me, still grinning inanely. "Nah."

"White Sox fan?"

"Not that I know of."

I'm getting irritated now. James has always known how to push my buttons with an artfulness beyond his years. When he was eight and I was ten, he mixed up the cataloging order of my Spider-Man comics. It took me two days to fix them, and he accepted his deserved ass beating with astonishing equanimity. He's also a withholder of information, which pisses off the lawyer in me to no end.

All this time, I've been making a conscious effort not to pay attention to Pink and BB, though I have to admit a certain satisfaction that James confirmed her single status. But then I make the mistake of looking and catch BB's hand on her thigh, the same thigh my hand was exploring a moment ago in my fantasy. My heart jerks and, as if to appease the *th-thunking* little bastard in my chest, she removes the offending paw and places it on the bar.

Hands where I can see them, asshole.

This would make me laugh—sometimes I crack myself up —if I wasn't still annoyed with James for being such a withholding dick.

"You know this woman how?" It emerges sharp and lawyerly.

"She's a business associate."

James works in IT at Chase in the Loop because *(a)* he's a nerd and *(b)* he's a nerd who makes a shit ton of money for knowing his way around computer servers. Or something. I know enough to set up my wireless router but it's not paying me 150K a year.

Pink doesn't look like a nerd, but Chase is a big organization so she could be doing anything. I don't care as I don't imagine we'll be discussing our days.

"And she's not my type again because?"

"You're a cynic."

Ah, she's one of those. A believer. Okay by me. As long as she understands the expectations—fun while it lasts but don't get attached—then I could be a believer, too. I hold a firm belief in my ability to fuck this woman until she's forgotten why I'm not her type.

"Cynics need blow jobs as well," I say in my most pathetic voice.

James laughs and shakes his head. There's that mouth-twitch again, and this time, I zero in like the good little lawyer I am.

"What's going on, Jim-Jam?"

He blows out a breath, then another, clearly building to some great reveal. Shit, I'm worried now. Is he sick? Is something up with Mom or Dad?

"I wasn't going to mention it, with you being such a hater and all, but you're going to find out anyway as I'll be telling the parental units tonight."

Alarm bells go off in my skull, and I already know the three little words he's going to say before they exit his mouth.

"I'm getting married."

CHAPTER 2

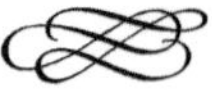

"Marriage is a fine institution, but I'm not ready for an institution."

— MAE WEST

Max

I simply stare like this could roll back the last ten seconds to a time when my brother is not about to change his life indelibly. My opinion on the state of holy matrimony is well known in our immediate circle. Sure, it works for some people. Take the parents. Jack and Susanne have been married for thirty-two years and still act like hormonal teenagers. These days, it's either announce my presence loudly every time I visit or risk walking in on Dad with his hand inside Mom's blouse. (I really should be in therapy.) Essentially, my parents are poster kids for happily-ever-after, still-doin'-it-at-sixty in the burbs.

I prefer to think we boys gave them so much damn joy they couldn't help themselves, but they married during a simpler time when people took their vows seriously. These days, no one wants to put in the effort, not when they have so many distractions and temptations. (Netflix has broken up more marriages than you'd think, friends.) Another check in my parents' favor is their long courtship of three years. Probably sex-free, too, so you know it was the real deal.

James has known Gina for three months.

Still, I'm not loving that look he's giving me, like he's checking off the *Max Henderson Reaction Playbook* in his head. Determined not to play to his assumptions, I take another tack.

"Knocked her up, then?"

"Asshole," he mutters, but he's good-natured about it because that's his way.

"Then why now? You're not even living together." Jesus, if I was to write a listicle on how to kick-start a successful marriage, that would be rule number one. Figure out how much you hate each other *before* you say "I do."

"When you know, you know," he says, all Zen master.

Each word is a stake in my heart because it's meaningless. It's like some Yogi Berra BS that sounds philosophical, but it's not.

It. Is. Not.

There's still time to figure this out. Most weddings are hijacked by the matrimonial-industrial complex and take a year to plan. A long engagement with cohabitation will give them plenty of time to sour the deal.

"Set a date yet?"

"July."

"Next year," I say. Hopefully.

"No, this one." He does the mouth-twitch again, which I'm starting to hate. Busy cycling through all this information in my head, I try to piece it together. Three months of dating, three months to the wedding, no fetus a-growin'...

I cannot in all good faith dissuade my brother from marrying Gina. I have no jurisdictional standing here. His life is not my life, and while I would give anything to have him reconsider this rash decision, I'm not going to turn on him now.

One last hope is all I have. "July," I muse with a nonchalance I'm mighty proud of, considering the way my heart is taking a crap in my chest. "So, city hall."

If you're going to marry someone you barely know, then do it on the cheap. When it all goes south later, this minimization of the big day will be one less thing to impede the dissolution process. In my experience helping clients sever their matrimonial ties, I'm always surprised at how often the wedding day gets mentioned. No matter that it's three or thirty years ago, every client harks back to this golden time as the high point. This one day when hope sprung and lambs frolicked and everyone was the best version of their usual self.

It was at The Drake, Max. Oprah was one of our guests.

The cake was perfect, Max. Five tiers, so pure, so representative of our love.

Carolina Herrera's assistant designed the dress, Max. We saved ten percent.

And when you think how much money is spent weaving this ridiculous fantasy . . . well, there ought to be a law against it.

This is why I ask my brother about city hall. Gina's a beer-drinking, hockey-watching prep school teacher who has an unhealthy obsession with the Penguins (she's not even from Pittsburgh, so I'm guessing it's a Crosby thing). James is a nerd who I'm pretty sure has zero interest in fancy nuptials, unless it's themed with him dressed as Legolas and Gina as a hobbit. They allow interspecies marriage in the Shire, right?

If they're in such a hurry to tie the knot, then the trappings shouldn't matter.

"Well, there's an opening at . . ."

He hesitates. I pounce.

"At?"

"The Peninsula, on Michigan Avenue. Someone canceled—"

"You mean realized their mistake."

That should set him off, but no, he's a man in love and he's impervious to my blows. Torn between pride that he's sticking to his "ain't love grand" guns and annoyance that he's not seeing the bigger picture, I grind my teeth and remain silent.

"And we were able to get it. So July 15. Save the date." He clinks his glass against mine. The boy's messing with me now, and he's enjoying the hell out of it. "You should see your face, Max. It's like that time I screwed up your Spider-Man comics."

"Remember what happened there. You got your ass kicked."

"So worth it."

I consider him. "Is this a hoax?"

A small, pitying smile lifts the corner of his mouth. "Do you really want me to *not* get married that badly?"

"I just . . ." I halt, thinking through my reasoning here. I'm not completely opposed to true love. I don't have a string of broken relationships or some Mary Sue clutching my pulpy heart with her skeletal hands in my closet. Or, not exactly. A flash of Becca's face tries to take hold but I will it away. One broken engagement has not defined me.

What has, you might ask? The wealth of bat shit I see in my day-to-day. I want better for him. "It's happening sort of fast. I just don't want to see you get hurt or taken for a ride."

"By Gina?" he asks, with a teenage boy's chuckle at the imagery conjured up by "taken for a ride."

"By anyone. The Peninsula isn't cheap. Why the hell are you shelling out this much cash on one day?"

"The wedding planner—"

I hold up my hand as if he's a client about to offer unbidden the Saugatuck vacation cottage to his ex. I *knew* there was something shady about this whole thing. "There's already a wedding planner involved? When did you get engaged?"

"Six days ago."

Fuck. We met last week when he must have been planning this, and he didn't say a word. He waited a week to tell me because he knew I'd be an asshole. And I feel like the asshole he knows me to be.

Guilt shadows his usually open features. "I was going to call but I wanted to tell you in person. I know you don't deal with change well." He looks down at his scotch, then flashes a cheeky peek, checking out my reaction.

The change comment might be said in jest, but it's not totally untrue. I'm a man of routine and big life events tend to impact that. I run the same path in Lincoln Park, I eat at the same restaurant every Sunday night, I wear the same suit to court (Ermenegildo Zegna, tonal plaid wool two-piece in slate blue). But I can't use the "change bad!" notion to dictate the lives of those closest to me.

"Congratulations?" I offer, five minutes too late. Then to underscore my unbridled enthusiasm, I clink my glass against his and throw down the scotch.

It burns.

"Now that wasn't so hard, was it?" The little prick is having a blast. "And I really don't need a grouchy best man standing up with me."

I grin because I may not be totally on board but I'm going

to be my little brother's best man, and the thought makes me warm.

"I'm not sure three months is enough time to plan a bachelor party, never mind a Peninsula-worthy wedding." I'm still a little bit touchy about the location. It's so over the top and I wonder if this wedding planner he mentioned is bamboozling them. That's this chick's job—smoke and mirrors, upselling on everything, creating the fairy tale while you flirt with bankruptcy.

James pretends not to notice my testiness. He's good like that.

"I'm sure you'll think of something. Remember Toby from the Patterson?"

This kicks off one of our favorite stories about Toby, a guy we know from a neighborhood watering hole, who had his bachelor party at a sex dungeon. We've re-told this tale to ourselves and others several times but it never gets old, and by the time we get to the part where an Arby's roast beef sandwich was used in a fetish simulated sex scene (I kid you not), my bad humor is, if not exactly a thing of the past, making a halfhearted effort to not harsh the vibe.

His phone rings and a goofy smile overtakes his face. With a "gotta take this" nod, he makes to leave the booth, but I stay him with my hand.

"I need to take a leak. You talk to your . . . fiancée." That sounds weird.

But not to him. I'm already forgotten and with a smile that could power the city grid, he answers with, "Hey, honeybear."

Ker-ist.

I head past the bar toward the restrooms, vaguely aware that the goddess who's not my type is no longer here. Neither is Brooks Brothers, so I guess I missed my shot. Hot Server smiles at me and I almost stop. Almost.

I need clarity here more than I need a quick fuck.

I'm still on edge about James's news, and I'm thinking about ways to ensure he looks after himself. I'm not saying Gina's a gold digger, but she sure as hell isn't making bank teaching whiny eighth graders, no matter how nice the prep school. Educators are never paid what they're worth, though if she's showing up hungover every morning, everyone's probably getting what they deserve.

James will go ballistic when I mention a pre-nup but I have to do it. Not because he makes 150K playing at nerd but because my little brother has a net worth of about ten million. I used to be in the same boat, but that's a story for another day. You might know the name of our great-grandfather on my father's side—Hank Henderson. As in Chicago pig baron, Hank Henderson, the slaughterhouse king who made his fortune in the early twentieth century. Those little squealers were good news for my family's financial well-being, and while we're no longer in the business of spilling porcine blood (except for when I use the law to eviscerate my opponents, natch), the trust is still ticking over and compounding interest at a healthy rate.

You could say we're targets for women of a certain mind-set, not that I think Gina is like that. I'm exceptionally fond of her but—

"Hey, watch where you're going!"

I stop, too late to watch where I'm going, but just in time to see where I went. Or rather what I stepped on.

My goddess.

She's holding and rubbing her foot while standing on her other heel. Her face is scrunched up, more annoyance than pain, I'd wager, and I realize now that she was walking out of the ladies' restroom when she crashed into me. My thoughts might have been elsewhere but I'm pretty sure I had the right of way.

I could notify her of this but she's currently hunched over, so I'm not going to assert my case yet. Besides, this position gives me the perfect opportunity to finish that inventory I started earlier.

The pink dress has a subtly deep V that reveals a perfectly proportioned rack and a lush expanse of smooth, golden skin I want to lick. Freckles dot her shoulders like a night sky, leading me to plot a course to pleasure. Who knew an overproduction of melanin could be so damn sexy? My reaction is unstintingly visceral. It surprises me because, while I'm a healthy red-blooded American male, I'm not given to instant hard-ons at the sight of an attractive woman.

Finally, she peers up through long, golden lashes and I'm heat-blasted by a singular beauty. Green-not-blue eyes, cherry-red lips, a Cindy Crawford beauty mark.

She is absolutely gorgeous.

She is also absolutely pissed.

"Nothing to say, big guy?"

Now I'm not that big. I clock in at six feet and change but I look taller because I have broad shoulders from swimming all winter long every morning in the pool at my building. But I'll take it because it sounds like she's hovering on the edge of flirting.

"Let's check the damage." I jackknife to the ground outside the women's restrooms at the Gilt Bar.

This surprises her so much she straightens and jerks her foot back.

"May I?"

This surprises her more. "I—" She blinks.

"I just want to be sure your foot is okay."

"Um, sure."

Before she can second-guess that excellent decision, I take her allegedly injured foot in my hand. Shoe off. Palm around her heel. Gaze avid, searching for the imprint of my Ferragamo cap-toe Oxfords.

I glide a thumb over a slightly darkened patch of skin, along the knuckles of her toes, gratified to feel her shiver. Her nails are a pearlescent blue, sort of surprising given the womanly sophistication of the pink dress and the quality of her footwear.

"Still throbbing?" I ask, all cheeky innocence as I peek up.

Her lips *almost* curve but she fights it. "Just a shock, that's all. You really need to pay attention to where you're walking."

"You crashed out of the restroom without heed to the main thoroughfare. When entering from a side street, it's incumbent on you to check for oncoming traffic."

I don't know if she crashed out of anything, but I'm sure enjoying her disbelief.

"*You* collided with *me*. If it was the other way around, *my* heel would be embedded in *your* foot." In my mind, I hear the word "dickhead" tacked onto the end of that and the implicit wish that her heel was embedded in a more sensitive part of my anatomy.

She has a point but I refuse to concede. Instead I obfuscate because that's how I make my goddamn living.

"What can I do to make it better?" No admission of guilt, but an offer to settle in a way that will satisfy both parties. I smooth my thumb over her foot again, outside-in, lingering on the arch. The little hitch I hear in her breath turns me rock-hard. *You are eventually going to have to stand up, Maxie-boy, so why are you making it so difficult?*

She pulls away and fumble-feels for her shoe, but I'm there like a psychic Prince Charming sliding her into it. *That's right, my slide action is a thing of beauty.* Cheesy, but as long as it's in my head, I can be as cheesetastic as I want.

"I'll live," she murmurs.

I stand and, even in her heels, she's a good six inches shorter than me.

"Should we exchange insurance information?" I ask.

"I think we can handle this without getting all that bureaucracy involved."

"Right, wouldn't want our deductibles to shoot through the roof." Meanwhile the deductible in my pants is angling for an introduction.

We hold the moment, and it's not awkward. It's pretty nice, actually. The insurance metaphor has run its course but it was kind of silly to start with.

She peers up at me, waiting for something though technically it's her turn to talk. For once in my life, I don't want to talk. I just want to soak her in. She's as flawless as my first impression, with lips that are newly glossed, probably while she was in the restroom. This reminds me of Brooks Brothers, and he's the last guy I want polluting my brain.

As if I can shield her from the rest of the bar, I raise an arm and lean it against the wall. It makes my biceps bulge against my suit jacket and while she doesn't look, I know she sees. She inhales a quick, tight breath and magnetizes me with those emerald-fired eyes.

I can't believe I'm going to say this . . .

"So how does a girl like you get to be a girl like you?"

Slight eyebrow tilt (her). Epic held breath (me).

"Good line."

"Thanks," I say around my disappointment.

The "good line" is from my favorite Hitchcock movie, *North by Northwest*, and sounds better when spoken in that weird, clipped accent by dapper god of screen Cary Grant. When I'm interested in a woman, I throw it out—okay, ya got me, it's sort of a test. I'm not expecting an answer, per se, but some inkling that its awesomeness is appreciated.

If she had said, "Lucky, I guess," which is Eva Marie

Saint's response in the movie, I probably would have dropped back to my knees and proposed. I love a woman who can appreciate the classics.

Hold up there, Henderson. My brain screeches to a halt because I'm running away with myself here, pretzeled in knots by this woman. I certainly do not want to cuddle up with her on the sofa watching Jimmy Stewart stalking Kim Novak or Anthony Perkins undergoing a Mommy-induced identity crisis.

I date but I'm not interested in anything long-term, at least not now. My partners at Wright, Lincoln, and Henderson pick up the slack in that area. Lucas comes off like my brother, an über-romantic who plays the field but who I suspect is heading for a fall one of these days, while Grant is getting back on the dating horse after the hell of his divorce from one of my best friends, Aubrey, aka the Ball Crusher. My heart squeezes thinking about these people I care about in pain—and for what? The cause of true love. It's enough to make anyone a skeptic.

Suffice it to say I'm not in the market for a relationship and, if my brother is to be believed, this green-eyed goddess is a relationship sort of girl. Which means I need to set the stage.

"Did you ditch Brooks Brothers?" I say it roughly, a low rumble of sex so she knows that playtime is over. Down to brass tacks.

I expect her eyes to widen at the admission I've been tracking her all evening. Instead, she accepts it as her due that every man in this place was likely eye-fucking her over his Manhattan.

"Maybe he's in the restroom," she offers.

"Maybe he shouldn't have left you alone."

"Maybe this gal can handle herself."

"Maybe she should let herself be taken care of by someone who knows what he's doing."

She's having a hard time settling on amused or irked. "Does this work for you?"

"What?"

"The cocky player, shock-and-awe approach."

That brain screech from a second ago has turned into an Aston Martin crash into a tree. Here I thought we were rocking the fun flanter and now I sense some attitude.

I decide to go all in. "Every. Damn. Time."

Confidence is ingrained in me. It took a while, given my distinct lack of poise as a child, but I've worked hard to overcome my early deficiencies. Now I'm the guy who knows how to please a woman—my clients, of course, but most especially the women in my bed. (In case you're wondering, those two categories never intersect. I love my job too much.) If I were to hand off an exit survey to a woman leaving my bedroom, I'd be getting all fives on the Likert scale. Meaning "Fuck Yeah Satisfied."

My cockiness might throw off a certain kind of woman. But *this* woman? She's into me but something—her wise old grammy or a still hurting heart, perhaps—is telling her she needs to put up a show of resistance.

"No, thanks," she says.

"No, thanks, what?"

She waves a hand between us. "You're not my type."

"You sure about that?"

Her luscious lips form an O. "I don't have time for this. I'm really looking for something a bit more . . . compelling."

I'm tempted to say that she'll never have a more compelling time than when she's screaming for me to do her harder, when I hear, "Max," in my brother's voice. Reluctantly I drop my arm, which places the goddess's perfect profile in James's sight line.

"Charlie!" James steps in—between us, mind you, which requires I move back—and hugs her. Hmm. A bit more than I'd expect of a relationship between business associates. Maybe they chat about geek code over the water cooler at Chase.

And Charlie. Short for Charlotte? It suits her. Hitchcock would be proud.

How does a girl like you get to be a girl like you?

My brother is speaking to her and ignoring me. "I saw you earlier, and I was going to come over and say hi, but—" He looks at me and cocks his head, that amusement back. "I see you've met Max."

"Max Henderson." I offer my hand, and she hesitates for a split second, but then takes it.

"The brother."

Uh-oh. Apparently I'm on her radar and have already failed the big test. I'm confused now, so confused that it takes a moment to realize I'm still holding her hand.

I let go, annoyed with myself. I'm usually a lot smoother than this. Hell, I was ten times smoother ten seconds ago.

"I just told Max about the engagement," James says, again in a tone that makes me think I've completely mischaracterized their relationship. This isn't business-casual. These two are friends.

Two questions bubble up. Why the hell have I never met her, and why the double hell is my brother warning me away? My curiosity about her is pounding at my insides and I look at him, only to find he's smirking. I don't like being at a disadvantage around anyone, especially not my baby brother who seems to have the jump on me in all things today. *Prepare to be nuggied later, little one.*

I don't care that James thinks she's not my type, but I do care that she's in agreement. I want those honey-skinned thighs around my hips, to feel those perfect breasts on my cheek, and to taste all her smart mouth has to offer.

"So how do you two know each other?" I ask, super casual.

"Charlie's helping with the wedding."

I nod, working my head around that. If she works with him at Chase, then maybe . . . "You fronting the cash for the wedding of the millennium?" It's a joke because I know she's not but I'm waiting for someone to clue me in.

"Oh, I don't front cash. I spend it." She winks and it's a beautiful thing. "I'm their wedding planner."

James laughs because he knows what I think of weddings. Just as he knows what I think of parasitic, blot-on-society, spend-other-people's-money wedding planners.

Oh, I'm not enjoying this at all.

CHAPTER 3

"I love being married. It's so great to find that one special person you want to annoy for the rest of your life."

— RITA RUDNER

Charlie

"So how did he take it?"

Initially James rocks a careful neutrality on hearing my question, and I wonder if maybe I've misjudged his relationship with his brother. When I sat down with him and Gina last week, I asked about family members. It's standard on my intake because I like to know if I'm dealing with evil stepmoms or squabbling parents who need to be seated in different zip codes, and the first person they mentioned was Max.

The divorce lawyer who I've been warned is not a fan of weddings. Or marriage. Or love, it seems.

And who is now sitting across from me in the booth I'd decided to visit for a round of drinks at James's invitation.

After that little flirtation in the hallway—*you let him fondle your foot!*—I really should be out of here. But there's something about Max Henderson that ticks me off. He's far too hot, too cocky, too *everything*. I want to seriously mess with his—uh—mind.

"I'm right here, you know," he mutters before James has a chance to answer. He's annoyed, and while any number of reasons could be to blame, I'm going to hazard a guess at three. (I like lists.)

1. I threw his Cary Grant *North by Northwest* line back in his face. (God, was I impressed, though. Really impressed.)
2. I made sure he knew I was onto him and his player ways.
3. I represent everything he despises—i.e., belief in the lasting power of true love.

Of course, a cynic like Max Henderson will say I believe in the *cost* of true love, the more expensive the better. I refuse to apologize for making a living, not when people are willing to pay highly for the services I offer.

I am excellent at what I do.

"He took it about as well as I expected," James says with a grin that includes his hot brother. The hot brother doesn't grin back, but the scowl really works for him.

"Pulled out his hair in clumps?" I assess his dark hair, which is pretty perfect and could do with a thorough mussing. "Crumpled his bespoke suit while on the floor throwing a tantrum?" The suit is impeccably pressed and distinctly uncrumpled. I take a few seconds to consider my next words. "Oh, I know. The lawyer is more of a verbal guy. He probably made a few snide comments about—"

"Gina being knocked up," James says cheerfully.

I shake my head in mock disapproval, which makes Max frown even deeper. There's an intensity about him that I imagine works to his benefit in a courtroom. Or a bedroom.

"That's not very nice," I chide.

James is laughing now. "No, it's not, but that's my brother. He doesn't pull his punches."

"I was just surprised, that's all," Max says begrudgingly.

James rolls his eyes affectionately and turns back to me. "How's the hunt for Mr. Right going? Was that a date you were on earlier?"

I'm amused and a little touched that he remembers our conversation from a few days ago. Gina is in my book club, which is how we connected, and when I met her and her fiancé—who are so damn cute together, by the way—we hit it off. Later, the subject of dating came up. My dating. Particularly how I'd decided to get serious about it now that summer was almost upon us.

No one can truly enjoy summer in Chicago without a little arm candy. If he owns a boat, all the better.

Truth be told, I'm looking for more than a casual dalliance. Constantly surrounded by happy couples in my job, I see love in all its forms, both obvious and subtle. From the attentiveness of a guy touching his fiancée at every available moment to the willingness to compromise over "band versus DJ." She wants the band—give it to her! Happy wife equals happy life.

I'm ready to be a happy wife.

I came close about eighteen months ago, and that experience taught me a lot about what I need and shall we say, the *parameters* of the husband hunt. I won't settle but neither will I shoot for the moon.

"Tonight was not the one." Tonight was a guy who clearly wanted to bypass the dating phase for the bedding phase, as his wandering hands affirmed. And that was before I let Max Henderson play sexy podiatrist in that hallway.

It might be worth it for the foot rubs . . .

"Maybe Max can help you out."

"I doubt it." This comes off ruder than I intended, mostly because I'm annoyed at my apparent willingness to compromise my principles for a semi-decent massage of my tired arches.

"Oh, I don't mean personally," James says with a sly look at his brother. "But he knows where all the newly single guys are—and their net worth."

"So a recently divorced guy with a shitload of baggage who feels his ex has screwed him into the grave? Sign me up." *Charlie, what is wrong with you? Do not bait the bear.*

Max doesn't look affronted but then a divorce lawyer must be used to slings and arrows about his job. For a moment I feel sorry for him. He's forced to deal with all that negativity on a daily basis.

Any sympathy I possess leaves the bar in a flouncing huff when the man speaks. "I'd probably advise my clients not to jump into a relationship so quickly. Especially not with someone who appears so desperate to get hitched."

My pulse spikes. "Ready is not the same as desperate."

He circles a finger around the rim of his glass and remains silent. This is likely some trap to make me defend myself and look like an idiot in the bargain.

I tumble right into it.

"Just because a woman is looking for a serious relationship, she's automatically labeled as desperate?"

Instead of answering, he poses a question. "How old are you?"

"Twenty-nine."

"Your parents married at what age?"

"Dad was twenty-six; Mom was twenty-four."

He nods, filing that away. "And you see all your friends from college and your current circle pairing off for the long haul?"

I squirm in my seat, not especially enjoying the cross-examination. At the end of whatever this is, he'll likely wow me with some learned conclusion about how I worry I'm a slow starter. How my parents are constantly hinting that I need to settle down. How my two closest friends are married. To each other.

So what if it's true. I don't need to hear an argument I can make so cogently myself.

"I know where you're going with this. Yes, I come from a family that values marriage and children, and they want that for me. Yes, I'm ready to find a man who's not a commitment-phobe and who holds similar ideals and values. And yes, I'm tired of the dance, and I'm ready for something deeper than casual dating and one-night stands, no matter how amazing the penis on offer. Does that count as desperate in your world, Mr. Henderson?"

He maintains that aloof cool I'm starting to despise. "Mr. Henderson is my father. I merely wanted to point out that you can enjoy yourself while waiting for Mr. Right."

Ah, still miffed at being rejected. I wink at him. "I've enjoyed myself plenty."

"Enjoyed" might be a stretch but I have had three semi-decent lovers in the last two years. Ready for another list?

1. Gaston Ramirez (Yes, his name was actually Gaston.): A player, just like Max, though he exuded nowhere near as much confidence as this streak of handsome sitting across from me.
2. Jase Colfax (Sounds like an international spy, doesn't he?): Finding him getting bendy with my yoga instructor had hurt, no denying it, but I'd

never considered him serious husband material anyway. Bonus fact: hair-trigger dick.
   3. Jeremy Craven: the closest I came to saying "I do." I'll admit the end of this relationship sent me into a funk from which I've only recently emerged.

The take home here? I don't have time for guys who aren't ready to game up (or don't have the stamina to stick with me in the bedroom). Besides I promised my dad I'd find the one.

Max is assessing me with crystalline blue eyes, so sharp I feel them cutting into my body like lasers.

"So while you wait for the one"—*get out of my head, playah!*—"you live vicariously, setting up lavish matrimonial monstrosities and selling people an impossible fantasy. Overcompensate much?"

"Maxie," James says. "Play nice."

I've met this guy before—not Max specifically, but the guy who would prefer to focus on the worst life has to offer. They call themselves "realists," which we all know is code for "cynical assholes." I get it. Humans are hardwired to dwell on negative experiences, which are more likely to shape us, stick with us, and shut us down to the possibilities.

I refuse to be sucked into that vortex.

"You know what, Mr.—"

"Max," he interjects.

"You know what, Mr. Max? I'm putting together a wedding for two lovely people in the space of twelve weeks. It's going to be a lot of work but it's also going to be a blast because nothing thrills me more than giving a couple the day of their dreams." I turn to James, who's grinning up a storm. Evidently, he enjoys when his brother's worldview is challenged. "Screw this guy and the apocalyptic horse he rode in on. This is about celebrating you and Gina and how fucking awesome you are."

I refocus on Max, whose eyes have darkened so much that they've swallowed all the blue. A slight muscle tic is hammering away in his jaw. I wonder how it would taste.

Like do-me-against-a-wall sex and morning-after regrets, I bet.

"I'm guessing that a busy guy like you won't have time to worry about the finer details of wedding planning," I continue. "Just show up for your tux fitting and stow your hate at the chapel door."

Booyah! That's a pretty great exit-stage-left line so I stand to leave. But I should have known that a guy as verbal as Max Henderson would have to get in the last word.

"That sounds like a challenge, Charlie." He says it quietly, like *he's* issuing the challenge. My name on his lips is sex in two syllables. "You think I can't be the supportive brother here? That I can't put aside my concerns to make sure James's marriage gets off to a great start?"

"I doubt it. Your cynicism is bone-deep, and you can't help that it's seeping from your pores every time you open your mouth." *Along with your testosterone.* I smooth out the skirt of my Tory Burch dress, though really that's a ploy to stop my hands from shaking.

Max stands and pulls on his cuffs, a motion I love seeing in a man. Diamond-studded cufflinks glint in the light streaming in from the entrance and a ridiculously cooperative ray catches his hair, giving it a blue-black shine. *Come on!* Even the sun is conspiring to ensure that Max Henderson is the hottest guy I've ever seen in person.

He stares at me, into me, which I suppose is a strategy he uses on discarded wives in courtrooms. (*Tell the truth, Mrs. GoldDiggah. You trapped my client into this sham marriage and now you want the Lamborghini? No dice!*)

"For the next three months, I can stow the cynicism. This is important to James and Gina, so whenever you see me, I'll be a Disney fucking prince."

I battle my smile. Hold on by a thread. "Breaking into song during the fittings? Belting out ballads at the rehearsal dinner?"

"I'm already composing the tunes."

Laughter erupts from somewhere close. I'd completely forgotten about Max's brother—I mean, James, my client. Max Henderson is so maddening he'd make a girl forget that the bar was burning down around her.

"This should be good," James says, his amusement plain, and then to me, "Charlie, how the hell did we manage to land the best wedding planner in Chicago?"

I hold his gaze, though what I'm about to say is really for his obnoxious brother. Channeling my best Eva Marie Saint from *North by Northwest*, I consider Max's question from earlier.

How does a girl like you get to be a girl like you?

"Lucky, I guess."

I take just a second to absorb Mr. Hotshot Lawyer's obvious surprise, smile my goodbye at James, and head out into the April sunshine.

Now, *that* was an exit.

CHAPTER 4

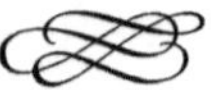

"Ah, yes, divorce from the Latin word meaning to rip out a man's genitals through his wallet."

— ROBIN WILLIAMS

Max

I'd rather be swimming.

Instead I'm running in Lincoln Park listening to Lucas, one of my partners in Wright, Lincoln, and Henderson *not* tell me about the woman he met last night. This is par for the course with the guy. God forbid he actually impart any salient facts.

"I didn't get her name, but I think it's better this way."

This is where I'm supposed to ask, *Why is it better?*

I elect not to. Makes no odds to Lucas, who once talked a judge into a stay he had no right receiving. Just before he talked his way into Her Honor's panties in chambers. He's the chattiest guy I know, and while the British Empire may no longer be the force it once was, that limey accent of his is a weapon of mass destruction.

"It was one of those never to be repeated moments," he continues, oblivious to my lack of interest. "Dark bar, eyes meet, my favorite parts get acquainted with her favorite parts on top of the restroom sink."

"Germ-ridden surfaces, bodily fluids mingle, a lifetime of venereal disease is your reward."

"Ever the romantic, Maxie."

I snort and pick up the pace, my annoyance on the rise. Maybe it's how Lucas is shoving his sexual adventures in my face—about sex in public restrooms no less—while I had my own less than satisfying encounter *outside* a restroom just yesterday evening.

I'm still ticked off at Charlie Love.

Even her name chaps my dick. It sounds invented, like a stage name for a woman who sells romance. It might be in everyone's best interest if I run a background check on her, see if she is who she says she is.

"So, awesome news about James," Lucas says.

"Yeah, it's great."

There's no missing his sidelong glance. We know each other pretty well, having met six years ago straight out of law school while we worked at a big firm downtown. We put in our grunt time together, and when Grant and I decided to open our own practice, Lucas, our cheeky chappy Brit pal, was a natural fit.

Somehow the fucker talked his way into getting his name listed first. Said it was more musical to have the names go in order of one syllable, two syllables, three syllables. That the last name of the trio would be remembered most. I fell for it because he's that good.

"Now, we both know you're not a hundred percent on

board with this, Maxie. Talk to your uncle Lucas."

I stop because standing still is necessary for what I need to get off my chest. "It's kind of soon, don't you think?"

Lucas gives me the respect of not dismissing my concerns with a derisive look or a weird noise. "I'd say for some people, yes. But James has a good head on his shoulders."

He does. And Gina's a nice girl. It's the wedding planner. That's what's turned this from a low-level hum of irksome into a full-scale throttle of annoyance. I understand that some people might view my job as feeding off the misery of others, but I'm performing a necessary service. This woman —Charlie Love, if that is her real name—is sucking at the teat of people's pseudo happiness. Not just that, she's manufacturing a need that doesn't exist.

"They have a wedding planner."

"I heard. I also heard you kind of got into it with her."

"You and Jim-Jam are awfully chatty, Wright."

"He thought you might need a shoulder in your time of sorrow and called to prep me for the waterworks. We all know how much you hate change."

While it's annoying to be so easily pegged, he's not far wrong. I had to be dragged into leaving my old firm by Grant. I have routines I like, a life I've honed to stability. The one time I stepped out of my comfort zone and invited someone in ended in disaster.

"I like what I like," I mutter. Maybe it's boring, but I don't enjoy surprises.

"You need to have your life shook up, mate," Lucas says. "Get you out of your rut."

I need nothing of the sort. I quickly change the subject.

"My parents are thrilled." They see nothing but promise and joy ahead. I love them dearly but their naïveté about how life works worries me.

"And you don't have to perform. Number one son is off

the hook!" He squints over my shoulder. "What's the name of that woman you took to the bar association ball in December?"

I'm already running before he can even finish the query. Some people might call it cowardly; I call it a distinct case of self-preservation.

Mitzi von Stueben is a lovely girl, far too nice for the likes of me, which I found out after I took her on two dates and she started talking pets. As in which type of dog we should be getting because apparently sharing custody of a dog is a clear indication of a man's readiness to settle down. Though it pisses me off to change up my regular trail, I've been taking a different running route because since I told her we're not going to work out, I've crossed her path "accidentally" approximately six times in two months.

"She still there?" I ask Lucas as I sprint like my freedom depends on it. He's doing a fine job of keeping pace with me. The Lucky Escape Fitness Regimen.

"Nah, she turned off the path and headed over to the zoo."

Good. Maybe she'll find a monkey she can adopt.

I SHOULD HAVE stock in Kleenex.

I hand the box of tissues to Mrs. Steven MacKenna—she still goes by this name even though the next Mrs. Mac is metaphorically cocking her hip and tapping her wristwatch in the Gold Coast pied-à-terre. It's one of the things that can often impede a fast and efficient dissolution: the knowledge that someone's waiting in the wings, already measuring the closets.

"I don't see why he"—read *she*—"gets to keep the condo on Schiller," my client croaks out between sobs.

"We went over this, Elizabeth. You're getting the house in

Lake Forest. Ten thousand square feet and eight million buckaroos is always going to trump a pokey seven rooms worth a paltry 3.9 mil." In this market, more like 4.2 million, but I'm playing it down because the slightest encouragement will launch her into a spiral of indecision. "With the alimony settlement, you're doing very well out of it financially."

I use the term "financially," though I know she's not quite at the stage where this is a transaction yet. I can get her to a place where she'll be doing better emotionally, but we need to get closure on the assets first. Elizabeth is a friend of my mother's and was initially resistant to using me as her lawyer because I peed in her swimming pool at the age of three. She's since come around, but in her mind, I'll always be the Little Pee Boy of Winnetka.

A gentle knock that I know to be Sadie, our office manager, is a natural stopping point in our conversation.

"Come in."

Sadie walks in with a silver tray laden with a full French press, cups, cream, and double-baked almond and apricot biscotti.

"Right here, Sadie, thanks." I gesture to the coffee table in front of the sofa where I'm sitting with Mrs. Mac. For these emotional conversations, I prefer to treat the exchange as a cozy chat.

Sadie is a model of discretion. A pretty Black woman in her early forties with short black hair and chocolate eyes, she's been with us from the beginning. Her firefighter husband and five-year-old twins keep her busy—*they're more mature than the three of you,* she likes to say. I don't doubt it.

She leaves as quietly as she arrived.

"Want to hit the plunger, Elizabeth?" I motion to the French press. "It can be amazingly cathartic."

Her mouth pulls up slightly, attempting a smile. She's

really quite attractive, barely past fifty, with a rosy future ahead of her. She will get through this.

Taking me up on my invitation, she palms the plunger and depresses it with a satisfied exhale.

"Her or him?" I ask.

Her smile shines brighter, more self-aware. I like knowing smiles on my clients' lips. Knowing smiles imply humps being hurdled. "You think I should be imagining crushing his balls into coarse coffee grounds, I suppose. I understand that he's to blame and she's just a symptom, but . . ." She turns astonishingly clear green eyes on me, and I'm reminded for a moment of Charlie Love, though Charlie's have golden flecks shot through the irises. "I really feel if given another month, he'll grow out of this nonsense."

Steven MacKenna has had eight months to grow out of this nonsense. He actually prefers it and has the resources to indulge his late-in-mid-life crisis.

I'm going to need to take this one to the next level.

"Coffee, Max?"

"Please. And when we're done, I have something to show you."

"A GYM?" Elizabeth gazes around in wonder at the room we've just entered. "Why have you taken me to a gym in your office suite?"

"Do you work out, Elizabeth?"

"I go to Zumba classes like a normal person."

"No Zumba here." I give an all-encompassing wave around the room, taking in the punching bags, the grappling dummies, and everyone's favorite, Bob the Torso. There's a notable lack of traditional gym equipment such as treadmills or the like. This is not a get-fit kind of place, it's a get-even kind of place.

"When you said 'Punch Palace,' I assumed you meant a place to drink punch." Only a woman who runs in the society circles Elizabeth MacKenna does would jump to that conclusion. She completes a small circuit, stopping at Bob, who has a Popeye cast to him, her expression one of curiosity cross-bred with distaste. "That is one ugly son of a bitch."

"He can always get uglier." I walk over to a cabinet and open it up. Once I find what I need, I join her in front of Bob.

Her eyes widen at what I'm carrying in my hands. "You're kidding."

"Nope. Let's see how it looks." Thirty seconds later we're staring at a scarily accurate facsimile of Steven MacKenna III above a naked torso on a polyethylene sand-filled base.

Elizabeth raises a hand to her throat. "It's so . . . I refuse to say lifelike because that implies the bastard is human, but it's quite remarkable. Creepy. Where did you get it?"

"We have a company that makes the masks for us based on photos we send them. Not everyone gets the treatment but I try to anticipate who might need a helping hand—"

"Or fist."

"Or fist, to get them over the hump. Right now, you're caught in no-man's-land. You hate him but you think there might be hope. From a legal perspective, I think you know that this marriage is over, but your brain isn't there yet."

"You think punching a dummy with my husband's face on it will get me past this?" She hasn't taken her eyes off fake Steven since the moment I put that mask over Bob's ugly-ass mug. Stevie's not much of an improvement.

"I think it can't hurt to give it a shot."

"I assume I'm getting charged your full rate while I'm indulging in this ridiculousness." She can't decide if she's impressed or disgusted. "And to think you used to have poor bladder control."

My three-year-old self still haunts me. "Some of my clients tell me they would happily pay extra for this service."

Sometimes it has a fortunate by-product. Not only does a discarded wife get to punch the living daylights out of her ex, she often finds the activity addictive. Losing those pounds she acquired in middle age, the ones her ex-husband couldn't appreciate as the sacrifice she made to bear his children, is the ultimate fuck you to the prick who's moved on to a newer, shinier model. I get an uncommon kick out of watching a former spouse's jaw drop to the courtroom floor at the sight of the new and improved woman he trashed for the crime of a too-large booty and her inability to surprise him anymore.

Elizabeth looks down at her elfin, have-never-done-a-day's-work hands and curls them into fists. "Do I just—"

I place my hand over hers before she can connect with fake Steven. "A broken finger isn't going to make you feel better." And will likely result in me getting sued to hell and back. "Let's get you a pair of boxing gloves."

CHAPTER 5

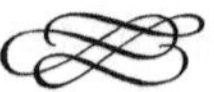

"I promise not to keep score, even if I am totally winning."

— UNKNOWN

Charlie

"She won't talk to me," Nathan says. "She said you either call her back within ten minutes or she's walking."

I growl into my phone.

"Down, girl."

"Nat, why did I hire you?"

"Because I'm your best bud from college, handsome as fuck, and hung like a Kentucky Derby winner."

"No, my sweet, I hired you because you flirt like there's no tomorrow and that's what I need to calm all the diva brides. Now why aren't you doing what I hired you to do?"

I check my watch, noting that it's five minutes past the

40

time I've arranged to meet Gina and James for the menu and table settings selection at The Peninsula. Beautiful people float by me in the lobby on their way to glamorous lives and afternoon tea.

"I tried everything, but it's hard to do my best work on the phone," Nathan says. "You know I'm more effective when I can employ my dimples to maximum capacity."

I can't disagree. Nathan is a magical unicorn in the wedding planning industry: a heterosexual man who loves the thrill of putting together a couple's dream day. Everyone assumes he's gay and then gets annoyed with him on behalf of all the gay wedding planners he's supposedly rooking out of jobs. We met in college and after a short stint in events management for a large hotel chain, he joined me when I broke out on my own two years ago with Perfect Day, my wedding planning company.

The client he needs me to talk down off a ledge is Kennedy Faulkner, who has taken the role of bridezilla and decided to ramp it up to Oscar bait levels. I'm usually exceptionally present for my clients but Kennedy . . . I missed three of her calls while I was in a meeting, then ignored two more because I suspect it's a storm in a teacup. And I'm right. According to Nathan, the bride-to-be is worried that the foie gras on the wedding reception menu *might* be produced from natural feeding instead of the traditional means of force-feeding that all foie gras aficionados know and love. In other words, Kennedy needs an assurance that the most barbaric and cruel practices possible were employed to produce her first course.

"I already called the chef," Nathan says. "He said he only ever uses the real thing—in fact, he sounded insulted I'd even ask—but she needs to hear it from you. Says her father won't eat anything else, and he's concerned someone will slip in some 'faux gras.'"

My time in group homes where a PB&J was considered gourmet didn't prepare me for this. "Give her Chef Fontaine's direct number."

"Really?"

"Yep. She might say she wants to hear it from me but really she wants to vent, so she may as well do it in his ear."

"Atta girl."

We chitchat about a few outstanding items on our lists, then I sign off. Ten minutes late now. I'm not pleased about this because the timeline on this wedding is much more contracted than usual. I pride myself on being able to pull off anything but I need client cooperation.

My phone buzzes with a text from—uh-oh—Gina.

> Sorry, my car broke down on Lake Shore and James got stuck at work.

Damn, a complete waste of my time.

Typing . . . typing . . .

> I can get there in about twenty minutes, but in the meantime we've sent someone to get us started.

Typing . . . typing . . .

I don't need to read the next message because my skin is already goosebumping with awareness. *Asshole Alert!* Apparently I must have crapped on a god's head in a previous lifetime. I look up just as The Cynic™ appears.

"Ms. Love."

Guys have tried to speak my name knowingly, even flirtatiously before. I'm used to men digging deep for their inner Barry White, drawing out that single syllable, and inviting me into a world where the husky pronunciation of this one word is supposed to make me cream my Vicky S high-cut bikini.

It's never worked. Until now.

And boy, does that get on my tits.

Max Henderson says my name like I should fall to my knees and praise the deity who chiseled this man from angel poop. While I'm at it, I should probably unzip, untuck, and unhinge my jaw to show my true gratitude. And now I have no choice but to stare at his zipper and all the business that surrounds and strains against the zipper. Strong thighs, trim hips, narrow waist, all encased in a navy pinstripe suit that fits him perfectly.

"Mr. Henderson." I stand because I feel at a disadvantage while sitting. Upright isn't all that much better but at least I'm no longer eye-level with his crotch.

"Call me Max. Did you hear from Gina?"

"Just now. We can probably reschedule for another time—"

"And have you add this to your bill? I don't think so." He looks at his watch, something incredibly expensive peeking from the cuff of a shirt that probably cost several of my monthly mortgage payments. "I already said I'm happy to help, and Gina should be along soon enough. How about we get started?"

I pin on my fakest smile. "Sure, why not." As I lead the way, I speak to him over my shoulder. "I'm not sure how much Gina and James filled you in. Today we're going to choose table settings and try a sample menu. Do you know if anyone in the immediate family has food allergies?"

Max Henderson is busy looking at my legs.

I stop so he can come alongside me.

"Spoilsport," he says with a tip of his mouth up at the corner. He's really far too attractive for my own good.

"Food allergies?" I prompt.

"Rubbery chicken priced over a Benjamin per plate."

I make a big to-do out of noting that in my phone. "That didn't take long."

"What didn't?"

"You reverting to type. Scroogy MacScrooge Pants and Bah Humbug 'are there no poorhouses?'"

"Now how did you know my nickname in high school?"

"Oh, I bet that wasn't it."

He leans in and, holy pinstripes, he smells incredible. Like a manly orchid. A manorchid.

"You're right, it wasn't. Maybe I'll tell you one day."

Max Henderson hit on me pretty hard at that bar a week ago and turned cool when he found out who I am and what I do for a living. But I suspect he's gotten over his initial gripe. After all, why allow principles to get in the way of the needs of your penis?

It would be so easy to fall into those dangerous blues, let myself be swept up in a torrid exchange of bodily fluids with no strings. But I'd hate myself in the morning.

"I hope you're hungry," I say. "The food here is divine."

His eyes stay fixed on my lips, then snap to my eyes. "What's your favorite Hitchcock movie, Charlie?"

The change of subject and caress of his tongue over my name send my pulse rocketing.

"What makes you think I have one?"

His eyes crinkle in a "come on, I know you do" way. There's something soft in that eye crinkle, something that speaks of a man who might have the capacity to surprise me.

"*Rear Window*. It's perfect."

"It is."

A shiver of excitement thrills through me that we agree on this—or perhaps he crafted the moment so we could agree on *something*. It's silly, really, because lots of people like Hitchcock movies.

"We should . . ." I thumb over my shoulder.

"Lead the way," he murmurs.

The menu tasting is far more intimate than I'd like. Melissa, my contact at The Peninsula, usually sets it up this way to create a sensual atmosphere conducive to the happy couple. *Sexy food puts the marks in a good mood,* she once told me.

The lighting may be muted, but it's plenty bright enough for Melissa to get a good gawp at Max. On hearing he's playing proxy for the groom, the woman promptly forgets that she is herself engaged. But then Max seems to have that effect. Common sense, self-respect, and knickers fly out the window whenever he's near.

"The bride is running a little late but Mr. Hend—" It feels odd to call him that, especially when Melissa is blinking at him like he's God's gift. A surge of possessiveness takes charge of my tongue. "Max is pretty sure he can guide the choices here."

"Of course," Melissa says, never taking her eyes off Max. "How about a little champagne to start?" Another tool in Melissa's box. Ply the client with bubbly to get them to agree to the higher-priced bar packages with top-shelf liquors and wines. I prefer to keep a clear head, which Melissa knows too well. She eyes me, and I eye her right back. I won't allow my clients to be cheated.

She pulls a bottle of Californian sparkling from a bucket on a side table, but before she can uncork it, Max raises a hand.

"I think we can do better than that, Mel. What's the best vintage you have on the menu?"

"Moët & Chandon, of course."

"I prefer Veuve Clicquot but we'll take the Moët if that's all you have. My treat." He smiles at her, and wow, the low-light romance of the room brightens to megawatt sexiness.

She nods, a little dumbstruck by Max's smoothness. I, on

the other hand, am restraining myself from a considerable eye roll. Melissa practically runs off to the bar to grab the champagne.

"And there I was thinking you had concerns about the budget."

"My concern about drinking piss-poor champagne will always trump budget concerns."

I laugh, reluctantly amused. "That wasn't pretentious at all."

His grin tells me he knows it was, and hey, isn't this fun how we're all in the know? Again, I'm struck that maybe there's more to Max than he's chosen to present.

"I'd think you'd want to add on as much as you can. Getting the clients toasted on expensive booze can only help your case and increase your kickback."

"That's not really what this is about. At least, not from me. I'm here to protect my clients from predatory behavior."

"Right."

"Just admit it, Max. We're both part of the rich cycle of love and marriage, only my contribution actually makes people happy."

"You haven't met any of my clients. Sure, they don't start off happy—probably something to do with the unrealistic expectations force-fed down their throat by unscrupulous hawkers of love and marriage. By the time I'm through with them, they're a little bruised yet at peace for the first time in forever. Your contribution gives them a false sense of security. Mine restores the balance you and your ilk have thrown off."

What utter tosh. I open my mouth to say so, but am interrupted by Melissa. "Let's get this party started, shall we?"

Fifteen minutes later, I'm halfway through the glass of champagne I swore I wouldn't let pass my lips. It's Moët & Chandon, on Max, and I took an Uber here, so why not?

We've already cycled through four appetizer choices: shrimp with chives, ricotta ravioli, a crab thing, and an asparagus thing. The fact I'm calling them "things" means my alcohol tolerance clearly needs boosting.

"The crab thing and the ravioli," Max says.

"Agreed. The chives overpower the shrimp—"

"And the asparagus is just blerg," he finishes.

My thoughts exactly. Well, sort of. "Blerg?"

"Legal terminology for indifference to asparagus appetizers. I'm only surprised the chef hasn't thrown out Brussels sprouts. Christ, I'm sick to death of seeing those on every menu." He tops up my champagne. "So, Mel, what are we looking at here? Give me some numbers."

Melissa slides a perfectly printed list of the packages with prices over to Max's side of the table. I watch his cool appraisal of the admittedly high cost per head. But this is The Peninsula, one of the world's top luxury hotel chains, with this branch located smack bang in the middle of Michigan Avenue, one of the most famous streets in the country. A wedding at The Peninsula—at *this* Peninsula—isn't going to cost chump change.

For all his bitching and moaning about wedding planners and the matrimonial-industrial complex, he's remarkably contained. I wonder what it would take to make him lose his self-control. When he goes to bat for his clients, does he get emotional? When he beds a woman, does a different Max Henderson come out to play?

I doubt it. The man I see is slick and centered and a little bit *plastic*. The law suits him.

He looks up, and for a moment I feel caught in a trap of my own making, as if he knows what I'm thinking and he's saying, "All wrong, Charlie!" His eyes skitter over me before landing on Melissa. "I think there's a little wiggle room here, don't you, Mel?"

Melissa simpers in a most annoying way. You are engaged, woman!

A loud crash sounds behind her, and all eyes whip to the source. Gina is standing over a stainless steel cover, looking absolutely mortified.

"I am *so* sorry!"

Before a glaring Melissa can put her foot in it, I jump up to greet the bride. "It's fine! Just glad you could make it. How's the car?"

"Towed. I cabbed it." She takes my arm like we're old friends. Wild, mahogany curls fall over her bright hazel eyes and smooth olive skin. "Hey, Maximus, thanks for keeping Charlie company." At the table, she lifts my glass and downs the rest in one swallow. "I soooo needed that!"

Max stands and gives her a hug while I watch carefully for evidence of disapproval on his part. I'm not sure why, but I want to protect this girl.

"I didn't get a chance to congratulate you, GeeGee," Max says. "Welcome to the Henderson asylum. You're gonna love it here."

Gina hiccups and squeezes him back. "I know you're not on board but I don't care."

"That's the spirit," Max says good-naturedly.

Introductions are exchanged, and Gina pulls up a chair while Melissa heads back to the kitchen to get more samples for the main course.

"I'm fucking starving!" Gina downs the remaining appetizers.

"Any thoughts?" I say, charmed by her attitude.

"The asparagus thing tastes like shit."

Max catches my eye with a twinkle in his own. "Also, a legal term."

I giggle stupidly. Damn top-shelf champagne—who's playing who here?

One bottle of Moët and forty-five minutes later, we've decided on a menu. When Max steps out to take a call, Gina leans in, her voice low. "I haven't seen anything about prices."

"James said not to worry. Just pick what you like." And I suspect Max is going to try to bargain the package down because it's the principle of the thing.

"All this . . ." Brow in a crumple, Gina looks around. "It's so over the top, don't you think? Well, of course you don't think that. This is perfectly normal for you but for me . . ."

I squeeze her hand. "Whose idea was it to get married?"

Her face lights up. "James. He said he wanted to ask me the first night we met but thought it might come off as stalkerish."

Lovely. "And whose idea was it to do the big wedding?"

"Okay, I see where you're going with this, but you don't know the kind of people I'm marrying into." She looks over her shoulder, and I follow her gaze. Max is over at the kitchen entrance, his head inclined while talking to Melissa. She's touching his lapel in a way that's really bothersome.

Ridiculous.

Me, that is. I'm being ridiculous.

"You mean because they're North Shore nouveau riche."

"Nothing nouveau about it. I mean, the money's been in the fam for decades. Millions of it from some pig baron or something. And here's little old Gina from Podunk, Nebraska, who crashes into tables and knocks back other people's champagne. Not to mention, Max hates the idea."

I wonder. "I think he likes you, though."

"He liked me better when I was just James's girlfriend. And there's so much to do—I haven't lived in the city for long and I don't know the first thing about any of this. I don't even have a dress. My sister is eight months pregnant and can't travel to help with bride stuff."

"How about your mom?"

"She's sort of busy with Husband No. 3."

Gina's not the first woman I've met with a poor female support network. "I can help with all the preparation. And you have friends in book club, right?"

"Casual. I only went to it because I saw a notice at the library and it was specifically about reading romance and not some highfalutin' snooty *New York Times* shit." Another look over her shoulder and again, I'm drawn to whatever Melissa and Max are up to.

Not that they're up to anything. They're only . . . negotiating. Outrageously, judging by that tinkling laugh on her side. It's enough to make someone throw up an asparagus thing.

"I don't want to let him down," Gina says.

"Max?"

She shoots me a weird look. "James. And Max, I suppose, because James does actually care what he thinks. They're very close. I want to make my fiancé proud."

"You will." So Gina is a little rough around the edges—it's all part of her charm. It wasn't so long ago that I needed a little polishing. Okay, a lot. Believe me, I was no picnic after my mom died and I ended up in foster care. It took a couple of special people to shape me into what you see now.

Of course, the new, improved me wasn't enough for my ex, Jeremy. I know what it's like to feel not quite up to par.

"I'm going to make sure your day is perfect. And a perfect wedding day starts with a perfect wedding dress."

Gina closes her eyes, and when she opens them again, they're shiny. "Thank God you said that. You're going to help gussy up this pig in shit?"

I think of all the wedding mags back at my office and my planner's heart grows three sizes. "Perfect Day is on the case."

CHAPTER 6

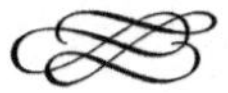

"The most important four words for a successful marriage:
'I'll do the dishes.'"

——UNKNOWN

Charlie

"*A*re you hiding out in here?" a soft voice inquires behind me.

I take a slug of the nice rosé I brought, but it goes down the wrong way. My choked out "no, no, I'm not!" sounds desperately false.

Of course, I'm not hiding out in my friends' kitchen! I'm *recovering* after spending the whole night in performance mode. I did my duty, waved goodbye to the poor stooge who was rolled in for inspection, and now I'm letting the man leave in peace.

Penny Kim, bestie and date-hawker, narrows her eyes at me, clearly not buying what I'm selling. Pushing back her glossy fall of black hair, she lowers her voice. "I thought you'd like him. He cures cancer. Kid cancer."

She makes me sound like a monster, but she's not wrong. I am. An ingrate who can't appreciate when her friend invites the most eligible men in Chicago to perfectly appointed dinner parties in her perfectly appointed Wicker Park home where she lives with her perfectly appointed husband. Who I introduced her to, by the way.

Mr. Perfect—Penny's boo and my other bestie/co-worker, Nathan—walks in and circles her from behind, landing a kiss on her exposed shoulder, though he has to bend because he's six feet two to her five feet squat. I inwardly sigh my appreciation at their adorableness, but outwardly grunt my discontent.

"Uh, do you mind?"

"Aw, you jealous?" Nathan grins while Penny looks at me with a head tilt of *poor Charlie.* "Guess you shouldn't have set us up. Now we're trying to return the favor and do you appreciate it? Not one iota."

More wine, more of my shoulders sinking in dejection. "He's very nice but he's so . . ."

"Good-looking?" Penny offers.

"Upwardly mobile?" Nathan's contribution.

"Flawlessly sainted," I finally say now that I'm allowed to. What use would I be to a pediatric oncologist? The man's saving lives while I'm—damn, here I am letting Jeremy into my head. He never considered my job to be important enough, and while I talk a good game to the likes of Max Henderson, familiar doubts have a habit of dropping acid into the crevices in my self-assurance.

Time for a little build-me-up-Buttercup. *You're not a rocket scientist but you're creating memories. Crafting the happiest moments of a couple's new life together. This is worthy.*

"He's a bit too untouchable for me," I say, feeling my

tongue loosen now that I know the saint has left for the evening. "A really nice guy but I can't imagine us together. Maybe it's too soon."

Nathan frowns, recognizing that this is my fallback position when I feel cornered. "It's been more than a year," he says gently.

"Eighteen months," Penny clarifies, less gently.

"There are only so many Jeremy Cravens in the world," Nat continues. "Don't lump us all in the same basket."

I smile, uneasy at the mention of my ex's name. Jeremy did a number on me all right, but I'm determined to get back on that horse. Just sidesaddle for a while.

"If only you didn't kiss like an anteater," I tell Nathan.

"And if only you didn't taste so . . . bland," he returns with a pitying headshake. Our one attempt at romance in freshman year was a disaster but it led to this—these two people I love finding each other.

He pulls Penny into his side and kisses the top of her head. "I'm going to unsubtly leave the room and clear plates, so you can get a little girl time and not so surreptitiously check out my great ass."

"As if we'd bother," his wife says with a pat on his great ass.

We watch his exit, and I offer a whistle of appreciation. It's a thing we do.

Penny turns to me. "Is this really about Jeremy? I know he hurt you, but Nat is right. There are tons of guys who would be perfect—I've introduced every surgeon, anesthesiologist, and plain old doctor I know, as well as a few non-physician types. You're not bad to look at—"

I raise a glass in thanks.

"So what's the problem?"

"I'm trying to be open-minded." Penny works as a fundraiser at Lurie Children's Hospital so she has access to this great pool of dating talent. It's how I met Jeremy, at one of the galas she organized. "But these days every guy I meet makes me second-guess all my instincts. I used to be able to trust them. Now all they're good for is big, clanging warnings. Ding, ding, ding! Assholes and players at twelve o'clock."

Like Max. Every alarm in my body is telling me he's trouble. I don't like him, yet he's managed to carve a rut into my mind. Or somewhere lower. I'm not proud of it.

Penny waves in front of my face. "Hey, where did you go?"

"Oh, nowhere nice. Just thinking about this incredibly annoying individual I had to deal with this afternoon during a tasting at The Peninsula."

"A client?"

"Brother of a client, who's acting like I'm trying to cheat him out of the family fortune and spend it all on appetizers."

"The Henderson family fortune?"

"How did you know?"

She grins. "Are we or are we not in the same book club? Gina said James Henderson is her fiancé so I'm guessing you're talking about Max?"

I perk up, demonstrating a lot more interest than I displayed three hours ago when I was introduced to Saint Kiddie Cancer Doc. "You know him?"

"I know the name. The family has a wing of the hospital named after them. Max donated his trust fund about five years ago."

"You mean he's not rolling in it anymore?"

Penny chuckles. "Well, he might have kept a couple of mil back for pin money. Each of the sons came into a ten million dollar trust from the Henderson meat money when they turned twenty-five, but the family has a history of philanthropy, so rather than spend it on hookers and coke, Max turned most of his share over. He could've kept it and not worked another day in his life but I guess he likes coming down and breathing the air of the common folk every now and then. He's not a pauper by any stretch but neither is he the prince he could have been." Her eyes mist over in memory. "I met him once. Movie star handsome, but I hear he's a bit of a player."

"Yeah, but it's more than that. He's cynical with it. A divorce attorney who really relishes his work of ripping marriages apart." I shudder, preferring to think it's because Max's profession makes me ill, though I suspect it's down to my memory of how Max assessed me this afternoon before the tasting. Like he wanted to taste *me*.

"And?"

"And what?"

"You're attracted to him."

My laugh is nervy. "He's attractive. Objectively attractive, which is not the same thing as being attracted to him. I dislike him intensely. He represents everything I despise and has no respect for what I do. He made a pass at me the first time I met him and—and—well, I'll admit I was tempted for a smidge of a second. But I certainly don't like him."

I punctuate this last statement with a swallow of the final drop in my glass. So, there!

Penny is still staring, her navy-dark eyes over-bright, her lips in a curve. Here it comes . . . the finger wag.

"You want him."

"No, I don't."

"Oh, you do. You've never been so affected by a guy in all the time I've known you. Not even Jeremy. With him, you were so . . . careful."

"That's ridiculous." Not the "careful with Jeremy" observation because she's right. I maintained a very precise image around him. But we all do that until we're sure it's safe to show our true selves, don't we? Problem is, that as soon as I let him see the real me, he wasn't interested. "Did you not hear a word I said? Max Henderson is the complete opposite to what I want in a guy. Rich—"

"Not so much. Cancer wing, or at least a quarter of it, is Henderson money."

"Entitled. Cynical." I'm counting off on my hand, hoping I have enough dickish traits to make at least five. Coming up short on the ring finger is a little too symbolic and just won't do. "Smug. A player." *Yes!*

I could start a count on the other hand. *Charming. Attractive. Sexy. Funny.*

Just four, and at least two of them are synonymous. The cons have it!

"So he's interested?" Penny asks, just as Nathan reappears with a stack of plates. "Maybe you should use him to work out your sexual frustration."

"I'm not sexually frustrated," I insist, sounding very, very frustrated.

Nat snorts. "You've been snapping at people—i.e., me—constantly over the last few months, usually coinciding with the morning after a date," he says while loading plates in the dishwasher. Penny leads me to a seat at the kitchen island, our usual place to relax after dinner while we watch her husband clean up. "Dates where I assume you're not getting some," Nat finishes.

I suppose I have been a little irritable, but because I haven't had any in almost a year? That's ludicrous. Sex, or the lack of it, does not dictate my moods.

"How was she today?" Penny asks. "Later this afternoon, in particular."

Nathan folds his arms, looking thoughtful. "Prickly. I almost considered uninviting her to tonight's dinner but I had hopes . . ." He waves off to the living room and the ghost of Saint Kiddie Doc who my ungrateful, gagging-for-it self can't appreciate.

"She had a run-in with him today," Penny says to her husband.

"Who?"

"Max Henderson, brother of one of your clients. They have a sexy-hate thing going on."

Nat rubs his chin. "Oh, that's interesting."

"No, it's not!" I finally manage to get a word in. I should never have introduced these two who have this weird simpatico thing where they operate as a single entity. "If I slept with him, I wouldn't respect myself in the morning. In fact, I wouldn't have to wait until the morning. The moment the deed was done, I'd feel nauseous. Like I'd made a huge mistake."

"But you're already considering sleeping with him."

"No."

Penny grabs my hand and squeezes. "You've thought of the consequences. Weighed them. Made an assessment. Which means you've considered the hot 'n' filthy act that would lead to the consequences. Maybe . . ."

"Considered it in detail," Nathan finishes with a smile that pops the dimples beloved of my brides. "This Max guy is already featured in your dirty, feverish brain. That's promising."

"Is it?" I say, a touch hysterically. Where's the wine?

"Very," my former best friend and possibly former employee says. "When have you last shown any interest in a guy like that?"

"That's what I said!" Penny chimes in, and then they gaze at each other in appreciation of being completely in sync. Sickening.

"Now, listen, idiots-in-love, I'm not sleeping with the brother of a client. That has to be ethically dubious." Serious side-eye thrown my way at that. "And even if it wasn't, I don't like him. I can't sleep with someone I don't like." Can I?

"It would probably be pretty hot." Penny shoots a dagger of a look at Nathan. "God, I hate when you don't rinse off the dishes first, you dick."

Nathan blinks in surprise, but quickly catches on.

"Well, I hate when you nag me about rinsing off the dishes. If you despise my methods so much, why don't you do it yourself?"

Penny gives a little shimmy of pleasure. "This antagonism thing is kind of working! And we're just faking it. Imagine how sexy it must be when you really don't like someone."

"I'm supposed to be looking for the one." I think of my dad and what I promised him. "Not fantasiz—considering—a fling with someone who is such a bad idea I can't think of a worse one." It's also a little too close to what the man himself said, about how I could enjoy myself while looking for Mr. Right. Max Henderson basically offered me the use of his body for sexual purposes. Like he's performing a community service.

"And one shot—or two if he's any good or you need a booster—will put your pipes back in order," Penny adds cheerfully in her "problem solved" voice. "And make you less testy at work."

"Yeah, Charlie," Nat says. "Do it for your co-workers. Meaning me. Your only co-worker."

"I'm not screwing some guy I don't even like to make your life easier."

Nathan rolls his eyes affectionately at his wife. "Worst. Boss. Ever."

CHAPTER 7

"Marriage is a wonderful invention: then again, so is the bicycle repair kit."

— BILLY CONNOLLY

Max

I'm back in Lincoln Park just after six a.m. on an earlier-than-usual run, trying to get in shape for the marathon in October, which I'll be running on behalf of Mercy Homes as I do every year. Today is motions day and I'm scrolling through the list in my head, enjoying the quiet and the crispness of an early May morning. There's a low buzz of sound from the odd few cars on Lake Shore to my left and Stockton to my right but nothing that interferes with my well-ordered mind.

The very fine ass of the female runner up ahead does the trick, though.

59

This park is typically safe but I wouldn't want any woman I cared even the slightest jot for out here when there's hardly anyone around. Torn between thinking I should overtake her quickly so as not to scare her and liking how the distance gives me the perfect vista of that heart-shaped gift, I elect to slow my pace a little. Nimble and lithe, she's possessed of great form as she maintains a steady rhythm along the running path. Every stride of her strong legs seems to emphasize her musculature, particularly in her nicely shaped thighs, calves—*and* we're back to that ass.

My dick stirs, which is not my usual when I'm jogging behind an attractive woman. I expect it has less to do with this woman and more to do with the fact my mind has spent far too much time on one Charlie Love.

I have to admit I enjoyed that taste-testing business. It felt like we were a team—even though her goal is to take my brother for a ride, and my goal is to ensure he gets everything he's ever dreamed of since he was a little girl while *not* being taken for a ride. As you've probably figured out, these goals are mutually exclusive, yet I liked how we both agreed on the food. This, I know, is preposterous. Why the hell am I latching onto this island of consensus in an ocean of disagreement? I'm not interested in Charlie Love, except maybe I am—or I'm interested enough to have turned down a sure thing with a woman Grant introduced me to at an ethics update/wine-tasting event last night. A stunning redhead, an environmental lawyer, and definitely interested. However, when push came to shove, I shoved myself right out the door and made my way back to my apartment.

So involved am I in my thoughts that I don't realize I've caught up with the runner and done exactly what I'd sworn I wouldn't do—scared the crap out of her. She does a weird zigzag ninja move like a scalded cat and jumps three feet to the right, where she lands in the grass, right on that ass I was just admiring.

"Damn, sorry 'bout that," I say at the same moment it dawns on me.

"You!" Charlie exclaims, like I'm the 'stache-twirling villain of the piece.

"Hey, I had no idea that was you." I hold out my hand. "But I admire your reflexes. Much better than the last time."

"When you stood on me." She takes my hand, likely because it would seem churlish not to. Again, I feel the spark and the widening of her eyes tells me I'm not alone in this.

"I don't think we ever made a final determination on fault that last time. But for this one, I accept full blame and am willing to make restitution." We're still holding hands, and I pray she doesn't withdraw anytime soon. Continuing to babble—and this is what I'm doing—seems to be a most awesome plan. "In fact, I'll even stump for a post-run coffee."

It takes her a moment but finally she responds. "Do you live around here?"

"I do. Over in the Gloucester on Fullerton."

"Nice building."

It is. "You?"

"I live on Wrightwood. Just moved into a condo about a month ago." She says it with something that sounds like— pride? I guess her business must be doing well, or well enough for her to move into a nicer place in a better neighborhood. Maybe her first time as a homeowner.

Weirdly, I feel proud of her, and I think that inspires the next thing I say.

"You know, this park might seem safe but running when there aren't that many people about is probably not a good idea."

Her eyes narrow, and her hand drops mine like it's a

slimy rock. I don't care that I've offended her; she needs to hear it.

"I can handle myself."

"I don't doubt it, but it seems foolish to put yourself in a situation where you have to."

She can't argue with that, and she doesn't even try.

"Mind if I run with you for a while?" I ask. "I have about fifteen minutes left."

"So you can play bodyguard, Mr. Henderson?"

"We're back to the mister? Come on, Charles. Thought we'd moved beyond that."

In my head, I've moved way beyond that. I've moved so far beyond it we're not even finishing this run. We're heading right to a steamy shower and I'm soaping her up all over, my hands cupping those perfect tits, my cock stroking through the cleft of her heart-shaped ass as I figure out which position will get me deepest and get her off quickest.

After which I'll start all over again.

"It's hard to determine where we stand with the whiplash of moods you present, Max. One minute I'm the matrimonial Antichrist, the next I'm a damsel in distress."

"Can't you be both? And I wouldn't even limit you to those two roles."

She fists her hips, ready for a fight. "Oh? How else do you see me?"

"Savvy businesswoman, ninja jogger, smart, and sexy." I could add "the woman who would look amazing against my fifteen hundred thread count sheets" but I elect to stick with the romance.

"Just because you add in the words 'savvy' and 'smart' doesn't make your shtick any more palatable, Henderson."

"Just calling it how I see it."

Somehow in the last minute or so we've moved closer, each sexy little jab acting like magnets to bind us together. I know it's a cliché to want what resists you, but as she already thinks I'm a cliché, then I'm okay with playing that role.

She resists ergo I press on.

Or at least I think I'm okay with it, except there's a look on her face, an expression that tells me she'd like to think there's more to me. That maybe I shouldn't sell myself short as a fun stop on her road to the real thing. That maybe I could be someone's reality as well as a fantasy.

That maybe I could be hers.

This is confirmed with her next words. "Perhaps we should start over."

All my life I've been surrounded by strong women—my grandmother, my mom, schoolmates, and college friends, even my former fiancée. I want a woman who'll go toe-to-toe with me and keep me honest, who won't play mind games and will tell me when I'm being a jerk. My female role models would expect no less.

Charlie's different from any other woman I've wanted, so using the same tactics is foolish. Don't get me wrong—she's also annoying as hell, a bit of a pill, and snarky with it. But I think that would make the sex fantastic and the conversation spirited. I'd never be bored with Charlie Love.

A lock of hair has escaped her hair tie, and I fold it behind her ear. It's calculated, or at least it's always felt that way. A part of my playbook. But with Charlie, it feels like a tentative gesture toward a new understanding.

My heart beats wildly, knowing we're on the cusp of something important.

"I'm Charlie," she says, almost shyly. She senses the significance of what's happening here, too. "I make people's dreams come true."

I don't even smirk, so taken am I with this shift in our dynamic.

"Hi, Charlie. I'm Max and I'm—"

"A grade-A asshole!"

Now, this charming sobriquet does not emerge from either me or Charlie, but from a third person who's decided to crash the party. We both turn to the source of the insult, and my once light-as-air heart plummets to the running path at the sight of Mitzi von Stueben.

Mitzi, as you might guess from the name, comes from excellent Teutonic stock—tall, blond, with thighs that could crush a lesser man. She marches over, but because she's dragging a tiny little dog by a leash, this takes longer than it should.

"Mitzi!" I need to handle this carefully because—*too late.* She has already decided how this is going to go, and it's not going to reflect well on me.

"Did you think you could just string me along, promise me the moon, and then cut and run like a thief in the night?"

This is really over the top, even for Mitzi. I never promised her a thing, but I don't really plan to get into the he said/she said here in the middle of Lincoln Park.

"Mitzi, who's your buddy?"

Thrown for a second, a temporarily deflated Mitzi looks down at the tiny dog, then back up at me. Rebounding, she addresses Charlie.

"Whatever he promises you, don't believe it. Like lazy Sunday brunches and doing the *New York Times* crossword puzzle and getting a dog together!"

While Mitzi did talk about brunch to such an extent that every time I heard a word starting with the *br* sound, my brain did a control-alt-delete, I can't recall excessive mentions of the *NYT* crossword puzzle. Maybe sudoku. The dog thing, though—that's very familiar.

"So you got yourself a puppy, Mitzi. He's downright adorable."

"He's a fucking shit factory, Max. We were supposed to raise him together—"

I never promised that. Would I have actually promised Mitzi a joint dog-raising situation to get her into bed? No way. The woman did not need the incentive.

She did seem to have her sights set on me for a stroll down the aisle from the beginning. Now that I think of it, she was talking about getting a dog from date one along with copious mentions of eggs Benedict. When I fucked her, she *sounded* like a yappy little dog. I mean, it was sexy, but can you see why I'm confused?

"Mitzi, I work such long hours. There's no way I would have ever committed to a dog." Never mind the fact she and I aren't *actually* dating.

"Well, it's time you recognized that promises have consequences. He's a cockapoo, by the way."

"A cockawhat?"

But she's no longer listening as she's already shoved the leash in my hand. Shocked, I wrap my hand around it while trying to wrap my head around what's happening here. In a complete daze, I watch Mitzi turn tail and march off.

I look down at the canine interloper, then up at Charlie. "Did she just dump her dog on me?"

Charlie isn't even bothering to hide her amusement. "I think she dumped *your* dog on you."

No, no, this is freakin' bonkers. "Mitzi!" I call out but she merely gives me the finger. Hell, if she'd shown that much backbone while we were together, I might have continued with whatever we had going.

Peering down once more, I meet a pair of soft brown eyes with blond strands of hair sheltering them. The little beastie is one of *those* dogs, the ones that crap on rugs, bite small children, and then tilt their heads with a look of "who, me?" I'm not buying it.

"I know where she lives," I say to Charlie, but really it's to myself because I suspect I've lost the room. "I'll drop it off later. Unless you're in the market for a cute little doggie for your new place."

Charlie raises her hands. "Sorry, Henderson, you're on your own here. I've got a run to finish. See ya!"

And off she jogs, with her ninja reflexes and blond perfection and heart-shaped ass, leaving me with a pile of orphaned fur on a leash.

CHAPTER 8

"It's no good pretending that any relationship has a future if your record collections disagree violently, or if your favorite films wouldn't even speak to each other if they met at a party."

— NICK HORNBY

Max

If you look up the word "quitter" in the dictionary, you will not find a photo of Max Henderson. No, siree. I've never quit anything in my life, and hell if there hasn't been a metric shit ton of things I should have laid down tools for and given up the fight.

Courtney Ellison was one of those things. Well, not a thing, a girl, who told me in the fifth grade that she'd never sit with me in the cafeteria because I wasn't good enough for her. Yes, my friends, there was a time when I didn't have all my gifts working to full capacity, and this was largely down to the late development of one of my best attributes.

Get your mind out of the gutter. I'm talking about my gift of gab.

You see, I didn't always have this facility with the spoken word. I stuttered as a kid—pretty badly—and it took a lot of speech therapy and a whole lot more willpower for me to rectify that situation and become the smooth-talking guy I am today. It's one of the reasons why I chose the law. Words matter. Crafting words into a persuasive argument matters. Being able to talk myself into and out of anything is one of the hallmarks of my success.

When I was finally able to string a sentence together and speak it to Courtney Ellison without tripping over it, her attitude to me changed overnight. Or over mac 'n' cheese at Lake Forest High. She couldn't see herself with a guy who could barely speak, no matter how cute or rich he was. That's when I learned that looks and money mean nothing. What we say counts. How we use our words says more about a person than a square jaw or a fat wallet.

I wouldn't quit speech therapy because I was determined to win Courtney over. Once I had—once she invited me to sit with her and her friends in the school cafeteria—I never spoke to her again. I wasn't magically cured, and I still had work to do, but I would no longer waste my precious words on a girl who didn't understand sacrifice. Who didn't recognize their magic.

The reason I bring up the "never a quitter" thing is because I'm about ready to quit being a fucking dog owner.

So the dog's not technically mine, but I've been placed in loco parentis by its true owner, one Ms. Mitzi von Stueben, who has decided to flee the country rather than let me off the hook. I truly believe she planned a trip to Paris, bought the doggie, then waited until I was flirting with another woman in Lincoln Park before she dumped him on me. It's pretty elaborate as revenge plots go, but I've seen plenty of this bullshit in my job so nothing surprises me.

This puppy is a yapper. A yelper. A howler. Luckily I'm on the penthouse floor of my building and the insulation is decent enough so as not to disturb my downstairs neighbor, an oil commodities broker who I know would be doing the equivalent of a broomstick against the ceiling (i.e., sending up Benji the doorman) if he could hear the dog's screeches. The fact that my neighbors aren't being disturbed is no comfort. I am being disturbed. I am being inconvenienced but I can't do a thing about it until Mitzi comes back. "Drop it off at a shelter," Grant said, but that's not an option. The little bugger gives me The Eyes, knowing I'm another one of those suckers born every minute.

I expect when I return home he'll have crapped all over my Java hardwood floors—at least he would have if I didn't lock him in the guest room where he can instead crap all over the carpet.

Determined to forget my troubles, I head down the aisle at Wrigley on the way to my seat for tonight's game. I wouldn't mind but I was definitely making progress with Charlie before Mitzi dumped the beast on me. I didn't enjoy that smug look on La Love's face, a look that said all her suspicions about me had been confirmed. Suspicions such as: I'm a playboy cad who leads women into thinking they have futures with me that involve brunches, lazy Sundays in bed, crossword puzzles, and yippity-yappy balls of fluff. Not only do I lead these women on, I then crush their hopes to the extent they have no choice but to foist live animals on me in public places! This is not good for my reputation.

Not that I should really care what Charlie thinks of me. But I don't like presenting the wrong impression. I want Charlie—everyone—to see the real Max Henderson.

Sounding like a sap there, bud.

Tonight should be stress-free. Okay, a Cubs game can never be completely stress-free, but it's early enough in the season that I can relax with a couple of beers and some lousy ballpark dog, and kick back with James, Gina, and my dad. Jack's making one of his rare visits to the city because it's Mom's night to volunteer with her literacy group.

As I get closer to the Hendersons' usual seats in the third row behind home base (these season tickets have been in the family for three generations), a flurry corkscrews down my spine. Unless my dad has suddenly taken to sporting a blond wig piled high on top of his head in one of those sexy-messy buns, I'd say tonight will *not* be a night for the Henderson boys to bond.

We meet again, Charlie Love.

I take my seat on the aisle, catching James's eye as I do so and wishing I could wipe that superior smile off his face.

"Hey," I say to Charlie. Gina and James are on her other side. "You're getting better looking every day, Dad."

"He's got a cold," James says, "and Mom insisted on keeping him at home after the last time."

Last time, my dad got a nasty case of pneumonia which dragged on for a month. He's always been so virile that it's hard to imagine him as anything but. Mom's probably being overprotective, but I don't begrudge her this. I like that they take care of each other.

Charlie gives a little shrug. "Gina, James, and I were meeting a while ago to discuss the music for the wedding and they invited me. Hope that's okay."

"Why wouldn't it be okay?" I say in a way that implies I don't think it's okay. I'm not sure why I'm feeling so testy around her. Maybe because in all our interactions so far, she's managed to best me. It's not a contest except that it is.

I always win. I never quit. Words are my weapons.

Now how the hell can I put all that together and ensure I come out on top when it comes to Charlie Love?

On top. I like the sound of that, though to be honest I wouldn't mind which of us did the honors. Tonight she's wearing one of those blouses with long sleeves where the shoulders are exposed through slits in the fabric. It's black with pink and orange flowers on it, and I think I could spend all night counting each exposed freckle and inventing dirty tasks to get her off.

This little freckle sent my fingers delving.

This little freckle got a swipe of my tongue.

This little freckle made my mouth water.

This little freckle had a shitload of fun.

And this little freckle made Charlie scream, scream, scream while I pumped all the way home.

Her jeans hug her thighs, and I've no doubt they show the same love to her ass. I wouldn't mind showing her ass some love of my own, squeezing its perfection, slipping my fingers between her beautiful thighs to find her so hot and—

"Max." It would seem James has been trying to get my attention.

"What?"

"Beer, asshole."

Yes, bro, your beer is definitely more important than my fantasy sex life. James is sort of pissed with me because I dared to suggest that he consider a pre-nup. With his wealth, it's common sense, but raising the topic has created a weird distance between us.

I flag down the beer guy who usually trolls this section. After I get Buds for everybody, Charlie tries to grease my palm with a ten dollar bill.

"I can spot you a beer, Charles."

"Okay, but I'm getting the next round."

I don't agree or disagree. No woman needs to buy her own beer in my presence.

As we settle in, she asks, "How's your doggie guest?"

"Man's best friend. Where the best friend is a whiny little shit who scratches the furniture, pees on my hearth rug, and will only eat top-quality steak."

"Back up a second. Did you say hearth rug?"

She's amused, and I'm immediately on edge. Nothing good can come from whatever answer I give her.

"Yes, I did say that."

"I'm imagining the pelt of a tiger stretched out before a roaring fire. Maybe there's a button beneath the coffee table that, when pressed, reveals a hidden recessed alcove with brandy snifters. Another button shutters the windows and—"

"Drops the needle on an LP of *Neil Diamond's Greatest Hits,*" I finish for her.

Her mouth scrunches up in query. "LP?"

"Long-playing, Charles. That's what we used to call the music-making thingies. Frisbee-shaped gizmos that make sounds. Way before your time."

She grins. "That hearth rug must see a lot of action."

"Right now, it's seeing a lot of Cujo."

"Cujo? Are you kidding? He was so cute."

"Try living with him." The first inning's about to start, and my gaze is taking it all in. The usual suspects in my section, the batting lineup, the—

"Shit. That's all we need."

Charlie follows my gaze.

"Muller," we both say at the same time, then turn to each other, surprised.

"I fucking hate that guy," she continues. "Worst umpire in baseball."

"Worst official in pro sports," I offer, my heart beating in recognition. If this woman wasn't such a true believer in all that wedding mumbo jumbo I would be bringing out every tool in my arsenal: the hearth rug, the brandy snifters, Neil freakin' Diamond.

Two spots of color appear on her cheeks. She's felt that zing of connection, too, but she's torn. She's already made up her mind I'm a player and not worth her time, but every now and then I surprise her and put her on the back foot. For the next nine innings, she's going to be fighting her attraction to me and I'm going to be doing my best to make her lose that battle.

"Play ball," I murmur, then return my attention to the field.

By the top of the fourth inning, I'm two beers in and the Cubbies are three runs down. As foretold in the Book of Max, the losing situation is compounded by the presence of Lars Muller, the worst umpire in Major League Baseball. He's denied Rizzo a run, claiming an illegal slide that wouldn't have held up in a court of law but somehow made the grade tonight. The strike calls are a joke and Maddon's already gotten up in Muller's grille. It's only made the bastard more recalcitrant.

The game might be a farce, but every moment of pain is worth it because not only does it piss off Charlie, it gets her royally riled up. Now my section is filled with die-hard fans, some of them like me with third-generation season tickets. If one of us can't make it, he or she texts Casper (that's not his name but he's a pasty-faced Irish guy who has never missed a game). Casper fills in the section for births, deaths, unavoidable kids' concerts—you get the idea. Tonight the guy is in his usual seat, the row behind me, two seats over, and every decision that doesn't go the Cubs way is like the loss of his firstborn. It doesn't take long for him to recognize a kindred soul in Charlie, who is on her feet whenever Muller screws up.

"You see that?"

For the first ten times, I agreed with her that I had indeed seen it. But my reaction obviously wasn't enough for Charlie, which is when Casper steps into the breach.

"Guy's an asshole," Casper says encouragingly. "Remember when he screwed the pooch on the Crosstown Classic last year?"

Charlie turns, hands raised, her delicate features more animated than I've seen, well, anyone. "He's been screwing the pooch for thirty years too long. Should've retired years ago." She stands up. "You're a bum, Muller! A lousy, no good bum!"

This draws a cheer from our section and several other people nearby. A few scowls, too, but I'm having far too good a time to be bothered. Charlie in a righteous rage means Charlie getting loose. It means Charlie standing up so I get a great view of her ass. (I was right, those jeans were made to love that ass.) It means Charlie plopping down, shaking her head in indignation, her perfume mingling with the night air and making me hard.

The officials are used to a few heckles. They've got to be thick-skinned, but even Muller shoots a look over his shoulder at that one.

If I'd read the situation right I would have handled it differently but I'm too caught up in the glory of Charlie. It's not often you meet a girl who knows her baseball, can throw down beers with the best of them, and isn't afraid to take it to the mat. I'm so busy admiring her that when the next play kicks off I'm too far gone to foresee the situation in the making.

Top of the ninth, and the Cubs are leading 5–4, a miracle considering the level of umpiring we have to tolerate. The

Cardinals are at bat with two out, but have a player on third, a slowpoke called Pallas who really should lay off the hot dogs. We need one more out, boys. That's all we need.

Casey for the Cards hits a ground ball to second base and Pallas starts his lumber home, Frankenstein in cleats. Bryant scoops up the ball, throws it to catcher Contreras at home base and good ol' Will does his job: He tags Pallas out two feet before he reaches home.

That fucker Muller calls Pallas safe.

War breaks out in the ballpark, everyone on their feet, screaming their heads off. The bench clears, our section is in disbelief, but we've got the replay, right?

Wrong. Maddon is out of challenges, leaving it up to the crew chief to initiate a replay. Muller must have something good on him because the chief elects not to exercise his right.

No one who calls themselves a Cubs fan approves of this decision. No one. James and Gina are enraged in a cute couple kind of way. Casper is mumbling like he's about to go into catatonic shock. I'm pretty upset myself, but boy I've got nothing on Charlie.

She's screaming blue murder at Muller. This guy better have security leaving the park tonight because Charlie will have his balls for maracas if she gets close enough. Every name you can think of and a few I've never heard of are lobbed like grenades over the bull pen.

Yeah, it sucks because instead of the out that would have ended the game, we have the run that tied it up. Instead of everyone heading to Cubby Bear for celebratory beers, we've got to wait it out in the cooling evening and see if our boys can bring it home in the bottom of the ninth. Assuming we can get out of this half of the inning without giving up any more runs.

Spoke too soon, Max. Buoyed by their oh-so-lucky call, the Cards go on a streak, pulling in three more runs over the course of the next ten minutes. Each one is a stab to the heart.

"This is a travesty," Charlie says, then stands up and shouts, "You're a travesty, Muller! Take a hike!"

Thirty seconds later, she has the entire section screaming "Take a hike!" at Muller. He faces the crowd, hands on his wide hips, wearing the face of a bulldog who's just sucked down a catcher's mitt for a snack and enjoyed the hell out of it.

"Take a hike!"

Muller stares the mob down.

"Take a hike!"

He turns his back, but it doesn't stop the taunts. That's when security decides to get involved. A big bruiser of a guy stands in the aisle next to our row and calls out: "You need to quiet down."

It's said generally to the section but it's clearly aimed at everyone's favorite rabble-rouser, Charlie Love. Ignoring him, she continues with her campaign. "Get off the field, Muller. There are donuts in the clubhouse with your name on 'em!"

Of all the things to offend an MLB official, I would not have thought this was it. But Muller looks at Charlie and somehow telepathically communicates his displeasure at *this* particular heckle.

"All right, out," Security Guy says.

"What?" From her now sitting position, Charlie looks down her nose at him though he's a foot and a half taller than her. "You're making me leave?"

"You're disturbing the players and the fans in this section."

"Am I disturbing you?" She arcs a hand over the people in our section, all of whom have been greatly digging her enthusiasm. Sure, don't we all love people who express our sentiments in a way that's (*a*) hilarious and (*b*) ensures we don't have to put ourselves out on a limb?

"Leave her be," Casper mutters.

Time to unveil Chivalrous Max. "Any chance we could let this go?" I smile at Security Guy. I usually recognize most of the employees who walk this section, but I've not seen him before. "I'll make sure she behaves."

Yep, I said that. Have you met Max Henderson, stone cold idiot?

"*Make sure I behave?* What, keep the uppity woman in her place?"

I turn, imploring with my eyes. "That's not what I meant. I'm trying to get everyone back to the game."

During this hubbub, the show has gone on and you've guessed it: the Cards choose this inopportune time to score *another* home run.

Charlie screams an expletive, clearly aimed at Muller, who while not responsible directly for this run, is really the founder of all that is fucking fucked-up about this fucking game.

"That's it," Security Guy says and reaches across me—to lay a hand on Charlie's arm.

A fierce protectiveness rears in my chest, so sudden it surprises me. Security Guy doesn't make it so far as laying a hand on Charlie because I push back. I push *him*. Hard.

And that's how I get sent to Cubs jail.

CHAPTER 9

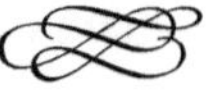

"Being married means mostly shouting 'What?' from other rooms."

— UNKNOWN

Charlie

I really should be angrier than this, but it seems all my negative emotion expired out in the ballpark. I spent a good chunk of my teen years managing my feelings, trying to channel my passion into appropriate avenues like ambition, productivity, and societal acceptance. When my mom died, I was left with a lot of grief which took the form of rage.

And boy, did I come up with some righteous ways to expend it.

No one could handle me. No one could stand to be around me. I would scream and curse and ensure I was unlovable because God help anyone who dared to think I might have a single redeeming quality. Everything sucked.

Everyone could go fuck themselves. Through two group homes and three fostering situations, I made myself impenetrable. I was a Teflon-coated anger monster.

Tonight, that monster showed herself and tonight, I experienced something sudden and bewildering: a feeling of safety. Max Henderson had stepped in to stop park security from laying a hand on me. Of all people, I would not have expected this man to come to my aid.

He doesn't look too pleased about it, though.

In the small room where security has stowed us to either cool off or wait for the police, Max is pacing, his ridiculously handsome face crumpled in annoyance.

"Do you want to call someone?" I ask.

"Like who? A lawyer?"

Sarcasm noted.

"I'm sure they'll let us go with a slap on the wrist. It's really not a big deal." Maybe he's worried about his reputation as an enforcer of the law.

"What the hell were you thinking, Charlie?"

"I was thinking Muller is an idiot." He was. He is. "The guy's blind!"

"But he's not deaf, is he? You can't scream insults at game officials and not expect consequences."

"So I should have just zipped my mouth and acted like the quiet little woman?"

"Don't do that."

"Do what?"

"Make this about feminism or getting beaten down by the patriarchy. It's about common sense and respect. Sure, Muller's an idiot and your running commentary was highly entertaining—"

"You thought so?"

He smiles. I wish he hadn't. I wish he'd keep that weapon to himself because it's lethal.

"I thought so. I'm not sure I'd heard some of those terms before. Douchewaffle was my favorite."

Now I'm smiling like a loon. "The truth had to be told, Max."

"Sure, but you had your fun and then when the people who control who stays and who goes got involved, then it was time to dial it back, oh, five hundred percent."

He's right. I know this, but I hate it. I hate feeling like that angry girl again, even if the stakes are as low as screaming invective at a ballgame official. I'm never going to find a man if I can't rein in that part of myself that's unpalatable to the segment of the human race I need to impress.

One of *them* stands before me. Not that Max Henderson is on my radar as husband material, but he is a sought-after member of the male species. Smart, handsome, upwardly mobile, a Ken-doll model for the guy I'd like to meet.

And Ken's looking at me now, his head tilted, his inquisitive blue eyes narrowing.

"What?" I ask, a little flustered at his scrutiny.

"Something happened just there." He does a corkscrew gesture with his index finger. "You toggled some sort of switch."

I swallow because that's a pretty accurate description of what I just did.

"Sometimes I need to make a conscious effort not to murder the person nearest to me, especially when he's a smug, supercilious, know-it-all douchewaffle."

He laughs. I like his laugh. It tickles a spot in my stomach.

"I'm getting the douchewaffle treatment now? Lumped in with Muller?" He steps in closer. "You know, that security guy had it coming. I just didn't want to see you manhandled."

"Even if I deserved it for shooting my mouth off?"

The mention of my mouth seems to act like a lever for his

gaze. It drops to the mouth in question, gives it an imaginary lick, and flashes with a flicker of appreciation.

"He had no right to touch you."

The words are said with an intensity that shocks me because one, it's ten minutes past the event, and two, this is Max Henderson, Mr. Smooth 'n' Slick, who seems to operate at a keel so even I'm not quite sure he's a hundred percent human. The only man in my life who's ever made me feel this protected is the one who saved me all those years ago, who saw my potential. I'm not used to feeling it with the guys I date and certainly not with guys like Max Henderson who are chronically undateable.

"You shouldn't have pushed him," I say.

"Because it landed us in here?" He's closer now, leaning over me like that moment when we met in the Gilt Bar.

"Because you could have gotten hurt."

"Aw, you care, Charlie?"

Yes. But I don't like the renewed smirk in his voice. Neither do I enjoy how his personality can shift so quickly between that drilling-my-soul intensity and the flirt he turns on for every woman.

"Because I'm sure you'd find a way to blame me," I say with a check of my nails. "Maybe sue me for your pain and suffering."

"Like I said, he shouldn't have touched you."

Which is when he touches me. Max rubs a thumb along my jaw, causing my entire body to ignite. My quickly drawn breath is necessary to keep me upright but it's also a mistake because it provides oxygen to that spark inside me and fans the flames of desire to the point I'm in danger of burning up. If this is the effect of one simple touch, how would I survive more?

"He was just doing his job," I murmur.

"And I was just doing mine." That thumb now moves over

my chin, trails down my throat, and hovers over the divot above my collarbone. As if he's trying to cover as much ground as possible without involving all his digits. Or his hands. Or all two hundred pounds of rock-solid muscle that I'm now imagining cradled between my legs as he slides in, deep, true, and to the hilt.

"Your job?" My voice sounds annoyingly breathless. "What job?"

"Protecting what's—" I think he rasps out the word "mine" as his mouth descends, stamping a claim over lips that are all too eager to part and let him in. I shouldn't allow this. I shouldn't cling to his hell-those-are-broad shoulders. I shouldn't be moaning my encouragement or reaching up to tunnel greedy fingers through his hair. I shouldn't be making an ass grab to pull him flush because I need that cock I've been dreaming about to notch between my legs and rub there, yes, *there*.

I've kissed my fair share of frogs, a few earls, even a prince or two. I guess that's all been practice as I worked my way up to the royal court of Max. This guy is King of the Kiss. It shouldn't surprise me that he does it well, just as it shouldn't surprise me that my body is reacting like it's a drought-riven land newly doused in water. Like Max is the answer to a lifelong thirst.

He's wedged his body between my legs, one very clever hand cupping my ass, the other holding my face at an angle that works for him. That theory I had before about him attempting to cover as much ground as possible with a single, teasing finger is now being put to the test. Max's body envelops mine in an all-consuming, cell-invasive manner. It should be terrifying, but it's not.

He's an amazing kisser. Not wet or sloppy, not pushy or aggressive. Max kisses me like this is important to him. To us.

"Charlie."

Max's kiss continues to drug me even while awareness of the world around us attempts to break through. Someone is saying my name. Not Max, who is definitely not talking, thank God, but someone familiar . . .

"Charlie!"

Our mouths separate like those of teenagers caught in a parked car. Oh, God. This can't be happening.

"Hey, Sully," I manage. The lips might no longer be *in flagrante* but the hands . . . oh, dear, I'm still enjoying a big, meaty handful of Max's most excellent ass. I let go and step out from behind him to greet the new arrival.

That guy I mentioned earlier, the one who saved me? Meet Frank Ignatius Sullivan.

Until Frank and Donna Sullivan came into my life, I was miserable on my rage-fueled island of one. Here were these two do-gooders pulling ashore with a raft and asking me to climb aboard. I stuck a pin in that raft. But they duct-taped over the hole and pumped the air back in and started over the next day. And the next. Wore me down.

I'd never felt more safe than when Frank took me in his arms and told me I could be a bitch for a while but eventually my real personality would want in on the action. The bitch took a hiatus, then a vacation, then a near-permanent leave. But she still comes back every now and then—this girl can gussy herself up with designer dresses and heels bought at consignment stores, she can turn herself into an in-demand wedding planner who deals with richer-than-Beyoncé clients, she can smile and simper at the sex-in-six-thousand-dollar suits she occasionally dates, but it doesn't take much to unleash her temper-induced potty mouth.

Frank raises one white bushy eyebrow to the ceiling at me, then abandons his disapproval to get a better look at

Max. You think my bullshit detector is finely calibrated? Frank taught me everything I know.

I'll give it to Max. He doesn't wither under Sully's stare, and before anyone gets into anything, I make the introductions, more so my foster dad won't think I'm snogging a complete stranger.

"Sully, this is Max Henderson. Max, Sully."

"Carter said you were making trouble," Sully says, referring to the head of security at Wrigley. He takes a long look at Max, source of the trouble. He's not wrong.

"I had a few choice words for Muller," I start in my defense.

"That asshole. I saw the calls on TV. Meanwhile, I'm up seventy-five bucks in a game, a queen short of a full house, when I get a call telling me my daughter has been arrested."

"Not arrested. Just detained. The security guy looked new, and he started to get a little physical at which point Max stepped in. I had it handled . . ."

Frank's no longer listening, his gaze having pivoted back to Max. "You were protecting my daughter?"

"Trying to. The calls were terrible, but Charlie crossed a line when she refused to back down."

"Hey, wait a second," I say, but Frank is already stepping in to shake Max's hand.

"She's got a temper on her, Max, but she usually knows better than to let it fly in my house."

Max is sizing up Sully. "Frank Sullivan. I know you. You used to run the Wrigley scoreboard up until . . . a year ago?"

"Yep, had to retire. Now I sit around, smoke cigars when my wife's not looking, and play poker. You a poker man, Max?"

I don't hear Max's answer because my brain is currently filled with a rushing sound I know all too well. The signal that I'm about to go she-hulk on these two idiots who are chatting as if I'm no longer here. The anger is a living thing inside me and then suddenly whoosh! it's receding like the tide.

Max's hand is rubbing slow, soothing circles on my back. It's as though he recognized I'm upset, even while engrossed in—still engrossed in—a conversation with Sully about how the scoreboard works. Of course he's a multitasker.

After a minute or so of me losing my mind in a new way, Frank steps in and cups my face.

"I talked to Carter, and no one's going to make any more of this." He kisses me on the forehead. "I won't tell Donna, either."

I sniff the air. "In exchange for keeping your cigar-smoking a secret? You know what the doc said."

Frank splits a grin between me and Max, then his eyes wander to where Max's hand is obviously still at my back. No longer circling, just in a holding pattern that feels much nicer than I care to admit.

"We've all got our secrets, Charlie."

I make a noise of discontent. Frank had a heart attack a year back that prompted his early retirement. Cigars are definitely not part of the recovery plan.

"All right, see you outside," he says. "Good to meet you, Max."

"Sully, you don't have to—" But he's already left. I turn to Max, who's got the megawatt grin on full force. "I don't know why he left first."

"Probably thinks we have unfinished business." His fingers dig into my hip. "You don't have the same name as your dad?"

"My foster dad. Since I was fourteen."

He betrays no surprise at the F-word. "So, you know your way around the park."

"Wrigley's my second home." I move myself two feet

closer to the door, ignoring the quick cool down of that hip indent where his fingers had fit a little too well. "And there's nothing unfinished about our business. What was happening when he walked in was not supposed to happen. You just caught me by surprise, that's all."

"Which is why you threw yourself into it like a nerd in a comic book store the day Stan Lee makes a visit."

"Don't make more of this than it deserves, Max. It was just a kiss. Pretty average, really."

He walks toward me, all that *Max*-imum intensity on display, looking like he's about to call my bluff and prove that kiss was anything but average.

I back up.

He reaches behind me with his hand and . . .

. . . opens the door.

"Don't worry, Charles, your lips are safe for now. But let's not pretend it wasn't amazing. I might prevaricate for a living, but I don't lie about the important stuff. Sweet dreams."

And then he's off, leaving me a little weak-kneed, to be honest. *I don't lie about the important stuff,* he said, and for some strange reason, I believe him.

CHAPTER 10

"Chains do not hold a marriage together. It is threads, hundreds of tiny threads which sew people together through the years."

— SIMONE SIGNORET

Max

"So, did you meet Maddon?"

Grant squints at me from the other side of the booth in the Legal Eagle, a bar we frequent near the law courts. I've just shared my Cubs jail story. It takes a lot to impress the boys, and my visit to the inner sanctum, albeit under less than ideal circumstances, has given me more street cred than I bargained for.

"Nope. But I met Frank Sullivan."

"Who?" Lucas asks much to Grant's and my disgust. Sometimes his Britishness really pisses us off.

"You need to assimilate to our ways, Wright," Grant says. "How the hell can you appreciate Henderson's tale if you're not even aware of who Frank Sullivan is?"

Lucas rolls his eyes so far into the back of his head all we can see is horror-story white. "So, he's a player?"

"He's the former manual scorekeeper," I say impatiently. "Of one of the last remaining manual scoreboards at one of the last remaining neighborhood baseball parks in the country. The guy's part of history." I clear my throat. "And he's the wedding planner's dad."

This makes Lucas smile, because "women" is a subject in which he considers himself an expert. Let me tell you more about our friend from across the pond. A boy genius, he graduated high school at sixteen with a full ride to Oxford. Can crush all comers in pub quiz trivia. Wears ridiculously jaunty hats and manages to pull it off. Has a *Doctor Who* fetish (for Classic Who, prefers the third over the fourth. For New Who, he'll take Capaldi over Tennant. I know, weird.). I have no idea what he's doing slumming with us. He's been a fixture in my life for years, yet I can't help feeling I've barely scratched the surface.

"So, you're defending this woman's honor," Lucas says, "then you get hauled off to Cubs jail, and you meet her father."

"Foster father, actually, but they're close. Very close. He walked in on me making out with her. I felt like I was sixteen all over again."

"Boners in the presence of father figures." Lucas shudders. "I'm getting a de-rection just thinking about it."

"Thought this woman annoyed you," Grant says, massaging us back on topic. "Like *really* annoyed you."

"She does. She really does. But there's something there."

Grant opens his mouth but Lucas holds up a hand. "Please. Let me." He turns to me. "Uh, what, mate?"

"She annoys me, and she interests me. The two are not mutually exclusive, Wright."

"No, they're not. But when you put 'em together, you've got the makings of a bit more than a bang-and-bolt situation." Elbow on the table, he holds his chin thoughtfully like a psychotherapist. Or maybe just a psycho. "Tell me more about the 'something.' Are we talking connection?"

"She's under my skin, that's all. You know what that's like."

Passing over Lucas, who probably doesn't know what that's like, I turn to Grant, who does. He watches me carefully, but elects to keep any comment to himself. My heart checks for him, knowing his pain is still a soul-crushing thing.

And then because it's not enough for the guy to be thinking about it, the embodiment of that pain appears before us.

"Gentlemen," a cool, moneyed voice says.

Aubrey Gates stands outside the booth, all sleek, dark hair, her lovely gray eyes assessing us. She's one of my closest friends—or at least she was until she and Grant officially divorced just over a year ago, though they'd separated a year before that. As a couple, they shouldn't have worked: Grant, the quiet, gentle giant from Georgia, and Aubrey, the Boston society princess who can enthrall a room with her laugh and biting wit. We met at Northwestern Law and became inseparable.

Married right out of law school, Grant and Aubrey defined opposites-attract. And then two years ago it came crashing down. Neither of them would tell me what happened. I assumed cheating but I couldn't imagine either of them sinking so low. After the failure of my engagement to Becca, I'd held my friends' marriage up as a shining beacon. When it dimmed to darkness, it sowed further evidence that love gouged too much from your insides.

I would normally ask her to join us—I miss her like hell—but I know it won't go over well.

"Hey, princess," Lucas says. "Heard you did good work for Gullickson."

Aubrey cracks a brief smile. "Someone had to. You boys wouldn't have been up for the task."

Peter Gullickson is a local news anchor who just went through a bitter divorce. He'd shopped around, coming to us for a consult, but ended up with Aubrey over at Kendall Inc., a big corporate outfit she'd recently joined as their star giant-killer.

"He needed a woman in his corner to make him look good," Grant says quietly to his ex-wife.

Aubrey considers this, waits a beat, and finally says, "All men do."

They hold each other's gaze for an unbearably long moment before she turns to me, as cool as can be. "Heard you got a dog, Henderson. *And* you were playing tongue hockey with a wedding planner in Cubs jail."

I turn slitty eyes of disgust on Lucas. "Really? I just told you. Like five minutes ago." He does have an uncanny ability to text and look like he's paying attention at the same time.

"Can I help it if word of your lawless deviance gets around? It was on camera, mate!"

"But not the fact I was kissing her. In private."

"With her foster dad in the room," Grant says.

"Sounds kinky," Aubrey replies, and Grant turns away slightly, hiding a smile. A flicker of light burns inside me at the thought there might be hope for my friends.

See, I'm not a complete asshole. I love these people, and I want the best for them. I truly believe the best is for them to be together because there are no two people who deserve more to be happy.

Unfortunately, we don't always get what we deserve.

CHAPTER 11

Charlie

"Oh, wow! This place is something else."

Gina takes in the vaulted ceilings, the dripping-with-crystals light fixtures, and the romantic ambience. Lili's Bridal, the salon in Lincoln Park, boasts beautiful windows with natural light and velvet-tufted couches, the perfect spot to get lost in finding a girl's dream dress.

Lili herself steps forward, kisses me on the cheek, and grabs Gina's hand.

"Congratulations! I can't wait to work with you."

Gina grimaces. "I know it's short notice. I really don't need anything too fancy." She looks around, her eyes troubled now by all the fancy. "I'm not really sure what I'd like."

I grip her hand and squeeze it. I know she's feeling out of her depth but I'm here to guide her through it. I can't imagine not having a friend or mom-figure to help me choose my wedding dress.

"Maybe a glass of champagne to get you settled?"

Gina nods. "That I can do."

Forty-five minutes later, I turn to Lili and pronounce, "That's it."

We've gone through two Olegs, a Zac Posen, and a Maggie Sottero, and arrived where I figured we'd end up: a strapless Vera Wang princess gown with a scalloped neckline and a beaded bodice. It has an understated simplicity that will highlight Gina's olive coloring, mahogany hair, and Hershey-drop eyes.

I stand to lead her to the triptych mirror. "What do you think?"

"I think it's four thousand dollars."

This is true, but we've already gone over this. The budget for this wedding can handle an off-the-rack Vera Wang.

"Do you like it?"

Gina rubs her tummy, then adjusts her stance to take in her reflection from a side pose. "It's beautiful."

"You're beautiful," Lili says, handing off another glass of champagne.

I frown at Lili, who merely shrugs, then I remove the glass from Gina's hand. She's only had one glass, but I don't want anyone accusing me of shenanigans later. And by anyone, I mean Max Henderson.

It's been three days since the Cubs game, and I can't stop thinking about that kiss. I've even been on a date since (a CPA who was "ready to go wild!" now tax season was over) and frankly it was ruined because Max was there in my head, telling me he's just doing his job. Not the one where he tears couples apart with relish but that side hustle of his, *protecting me.*

I know it's just a thing that alpha guys say to make a point or a girl swoon. *Well, point taken and girl toppled.* No amount of champagne can remove the taste of him from my mouth. I think of that kiss, and my taste receptors water with awareness.

With the mindset of someone who's tried the same thing over and over, expecting different results—you know, the definition of insanity—I knock back the champagne in my hand. I have no reason to see much of him until the wedding day in nine weeks. And not seeing him will return my taste buds to normal and kick-start my dating life to where it belongs.

Pleased with my determined approach, I redirect my attention to Gina. She's assessing herself in the mirror, but during my time-out to think on my Max problem, she's gone pale.

"Gina, are you okay?"

"I'm—" She swallows and screws up her face.

I recognize that look, but not in time.

She promptly upchucks all over the Vera Wang.

I hand Gina a glass of ginger ale and take a seat beside her on the couch in my condo. I still have some stuff in boxes, but I'm mostly unpacked. *My* home, bought with *my* money. It's an achievement I'm inordinately proud of.

But right now, I have other things on my mind. After Gina hurled all over the wedding dress—a sample (thank God) that can be cleaned (I hope)—we left Lili's Salon with the intention of taking her home. I'd assumed she was hungover because she'd looked a little peaky from the get-go, but Gina asked if she could go to my place, which I'd already mentioned was nearby.

Then she relayed another surprising request.

Now, if you haven't gotten this by now, I hope you realize that my client is number one. I'll accompany her to wedding dress fittings and cake tastings. I'll work my ass off to book that bluegrass-Zydeco band he *has* to have for the reception.

And I'll happily pop into Walgreens, buy an early pregnancy test, and hold her hand while she waits for the results.

"So, what makes you think you're pregnant? Other than the throwing-up-all-over-a-wedding-dress thing?"

Gina gives a tight smile. "Believe me, if I'd known, I would not be knocking back ballpark beer and bridal salon bubbly."

"Hey, I'm not judging."

She sighs. "I haven't felt well for a couple of days but I thought it was prep school flu. I pick up all sorts from the little bastards. I was okay this morning until I started trying on the dresses."

"It could be stress. I see it a lot. The reality of it all hits you and then—"

"The puke hits the dress."

"In a manner of speaking."

Gina covers her face with her hands. "I'm so embarrassed. Lili must hate me, and while I'd like to say I'll pay for it and buy another one, I'm not sure that's possible."

"Don't worry about it. They have coverage."

The timer on my phone goes off. Our joint gaze magnetizes to the bathroom door.

"Are you sure you don't want to call James? Maybe Face-Time him in?"

She looks at me in horror. "No, he's with Max right now, getting his tux fitted. If I call him, he'll be upchucking all over his Armani. Besides, Max is the last person I want to hear this."

I agree wholeheartedly on the Max comment. The Cynic™ does not need to hear about this yet.

Gina stands, a little sway to her frame I attribute to nerves. "Just don't let me do it alone, okay?"

"I'm here for you."

Thirty seconds later . . .

WE'RE HAVING A BABY! (Did you really think it would end any other way?) The tears arrive in full force along with recriminations and some fairly X-rated memories about when conception might have occurred. In a situation with a girlfriend in distress, I'd normally be offering quarts of wine. Instead, I'm the dispenser of ginger ale and back rubs and soothing words.

When she finally wears herself out and dozes off, I send a text to James, telling him to come to my place.

Alone.

CHAPTER 12

"Obviously, if I was serious about having a relationship with someone long-term, the last people I would introduce him to would be my family."

— CHELSEA HANDLER

Charlie

*J*ames and Gina left an hour ago, with Gina feeling a lot better than when she saw the plus sign on the pee stick. Her improved mood might've had something to do with James's reaction.

The man was happiness personified.

Witnessing his joy made my heart swell to epic proportions. He was so gentle with her that my faith in love—a little rattled lately by my own bad memories—was instantly restored. We'll just have to make sure the dress has breathing room and that she's well looked after for the next couple of months.

He and I also had The Talk while Gina was in the bathroom. (*The demon's already playing havoc with my bladder*, she said with a sniff.)

Him: *So, rules of the confessional here, right?*

Me: *I won't breathe a word to anyone, especially your brother.*

Him: *Cool.*

I'm settling in with a second glass of sauv blanc and what I figure will be an epic binge-watch of *Orange Is the New Black* (I'm two seasons behind!) when my phone rings.

The screen shows Donna's smiling face. My foster mom is one in a trillion and a saint for putting up with me. I know she's proud of me now, but I also know I put her through the wringer.

"Hey, Donna." I was fourteen years old when I went to live with Donna and Sully, too old to develop a habit of calling her "Mom."

"He's not eating, Charlie."

"You mean he's not eating salads and rice cakes." Sully's diet since the heart attack has left a lot to be desired. Donna is worried, and I can't blame her. "Is he there now?"

"Playing cards in the basement. Three nights this week, though he's usually over at Jimmy Finster's and ordering food from Portillo's!"

Hmm. Three times a week seems sort of excessive, especially if all he's eating is Portillo's dogs.

"What's on tonight's menu?"

"I've got a nice chicken breast with a wedge of lemon and a side salad, but he won't come up to the kitchen to eat it."

"Tell him you made pot roast. He loves your pot roast." It's the only dish she can make with any consistency. God love the woman, but she's a terrorist in the kitchen.

"I know! But he can't eat it anymore."

It's a tragedy, for sure. I wait for her to ask.

"Could you stop by?"

"And spy on him? Tell you how many cigar stubs I see,

how many French fries are lying around, how much money's in the pot?"

"He's always listened to you, Charlie. If you say you're worried, it'll make a difference."

I look at the TV screen, frozen on the rough, careworn face of one of the prison inmates they use in the credits. Real inmates, apparently. *There but for the grace of Donna and Sully . . .* I owe them so much, the least I can do is carry some food fifty feet and do a little snooping.

"Break out the Entenmann's. I'll be there in twenty."

~

I HEAD down the stairs to the den. The scent of cigar smoke should have me screwing up my nose in disgust but instead, it reminds me of those early days when I first arrived at the Sullivans, my fourteen-year-old self in a metaphorical boxer's stance with fists raised and ready. I was determined to make them hate me.

Sully was determined to teach me poker.

He didn't smoke fat stogies, but instead preferred cigarillos. Less ostentatious, he'd say. I didn't know what that word meant, but I liked it. I liked Sully, and I especially liked that he treated me as an adult. Poker was for grown-ups and it taught me a lot about strategy, patience, and expectations.

When Sully had his heart attack, the bottom of my world dropped out. Seeing him lying there in the ICU at Northwestern Memorial, tubed up and attached to machines, I almost faded out, unable to handle it. But I needed to be strong for Donna, who was staring down the possibility of life without the man she'd loved for over thirty years.

He made it through, but not before we had a few bedside heart-to-hearts, the upshot of which was I needed to stop working so hard and find myself a man. Sully wants to see me happy and for him, happiness doesn't come from a career, but from marriage and children. Old-fashioned, perhaps, but I took it to heart. I was already coming to that conclusion with each couple I helped on the road to their happily-ever-after.

I was ready. The dating pool of Chicago was not.

The scent gets stronger as I descend, my steps quiet on the carpeted rungs. I don't want to surprise anyone—these guys are in their prime heart-attack years, after all—so I call out.

"Get your pants on, gentlemen. You've got company."

On hitting the bottom step, I arc my gaze over the seventies-style decor, including a wall-mounted moose (not ironic), pennant flags of the Cubs, and the round table of graying, out-of-shape men amid Pabst Blue Ribbon bottles and poker chips.

Sully squints at me, knowing full well why I'm here, but he's not the player I'm focused on. That honor goes to the last person I expect to see at a poker game in my parents' basement.

The man, the legend. Max Henderson.

CHAPTER 13

Max

I could pretend that me playing poker with a bunch of old dudes I don't know is just another day in the life. Spinning it that way would certainly piss off Charlie, and I find myself wanting to piss her off. I'd like to see her lose her shit, especially as losing her shit will likely lead to us working our friction out horizontally.

Sully called me up at the office and asked me outright what my intentions were toward his daughter. That takes balls, especially considering said intentions could be readily inferred by the sight of my hand crushing her ass and my mouth eating hers alive. That's not to say I couldn't have more long-term plans, but this was his first impression. The man's not an idiot. He knows what I'm after.

She's my brother's wedding planner, I explained, as if there was some professional code of ethics that prohibited fraternization with the enemy. Then he asked me to hang with him and his crew playing poker.

I should have made an excuse, but I was curious. This guy spent twenty-eight years changing the score on the manual board at Wrigley. There are stories here. He also spent fifteen years playing dad to Charlie, and I know there are stories here, too. I find myself curious about those stories and about this woman who's keeping me awake at night.

The moose head on the wall had thrown me, but I'd recovered enough to weather cigar smoke and weak-as-piss beer and at least three fairly lethal farts from Finster to my right. A bit rusty, I lost the first couple of hands but I've made up for it and am now holding my own.

All the boys shout out, "Charlie!"

She stares at me, evidently wishing the moose head would fall on my head or at minimum, that I'd develop some god-awful disease. Preferably, of the scrotum.

"Ms. Love, you look well." Understatement of the century. She looks *fine* in red shorts that stop at mid-thigh. Up top she's wearing one of those halter thingies that require a strapless bra or no bra at all. She's stopped in place, not giving me a chance to assess jiggle quotient and make a definitive statement on the bra-or-no-bra situation. Her hair is in a messy pile on top of her head, as if she'd thrown it together quickly in her hurry to get over here.

I slide a look at Sully, who's sporting a frown.

"Yeah, you know why I'm here," she says with a hop off the last stair. Strapless bra is the winner. My dick doesn't mind because it's already imagining unhooking that halter, my fingertips skimming the side of her breast, my lips trailing shiver-shocking kisses over her collarbones.

Charlie walks in farther, passing me by and leaving a scent of strawberries and cream in her wake before Finster expels a puff of cigar smoke so toxic I'm pretty sure I just developed cancer. Standing behind her father, Charlie raises an eyebrow—whether at his hand or the "food" options on display I can't tell. The table is host to Chex mix, beef jerky, and oddly enough, olives, a contribution from Jerry, the guy who works for ComEd. I know this because he introduced himself with "I'm Jerry from ComEd." He's been chomping on olives and spitting the pits into a handkerchief, then stuffing it into his pocket. Kind of weird, but we're men doing manly things, and I've seen a lot worse.

"You still on the Mediterranean diet, Jerry?" Charlie asks.

"Sure am, Charlie. Keeps me in fine fettle."

"Did Sully eat any olives?"

Jerry looks uncomfortable at being put on the spot. Sully lets him off the hook with, "You know I can't stand 'em." He throws down a card and gets another from Finster. On sliding it into the fan in his hand, he sniffs and puts in five one-dollar chips. "Raise you five."

Thirty seconds later, Jerry has won this hand with a full house, tens high.

"What you got there, Charles?" I ask, jerking a chin at the plate she placed on a sideboard.

"Sully's dinner. Time for a break, gentlemen." Her tone brooks no dissent and sends blood shooting straight to my groin.

"We've already ordered—" Sully stops mid-sentence at the sight of Charlie's glare. Meanwhile my erection is showing no sign of minimizing. The woman's scowl is my personal Viagra.

Taking the hint, Finster stands and stretches. "Time for a leak." Jerry and the fifth in the group, Kovak, a Russian guy who has barely spoken a word, give Sully sympathetic looks and follow Finster upstairs.

Charlie looks at me. "Don't you need a potty break, Henderson?"

"Just fine here, Charles."

A very attractive crimp appears between her eyebrows. I want to kiss it and all her worry away. "Donna made you a nice salad with chicken, Sully."

"Salad?" Sully looks as if Charlie suggested he eat worms on a bed of rusty nails. "It's bullshit, Charlie. You know she's never been the best of cooks and now she's terrible when she can't make her staples."

"And you know what the doctor said," Charlie says. "You have to overhaul your diet, cut out cigars, start exercising. Even if it's just walking around the neighborhood." She picks up the ashtray where the boys had stubbed out their cigars and starts clearing away the worst of the mess.

The woman opens up her bag of tricks. Silverware and a bottle of light vinaigrette are brought out to play. Saran wrap is pulled back to reveal a grayish-pink slab of what I'm charitably calling "meat" on a bed of wilted greens—and not wilted in a haute cuisine kind of way.

"Fuck, no," I mutter.

Sully jerks a hand my direction. "Right? I can't live like this."

Even Charlie looks a little perturbed, but gamely she soldiers on. "Is this why you're playing cards more often? Getting out of the house to avoid mealtimes?"

"You try eating this junk."

"You've got to eat something. And hot dogs every night are not the answer."

I stand and stretch. This does not go unnoticed by Charlie whose eyes are drawn to the sliver of skin between the hem of my Cubs tee and the waistband of my jeans.

Father and daughter appear to be at an impasse so it's up to me to break the stalemate. "How about I make you a sandwich, Sully?"

"A sandwich?" He sounds suspicious.

"Let me see what the good Lady Sullivan has in her larder. Charles, care to join me and make sure this sandwich meets your approval?"

She opens her mouth. Closes it. Finally, she manages a testy "Oh, all right!"

I wink at Sully and get a grin of male solidarity in return, then I follow her up the stairs, taking a good look at her rear lovingly hugged by the fabric of her shorts. Ms. Love might be a hardass but there's nothing hard about that ass I want to cradle and stroke and knead. It had felt pretty goddamn right in my hands a few days ago in Cubs jail, and hell if I didn't want to experience it again.

The basement stairs lead right into the kitchen, and as I ascend into the light I have no choice but to get really close to Charlie, who's blocking my exit. My hands cup her hips and she jumps forward.

"Sorry," she mutters.

"'S okay."

I've already met Donna Sullivan over a cup of coffee and two slices of Entenmann's Cheese Filled Crumb Coffee Cake and now she looks defeated. Short, messy gray hair frames blue eyes and a lined face.

"He wouldn't eat it, would he?"

"It's okay—" Charlie starts, but I round her to give Mrs. S a pat on the shoulder. *I've got this, Charles.*

"No worries, Donna," I soothe. "How about I make him a sandwich? Maybe a nice grilled cheese?"

"Too much dairy," Charlie says.

"Got any light mayo?" I'm already rummaging in the fridge, which is packed with about eight different types of mustard and more gray chicken. Shuddering, I take out white bread, Dubliner cheddar, and miracle of miracles, light mayonnaise. "We won't use butter and we'll slice the cheese really thin." I grab a knife and start cutting the cheddar.

Charlie has taken up a watchdog position, leaning against the countertop, her gaze narrowed on me in suspicion. "So, care to explain why you're here, Henderson?"

Donna splits a glance between us. "Charlie, you know Max?"

"Vaguely. I'm planning his brother's wedding." Something passes over her face, a shadow I can't interpret. "But that doesn't explain why he's here."

"Sully called. Had a spot to fill."

"And you like rolling out to Sauganash to hang with strange men playing poker for peanuts?"

I scan the area and latch onto an apple. "I was hoping for some good stories. All I got was the one about how you painted Snowball, your fluffy white Siamese, with food coloring. Thought I'd at least hear about a fun dating debacle."

I add a couple of wafer-thin slivers of apple into the cheese sandwich then a barely there layer of mayo on the outside before lighting the gas under the frying pan.

"Charlie scared them all off," Donna says. "They're intimidated by her."

"I wonder why," I mutter, but not low enough to escape Donna's notice.

"Too bossy," she exclaims, a complaint I've no doubt is not new to Charlie. I feel a smidge of guilt for fanning the flames. "I tell her men don't want a woman who's always giving orders."

To temper the criticism, I wink at Charlie, whose cheeks are flagged with color. "I dunno, Donna. Some guys love being told what to do."

This makes Donna snort. "Not Frank." She assesses me more closely now. "No ring on your finger, Max." Lady Sullivan is not dicking around.

Charlie makes a sound of disgust, and after I defended

her, too. "Oh, Max doesn't believe in all that nonsense, Donna. He's anti-marriage."

"Never said that."

"Right, you need all those marriages for cannon fodder so you can tear them asunder in the guise of 'helping people.'" Air quotes with that.

"Exactly." I smile at Donna, turning it up a notch to piss off Charlie. "I'm a divorce attorney. A very successful divorce attorney."

"Oh, I see," Donna says.

And I see the appreciation in her eyes. She's already lining me up for her daughter to the slaughter, which I suspect might be Frank's end game as well. Not a problem as Charlie Love and I know exactly where we stand with each other.

I flip the sandwich, pleased with the golden crust and the sizzle I hear as the mayo-kissed bread hits the heat.

Donna blinks at me. "So you probably see some awful stuff? Really bad behavior?"

"Yeah, the breakdown of a marriage tends to bring out the worst in humanity. People usually start out thinking a divorce is the ultimate failure. No one wants to be associated with failure so no one wants to admit that they might be responsible for something that stinks to high heaven. My job is to try to give clients my most objective take, an emotion-free perspective. It's pretty rare for a marriage's failures to be the entire fault of a single person, so I try to navigate the blame game on my clients' behalf."

"Pretty sure Frank'll be one hundred percent responsible when I divorce his ass," Donna mutters, making me laugh.

Charlie's not amused. Instead she's staring at me, as if trying to puzzle me out. I like to keep her on her toes with a few utterances that shake up her preconceptions.

I pop the grilled cheese on a plate, slice up the rest of the apple, halve the sandwich, and arrange Frank's meal. "Dinner is served."

"That looks really good," Donna says with feeling. I don't mean to show her up but man, that chicken was a fright. "Right, Charlie?"

"Yeah, but will he eat it?"

He eats it. In fact, he asks me for another one but I tell him that's his limit. Charlie Love is not pleased.

CHAPTER 14

"A divorce lawyer is a chameleon with a law book."

— MARVIN MITCHELSON

Charlie

I am not pleased.

Of course I'm glad to see Sully eating something that's not deep-fried. I wouldn't wish Donna's cooking on my worst enemy—well, maybe on a certain blue-eyed, cocksure, too sexy lawyer who is a serious threat to the calm façade I've cultivated after years of practice.

I'm supposed to be at home binge-watching Netflix and kicking back with my third glass of vino (don't judge me!). Instead, I'm frozen in horror as my parents are charmed beyond recognition by the devil himself. The card game broke up thirty minutes ago, and everyone went home. Everyone, that is, but *him*.

Max stayed to help clean up. I told him there was no need

but he'd already loaded the dishwasher, insisted Donna put her feet up, and helped himself to more Entenmann's. That stuff is not much better than sugar-dipped shredded cardboard, but Mr. I-Once-Had-a-Trust-Fund is humming appreciative noises as if the most perfect morsel from a five-star pastry chef has slipped through his full, firm lips.

Now Donna shoves us all into the good room, the parlor no one ever uses. Max stands at the mantel, one narrow hip leaning casually, that ass-grabbing hand I intimately know the texture of wrapped around a coffee mug. He puts the mug down and picks up a photo of me, Donna, and Sully at my graduation from the University of Illinois.

"Happy day for the Sullivans, I bet," he says. "Your hair is darker here."

"She dyes it," Donna says. *So not the honey to catch the fly.*

I find myself holding my breath as Max moves along the mantel, this record of my life post-disaster—through my prom with Billy Foster, past one of the many times Sully took me to work at Wrigley. He stops at the photo of me with my biological mom, when I was about nine. I've always loved that Donna insisted it take pride of place.

"This is where you get those eyes from." He looks at me, then checks back with the photo. "The smile, too."

I assume so. I never knew my father and losing my mom in a car crash when I was thirteen seems like both another age and the life-changing event that happened yesterday.

As if reminded that a car wreck is the reason I came to live with the Sullivans, Frank cuts in.

"Charlie, did you get the tune-up for your car like I told you?" Not waiting for my answer, Sully speaks to Max. "She doesn't get her oil changed enough."

Max catches my eye, the glint of the devil in it. "That can be a *major* problem."

"Oh, shut up," I mutter, but there's little heat in it.

I catch exchanged knowing looks between Sully and Donna, that unfathomable language married couples speak to each other. Even though this silent conversation has a matchmaking sheen to it that I abhor, I love that they seem to be on the same wavelength. I've been worried about my dad, especially as he seems so desperate to spend time out of the house.

Donna and Sully's marriage has always been #RelationshipGoals for me. He buys her flowers once a week—cheerful yellow tulips tower above the photo frames on the sideboard. She gives him silly socks every now and then, his latest the Blackhawks ones he's wearing tonight. It's the little things, isn't it? I'm not so naïve that I think marriage is a cake-walk, but I need to know the love is still there, maybe because my job only gives me access to the start of something good.

"More photos, Max?" Donna makes a grab for the door to the sideboard where I know every awkward facet of my teen life has been meticulously recorded in photographic form.

I shoot up so fast I'm momentarily dizzy. "I have an early appointment in the suburbs tomorrow, so I should head out."

Photos forgotten, Donna is on her feet, heading toward the kitchen to wrap up a couple slices of Entenmann's. For Max, of course. "How are you getting home?"

"Uber," I say and immediately want to bite it back. I had already downed a glass of wine before I came over, so driving was out of the question.

"Max, can you take care of my girl?" Sully asks.

I practically screech, "No need!"

"Not a problem."

"I'm sure you have better things to do."

He holds my gaze unerringly. "Not at all. Especially now you've denied me a good photo-viewing sesh."

Two minutes later we're in his car, an Audi which, while

nice, isn't quite as baller as I expected. Not to say that if I'd spotted it parked outside earlier I wouldn't have bribed one of the neighborhood kids to key it.

I shake my head, annoyed that Max Henderson brings out such nastiness in me. I'm not like this, not at all. I have a temper but I work hard to control it, to present a cool and collected image to my clients and friends, and especially to the men I date. Spending time with Max unnerves me. Something about him feeds my inner rage monster, that girl who's all id.

"What's going on?" he asks as he turns off my parents' street, heading east toward where we both live.

"Excuse me?"

"I'm sensing a lot of hostility."

"Want to tell me what all that was about?" I wave behind me at the house where I lived from age fourteen to nineteen.

"You'll have to be more specific."

"Why are you here, Max? In my parents' basement? In their kitchen and parlor, yukking it up like you're all old pals?"

He waits a beat, a tactic I suspect he uses in court. "Sully called me and asked, Charlie. I could have made an excuse but he's an interesting guy, and I thought he'd have a few fun stories about hanging with the Cubbies. Not everything is about you."

Is that what I'm fishing for? An admission that Max showed up at my childhood home because he's interested in me?

Of course not. It's just incongruous to see this Mr. Entitled skimming his eight-hundred-dollar loafers over the will-never-be-clean-again kitchen floor, scarfing down store-bought coffee cake, and chatting easily with Sully and Donna.

Not only that, it's a little too close to when I brought Jeremy home to dinner. My ex's eyes flew wide at the working class quality of it all. I'd told him about them but the reality reframed his mindset in a way my stories couldn't. How could he use it to prop up his image?

Girlfriend /fiancée/wife with a compelling backstory: Chicago salt-of-the-earth types for foster parents, Cubs connection, adopted daughter made good in one of those "jobs for chicks" she can easily give up once we marry. Now to make sure there's nothing about Charlie that will throw off a run for Congress . . .

I want to protect my family and I'll scratch out the eyes of anyone who belittles them. Seeing Max hanging out at Chez Sullivan sent creepy crawlies over my skin.

At first.

Even more disturbing is how that incongruity quickly faded. How there was no awkwardness as he spoke with these people who mean so much to me and are clearly in a different stratum of society to him. There was no condescension.

Max Henderson continues to buck my worldview.

I haven't responded verbally to his defense of his presence in Sauganash, too busy thinking on what to say that won't make me sound petty and small-minded.

He speaks first. "My dad had pneumonia last year, a real nasty bout of it. Drove my mom crazy when he refused to take his recovery seriously. I know you must be worried about Sully's health, and Christ they don't make it easy."

"Well, Sully is so damn stubborn," I say, glad to be talking about something else. Complaining about one's parents and their foibles is good, innocuous car talk.

But then his next words damn that notion to hell. "What happened to your biological mom?"

Blinking, I speak to the passenger-side window. "A car

crash when I was thirteen. She was a nurse coming home from a shift when she got T-boned in an intersection. It—it crushed me. All my life it was just me and her, the Two Musketeers she used to call us. No dad in the picture." I try to smile, as if showing bravery will make my situation more palatable. No man likes a Debbie Downer, not that I need to impress Max. "There were no other close relatives, so I went into care for over a year. A few different group homes, a couple of nightmare foster situations where I was the nightmare."

"You? A nightmare?"

It's said with affection and warms my love-starved heart. "I know, can you believe it? I've always tended to let my passions override my sense, even my sense of self-preservation. Donna and Sully were willing to put in the time, and that's what I needed most. Time."

I slide a look, only to find him staring ahead, eyes on the road, keeping us safe. His profile is a thing of beauty, all superhero square-jawed with a shadow I long to run my fingertips over. His lips had tasted so good. I've no doubt the rest of him will give me some sort of Max-gasm.

This is the worst time to start feeling tingles along my thighs. But now all I can think of are Max's hands—the ones gripping the hand-stitched, leather-covered steering wheel with such authority. He did a fine job of cradling my ass in Cubs jail. Those hands would excel at exploring, at spreading my thighs wide and rubbing me wet.

Squirming in my seat, I clench my thighs together to stave off the ache. The car is quiet, the high-quality automotive experience doing a stellar job of cocooning us from the outside world. All I can hear is my shallow breathing, my erratic pulse, my throbbing flesh. I'm a one-woman band of heightened sexual responses.

Are we there yet?

Meanwhile, Max Henderson is silence incarnate. If I placed a mirror in front of his mouth, would there be a reflection or evidence of breathing? A sensual vampire, he's sucking all the oxygen from the small space. The man knows how to exercise rigid control—except I've seen it slip when his mouth met mine.

We turn onto my block, though I don't recall telling him exactly where I live other than my street.

"You can drop me off—" I'm about to say "here" when he pulls into a space half a block down from my condo building. I assume he's sold the soul I doubt he possesses to the parking gods because this good fortune is virtually unheard of at 10:27 p.m. in Lincoln Park.

"Thanks for the ride." I place my hand on the door handle, then think to ask, "How do you know where I live?"

"Easy enough to find out."

It hits me squarely in the solar plexus. I've been here before, and the last time someone did that, it did not end well. "You ran a background check on me?"

"You're providing a financial service to my brother. It's in my interest to know who he's dealing with. Who I'm dealing with."

Normally, I would understand this. Check me out with the Better Business Bureau. Look up my reviews on Yelp (all fantastic, by the way, except for one client who didn't like that I used Waterford instead of Baccarat). However, Max's investigation of me smacks of control and invasion.

"And did I pass the test?"

"Your business is booming; your clients love you except for Gale C on Yelp who was really pissed about the crystal flutes used for the toast. Kind of weird, but brides are in a review category of their own, I suppose. You pay your bills and taxes on time. You just bought this condo, your first property purchase. You appear to be a very productive citizen of our fine city."

I should view this as a boon, the perfect damper on all those pesky feelings running riot through my body. Or at least, a guy checking my financials to make sure I'm not a bad bet *should* be a vat of ice water on my crotch.

Why isn't it?

If he touches me now, I'll burst into flames.

I fumble for the car door and practically fall on my ass trying to scramble from the seat to the street. "Good night!" I call out, like I still need to be polite. It sounds weird, I look weird, and by the time I get to the front door of my building, I'm fairly certain I'm having an out-of-body experience. I'm floating above this city tableau, looking down on myself fumbling with my purse. Searching for my key. Shaking as I try to insert it.

This bird's-eye view shows a tall, dark figure behind me, not touching but I feel him all around like a fog.

"Charlie," he says. "If you're going to be mad at me, let's do it right."

I don't know what that means, yet I do. I resolve to hold my neck rigid, inhaling deep breaths, focusing on one thing at a time. Opening the door will allow me to walk inside which will allow me to escape which will allow me to be alone and dig out that vibrator one of my clients gave me two Christmases ago . . .

But I can't concentrate. He's too present, his scent a drug, his presence an anchor keeping me barely tethered to this world.

I turn my head slightly, and it's my undoing. His impossibly blue eyes seduce with purpose.

"I'm not mad at you," I say, the last gasp of a drowning woman.

"Liar."

"Maybe a little." If I can temper my emotions a notch, then I can reel in whatever it is I'm feeling. "I understand if James or Gina want to check on me, I just don't see why you need to stick your nose in."

"Merely looking out for what's mine."

The intent I hear in those words makes me shiver.

Flustered, I continue. "Not just with the checkup but you seem to be everywhere. I can't get away from you."

"The universe is telling us something."

"That you're a pain in my ass."

He shakes his head like *poor Charlie doesn't get it.* "Try again."

My heart is a thundering beast in my chest. I want to look away but he's made it impossible with his broad shoulders grilling my retinas, his perfect hair in need of a muss, his blue eyes darkening with each second I stand there frozen. I'm trapped in this no-man's-land of anticipation.

"You're not what I want," I blurt, true in one sense, a blatant lie in another.

He doesn't touch me. Instead it's a conquest with his eyes. "But . . ."

The bastard wants me to say it. To admit this is beyond my control.

I say nothing because if I open my mouth, it will be to beg for his touch.

"If you want this—if you want me—I'll need you to say so. I recognize that I've come on pretty strong, maybe too strong. Making you uncomfortable has never been my intention, but I think there's something here that's worth exploring. If I've misread the signals, I'll leave."

I swallow, because he's just made this so much easier. Nothing comes out of my mouth.

His smile is rueful. "Good night, Charlie." He turns to

leave and my heart leaps out of my chest with a desperate "noooo!"

I think of Penny's advice: an orgasm—or two or three—to clear the pipes. This doesn't have to be so complicated. It's purely physical, chemical, geographical. Nothing more. The decision needs no handwringing.

"Stop."

He stops, but doesn't turn. Max Henderson is a bit of a showman, I think.

"You haven't misread the signals. There's something here, but I meant what I said."

He faces me and closes the gap between us. "About what?"

"You're not what I want—I mean, for the long haul . . ."

"But . . ." he prompts, his mouth close to mine.

"You'll do the trick."

He blinks. *Gotcha.*

"Excuse me?"

I turn my body into his and place both hands on his shoulders, enjoying the flex beneath my fingertips. Exquisite. Even in heels, I need to reach, especially as he's still reeling from what I said and hasn't the wherewithal to lean down.

Poor, sexy Max.

My lips brush his jaw, and it's all I can do not to moan at the contact.

He's not so reticent. A throaty sound emerges that sets me all aflutter.

"You'll do nicely to scratch my itch, Max." I'm establishing the ground rules so we're both clear I don't want anything more than a night of sweaty, sheet-tangling passion. Max Henderson needn't think I have intentions beyond that. I won't be angling for follow-up brunches or lazy Sundays doing crossword puzzles or dog-sharing scenarios. I won't be asking for a second date.

Or even a first one.

There's a flicker of something in his eyes, but it dims to the dark desire he's been rocking since he approached me outside my building. Since I met him.

He heaves a breath and on an exhale, touches his lips to mine. "Let's hear more about this itch."

CHAPTER 15

> "Marriage is an alliance entered into by a man who can't sleep with the window shut, and a woman who can't sleep with the window open."
>
> — GEORGE BERNARD SHAW

I think I'm being used.

Actually, I know I'm being used because Charlie pretty much said so outside her apartment building.

This should *not* bother me. How many times have I told a woman that there's no future beyond a night, maybe two, with me? How many of my former lovers are given to understand the parameters of spending time with me? *All of them,* and I'm still friends with the majority, except Mitzi—but she's in a league of her own.

I should dig Charlie's refreshing honesty. I'm the guy who told her she could still enjoy herself while on the hunt for Mr. Right.

Is that what's bothering me? Her dismissal of me as husband material? Hell, I don't consider myself husband material for anyone, let alone Charlie Love.

Sweet, sexy Charlie. Her mouth is a sinful velvet, the perfect treat, made even more incredible by the fact her kiss isn't tentative. Now that's she's talked herself into doing this, all concerns about sleeping with me have been banished. I'm no longer on her radar as a likely mate. I am now a physical thing on which she can project her desires.

Pity I like her so much.

I'm not sure when this happened, probably some time between her screaming inventive insults at Lars Muller and shooting daggers at me while I grilled her dad a cheese sandwich. (Did I get a word of thanks? Oh, no, just snark.) It's kind of inconvenient to realize I have a crush on this woman who's viewing me as little more than meat, but I'm a big boy and expect I can handle it.

The elevator opens onto the third floor of her building, which looks like one of those rehab jobs of a twenties-era hotel. They probably joined a couple of units together to make one apartment, keeping the molding and nicer details of the old place.

She leads me down the corridor to her condo. That shake she had in her hands is gone as she hits the keyhole without a problem. Charlie is back in control.

I plan to change that.

I plan to make her swear like I'm a baseball official who's pissed her off.

I plan to have her asking—no, *begging*—for several repeat rounds.

Once inside her apartment, she makes a move for the light switch, but I pull her back against my hard-for-her body. Her sharp intake of breath goes right to my balls. I could do it quick. I suspect that's what Charlie wants, something slam-bang in keeping with the perception she has of me. But I'm all about upending perceptions tonight.

"Slow down, honey. Let me see what I'm working with here." I flip our positions so she's back against the door. Under-cabinet lighting from the kitchen to my right is enough to show me her expression.

"The bedroom's behind you," she murmurs.

"We'll get there eventually." For now, I have so much I want to do, to feast upon. There's a tempo to every sexual encounter, a rhythm that makes itself known. Charlie wants electronic dance music while I'm looking to ease in with a nice slow ballad. Acoustic.

She goes right for my zipper.

I swat her away, even though my dick is not happy with that decision. Nope, it's not liking my strategy at all. Fucker and his spherical friends will have to behave because I've got a woman to woo.

"Not yet," I murmur as much to my cock as to her before I capture her mouth in an all-consuming kiss. She moans, the sweetest sound of surrender as I ensure her mouth is loved to within an inch of its life. My hands skim down her sides, teasing, barely touching, my knuckles a gentle glance over her supple flesh.

"Max, I need . . . oh, God." She tries to get busy with my dick again and I do another cock block—I know, unbelievable—this time taking both her hands and holding them over her head.

"I've got this, Charlie. Let me take care of you."

"It's taking too long," she grates.

"I'll make it worth your while. Trust me."

Her body relaxes incrementally—this is Charlie after all, relaxation is not her jam—and she mutters, "Get on with it."

I chuckle and flip her around so she faces the door. I need both my hands free, and I can't trust she'll not try to lead this dance again if I don't make it a bit difficult for her. My body covers hers, finding that perfect fit as she slots into the concave space below my waist. For a moment, I let her feel how she's affecting me, first with a press then with a lascivious grind against her ass.

The hand above her head forms a fist.

Our own little *Titanic* moment right there.

I find the side zip to her shorts and ease it down slowly, every moment a tease, every inch a torture—for us both. I slide those shorts down over her ass. She steps out of them and I kick them to the side.

The kitchen light casts a glow over the curves of her rear, bisected by a sexy black thong. There's something both artistic and playful about how the light dapples her ass. I take one globe and squeeze while my free hand curls around her hip and skims the border of her thong.

Then inside.

Her breath hitches. Some time in the last few moments she's placed both her hands on the door and hinged her hips in invitation. Like I could possibly say no to that.

My fingers delve deeper, seeking her heat, that throbbing heart of her. I part her and sink in where she's so hot and wet. I shouldn't be surprised. The woman is unmistakably turned on and my moves are on the money. Yet a ripple of pleasure I don't immediately understand thrills through me. It's not lust. It's not even power.

It's recognition.

Like this perfect pussy has been waiting for me to stake a claim and I'm suddenly home.

I haven't even buried my cock inside her.

Yeah, I'm losing my mind.

She squirms against my hand and I push deeper. "Christ," I mutter. I dig my hand into her hip and pull her back so my mouth is at her ear. I'm panting like I've run a race and now

I'm wondering if I can keep up with this deathly slow pace I've set.

But I'll try my damnedest.

I turn my finger and rub against her clit, drawing a deep moan from her that starts a new conversation between us. Her body shimmies. I need unrestricted access. The thong is yanked halfway down her ass—it's hanging there, kind of sleazy, one of my favorite looks. Disheveled and desperate.

She moves against my finger, looking to create more friction, so I give it to her. A sawing motion through her slick heat, then I move my palm so it separates her thighs and makes her stance wide.

I grind my hand on her, spreading all that liquid desire around. She feels so damn good, and I want to tell her, but my vocal cords have locked up. Like I'm that stuttering kid who can't get the words out. Charlie Love has done it again —made me lose control of what's usually so easy for me. My words, my verbal dexterity.

Unable to speak, I do the next best thing to deepen the connection. I pull her back against my body, my mouth close to her ear, a low moan of pleasure escaping me. I still can't form words, but maybe it's not necessary. Maybe I don't need to be always in-control Max who knows what's coming next because he issues the orders and calls the plays.

I think I know how Charlie felt ten minutes ago when she realized letting go might not be so hard. I rub my cock against her bare ass while my hand continues to draw tight, erotic circles between her thighs. She's writhing now, close to going off, and I'm ready for her. So ready.

Her thighs shake, her body shudders, and her forehead dips to touch the door. It's stunning, yet the most controlled orgasm I've ever witnessed. That's okay. Some women are quiet but it doesn't fit what I know of Charlie Love.

I turn her to face me. Her expression is slack with pleasure, her eyes unfocused with desire. "That was . . . beautiful," I say. Because it was. I know I helped but I don't feel like I was truly part of it.

She blinks at my words, then seems to come back from wherever she went.

I know what's coming next.

Her hand on my zipper. An inquiry about condoms. A sequence to get me off and get me out the door.

I'm not quite ready to be dismissed.

True to my expectation, her hand smooths over my straining dick. I capture her wrist and hold her still.

"What's wrong?" she whispers.

Everything, I want to say. Instead I ask for directions to the bathroom and stumble off.

The man in the mirror looks the same, except for a little pinch of worry between his eyebrows. I have no idea of my end game here. Am I really trying to draw this out because I feel slighted by Charlie's attitude?

Hell, all I'm asking for is a little romance.

I chuckle to myself at the notion. *Extra! Extra! Read all about it! Max Henderson Needs Romance!*

I'm tottering on the edge of absurdity here. Outside that door I have a woman who is offering me the fantasy. Not even a fantasy, but the reality I live and have been enjoying for many years. No strings, no pressure, come fast and carry on.

Thing is: I think Charlie Love needs a little romance as well.

Not that I'm the one to give it to her—at least not the whole hog—but does everything have to be so transactional? Can't we enjoy the journey a little without the need to hurtle toward the destination at breakneck speeds? Sex doesn't have to be a race.

Satisfied with my well-reasoned conclusion, I turn to

leave and begin the woo. That's when I spot something designed to deflate the hardest erection. I pick it up and stare, trying to puzzle it out.

There's a knock on the door. "Max, are you okay?"

No. I'm not.

I open up, holding my find aloft. "Something you need to tell me?"

CHAPTER 16

Charlie

After what just happened, I need a moment to gather my wits because Max Henderson took me on a roller-coaster sex ride where the dips were as hot as the highs.

And then he stopped without pulling into the station, so to speak.

I thought that maybe he had a problem—if you know what I mean—but there was no denying that hardness I felt as he rubbed me all the way to orgasm. And when he opens my bathroom door, I can see he's still bulging. (So it was the first place I looked. Sue me.)

But my confusion is soon replaced by oh-shit panic at what he's holding in his hand: Gina's pregnancy test.

"That's not mine," I say instinctively.

What looks like relief softens his face. He nods. Waits.

"It belongs to a friend." *True.* "She's having a baby." *Your niece or nephew.*

"That's usually what the plus sign means," he says evenly. "Sorry, I didn't mean to be so nosy. It's just if you're pregnant . . ."

"I shouldn't be having sex with someone else?"

"I didn't say that. But it would complicate things."

It would. But I'm not. So it doesn't.

He throws the test in the wastebasket near the door, then washes his hands.

I relax enough to lean against the doorway.

"You redressed," he says, turning to look me up and down.

"I wasn't sure if you were staying."

"Do you want me to stay?"

Something wriggles in my stomach, a gut reaction to his question that wonders if it's a trap.

"Well, I had my fun and you haven't had yours yet," I say cheerfully.

Max dries his hands, then stands before me with arms threaded over his chest. "There are two things wrong with that statement. You're assuming I wasn't having fun while you were. Not true. And you're describing what's happening here as a quid pro quo. I scratched your"—he gestures to my shorts—"so now you have to return the favor."

I smile sweetly, unsure where he's going with this. "It's the least I can do."

He moves closer and my breath catches. "What if I told you I didn't want to play it that way? That I'd rather spend my time treating you right."

What nonsense is this? Why the hell would Max Henderson want to spend his time treating me right?

"I'm not looking for a relationship," I say, slightly on edge.

He stalks me, places his hands on my hips. "You mean, with me."

"Yes."

Any other guy would take offense, but not Max. Instead he does the sweetest thing: inclines his forehead to touch mine and whispers words every girl wants to hear. "Tell me what you need right now."

I need him to leave.

I need him to do me.

I need him to tell me everything and nothing.

The best way to get all these things is to get in bed with the devil. "I need you inside me."

It's a sexy thing to say. A dirty thing. But it also sounds surprisingly vulnerable on my lips because it's a plea not just for physical intimacy but for a visit inside my head with maybe a side trip to my heart and soul.

His hands slip from my hips to my ass, and then he's walking me back. His eyes never leave mine, his intensity a weight I feel to my depths. "Bedroom."

"Behind me. First door."

I want to kiss him, but I want to keep my eyes open. I don't want to miss a thing.

He backs me up against my dresser, then turns me around so I'm facing a floor-length mirror in the corner. I feel him hard and heavy against the top of my ass, his arms circling me, his chin resting on my shoulder.

"We look good together, Charles. My brooding good looks and your ray-bright sunshine."

We do, I can't deny it. But then this is the type of man who makes everyone he's with shine up good and proper. I refuse to take any credit for it.

"On the outside," I murmur, distracted by how his hand has snuck under the hem of my halter and is stroking my hip lightly. "Inside, you won't find Pollyanna."

His eyes flicker to mine in the mirror, something worrisome in them.

"I like your place," he says, the turn of the conversation taking me by surprise. "What I've seen of it." More of those delicious, erotic circles on my hip now moving toward my belly, fluttering up my rib cage.

"I just moved in. Well, a month ago."

"Bet your parents are proud."

That pulls me out of the moment. "They are." I stop there. He doesn't need to know what I put them through.

"Your own business. Your own place. Yeah, they're proud. Their girl done good."

My heart clenches. My whole life, I've wanted to make them proud and pay them back for saving me.

"Is that why you're in such a hurry to find the one?"

I pivot in his arms, needing to face him without the barrier of the mirror. "Did Sully say something?"

"Might have mentioned his wish for you to be settled. Happy. Thinks you work too hard. Wants to see you with a guy who'll treat you like a queen."

"You got all this over cards?"

"They're surprisingly chatty guys in between manly belches. You know what I think, Charles?"

"Bet you're gonna tell me."

"I think some guy hurt you and now you're making a list, checking it twice, and trying to figure out the minimum requirements for Charlie Love's future husband."

I find it both amusing and terrifying to be psychoanalyzed by Max. I'm curious, so I play along.

"And pray tell, what are these minimum requirements?"

"Kind, likes animals and children, unselfish in bed."

I make a play of looking over his shoulder. "Where *is* this paragon?"

"Not too flashy, will let you have your way, maybe a little" —he rubs his thumb and forefinger together—"boring. After all, anyone with too much personality might be a challenge."

"And I hate a challenge?"

"No. But I think you tried that and it didn't work so you're ready for an easier road, even if it involves compromising on what you really need."

"Which is?"

He takes a moment, which could be calculated to give whatever he's about to say a gravitas it no doubt doesn't deserve.

"The one who gets you. A soulmate."

I swallow because damn him, that pause works. Isn't that what everyone wants, a partner who fills their gaps, understands them, lets them run wild and reins them in when needed? I thought I was getting to that point with Jeremy, each moment we spent together a building block in our intimacy. I was careful not to reveal too much, to hold back some mystery and the parts of myself I didn't want him to see.

I don't need to be careful with Max, however. I suspect I could tell him every secret and I would never feel judged. No pressure because I'm not trying to win him over.

With such low stakes, Max would make a fun confidant and an even more fun lover.

"That soulmate stuff is overrated," I say, with a stress laugh. "But it's very seductive coming from a guy who doesn't believe in it for himself. Almost as if you're dangling a carrot of potential. No wonder ex-with-puppy got the wrong end of the stick. You gave off the vibe of forever, and you don't even buy a single word of it."

"I don't have to buy it to understand that it means something for others. Like any faith, if you believe in it, then it's enough to guide you. The problem is when people refuse to —or just plain can't—live up to this idealized version of a partner."

I throw my arms around his neck, strangely calmed by

what he just said. "Max Henderson, I believe we are on the same page in this."

"We are?"

"You don't believe that people can be happy in marriage. I do, but I also understand that happiness in relationships takes work. Along with honesty and communication. I have no expectations of you, Max. None whatsoever."

I'm telling him what every guy wants to hear, so why does he look . . . disappointed? Or maybe I'm projecting because I worry about disappointing him.

The politics of sex—even casual sex—are so damn hard.

Throughout this intimate conversation, which is pretty much hands down the best foreplay of my life, Max has been coasting his hands over my curves, such as they are. This measured approach is not what I expected but I find I'm loving it. Jeremy was very handsy, and not in a good way. I'm used to men pawing me in the name of unrestrainable passion, so coming across this rare unicorn who knows how to craft a moment is a revelation.

My shorts are pulled down slowly. Again. My halter is untied with reverence, slipped off with care. Max coasts his gaze down my body. I'm still wearing underwear, a strapless bra holding up nothing-to-write-to-*Penthouse*-about 34Bs and a silky thong that's damp but amazingly not incinerated to ash by now.

I should jot a note to Donna Karan. *Your panties withstood the onslaught of a Max Henderson seduction. Well done!*

He's silent, and it makes me nervous so I break it. "Cat caught your tongue, Max?"

The brief shadow that flits across his face like a dark-winged bird might be my imagination. He smiles. The shadows recede.

But still, no words. Either I've made him speechless or this is part of his playbook.

He unbuttons his shirt with a slowness that makes me squirm and the reveal is glorious. Hard and defined, with a light dusting of hair across his pecs and in a trail heading for the goods. It's really working for me.

Seems I want to be seduced.

"May I?" I touch the waistband of his pants. He nods.

In keeping with the moment, I inch that zipper down, a journey that takes ten seconds instead of the usually frenzied one. I palm the treasure behind the curtain and draw his groan and a choked out, "Ch-Charlie."

Peeling down his pants is another delaying tactic. I'm not sure why I'm taking this so slowly. He's already given me an amazing orgasm, but we've barely skimmed the surface of what's possible.

He steps out of his pants and places a hand on my shoulder, pushing me back on the bed.

"I have condoms in the—"

He cuts me off with a kiss, this perfect mating of mouths. My legs part to welcome him and he settles between them, the barriers to getting good and naked still on in the form of our stupid underwear. I don't mind, though. Not when Max is holding my face and exploring my mouth in a preview of coming attractions.

I thought I was in the mood for a quick, dirty encounter. It would better suit my state of mind but Max is sending my brain in a different direction, one where quick and dirty is replaced by slow and sensual. Romantic.

Max Henderson is courting me.

Before I can let that settle and find purchase in my heart, I grab his ass. It's the right thing to do to put a stop to my nonsensical thoughts.

He chuckles against my mouth, like he sees what I did there. "That's my girl. Tell me what you need."

I'm so confused. I want it slow and fast, dirty and romantic. It's not possible, but then Max makes it all seem possible.

"Need. You," I say. "Please." I'm a polite cavewoman.

He leaves my mouth and begins the all-important trek south. One breast pops out involuntarily, as if it sensed Max's devil lips were in the neighborhood. Now it's begging for his tongue and he obliges while its twin jealously strains against its lacy cup. Down, down, his wicked mouth goes and the next few minutes are a blur of sensation. My thong is pushed aside to make way for Max's tongue and God, that's so fucking good. Fingers, too, stroking and rubbing and slipping inside.

"Maaaax."

No verbal response from him, but it doesn't matter because I don't have anything worth saying. I buck off the bed for my second social orgasm of the evening.

This can't be real.

His big body hovers over me, his mouth near mine.

"Say yes, Charlie."

I appreciate his consent check-in, though I hear something else in those words. He wants more than my body, and when I murmur "yes" in return, I pretend that's all I'm giving him access to. It's necessary for my mental well-being.

He rolls my thong off, and something thicker than fingers slides inside my pussy. Damn, I was so dazed after coming that I didn't get a chance to see the Max Henderson weapon before he used it to blow my mind.

He cups my jaw and gives me a slow, deep, wet-with-me kiss. "Good?" A long stroke out, a deep push in, and I feel exquisitely full.

I want to tell him harder. I want to tell him faster. I want to tell him what I need in detail, but he's doing great on his own and why introduce that dynamic? I nod, letting him know it's all good, and he continues pumping into me, each glide long and liquid and deep. Yet all this time, he watches, assessing my reaction to each motion, adjusting the angle when he interprets some non-verbal clue I give him.

He's very intuitive, so intuitive that it isn't long before I feel that build of pressure low in my belly. Three times! This has to be a record but probably not for Max. He probably—shit, why am I thinking of Max giving some other woman orgasms?

I turn my head away, ashamed of where my thoughts have gone.

He turns it back, shakes his head, and—oh, God—smiles.

"Right here, lovely Charlie. Need to see you."

And I feel like he does. See me, that is. Now we're locked in a climb toward a place I'm desperate to reach, yet terrified at what it might mean. Every part of me is dizzying, fluid heat. Pure sensation. Max never wavers—in his thrusts, in his eye-fucking, in that intensity he exudes.

The orgasm crashes over me, and I bite down on my lip, stifling a scream, worried I'll scare my new neighbors.

Or myself.

His body tightens, and Max lets go on a long groan.

It's perfect, but then so is he.

CHAPTER 17

"My wife dresses to kill. She cooks the same way."

— HENRY YOUNGMAN

Max

I'm hashing it out in the Punch Palace. What do I mean by "it," you might ask.

Charlie Love's resistance.

For some reason, she thinks one time is enough. One time—with me! This is confusing for a number of reasons:

1. No woman has ever said no to a follow-up jump in the sack with me. Not one.
2. Even if I can't promise her that rosy happily-ever-after at the top of her list, I'm offering to be her fuck-toy for the foreseeable future. Sexy supply and delicious demand. Why would anyone turn this down?

3. We connected. Not just sexually, which was a
   chemical conflagration that made it the best sex I
   (and probably anyone) has ever had, but also on an
   intellectual level. I like talking to her. I like that
   sharp wit of hers, and I think she likes how I give
   as good as I get.

I suspect there's more to that last point, something buried in there that I need to poke around in, but I can't quite grasp. It's been two weeks since we hooked up—though "hookup" isn't even anywhere near the zip code of what happened. It was more than that. I *romanticked* the fuck out of that encounter.

Not that she appreciated it! She gave me the old "I have an early meeting" excuse to get me out the door right after. A couple of days later, I asked her to hit the Hitchcock festival at the Music Box with me, but she said no. I could have told her it was just a friendly evening out, but we both knew we'd be in bed five minutes after the credits rolled on *Vertigo*.

I punch Bob again—or rather, his replacement. This makes me smile, but it's a grim slash of my lips, little humor in it.

"Does Lucas know you're using him to get out all your aggression?"

I didn't hear Grant come in. For a guy who's six three and built like a linebacker, he skims the earth with a remarkably light step.

I walk over to the bench near the window overlooking the Chicago River and grab a towel. "You really shouldn't sneak up on a guy like that."

"Am I in danger of getting an ass-kickin'? From you?" His tone is one of such blatant disbelief that even I laugh.

"You need the room?" I down a half bottle of water.

"Nah." He waits. Grant's the kind of guy who takes a

moment before he unloads on you. It's a Southern thing, and despite being an impatient ass myself, I've always enjoyed my friend's slower, deliberate ways.

"What's got you all put out?" he asks. "Impotence, I assume."

I decide to shoot right to the heart of the problem. "There's this woman."

"The wedding planner?"

"How do you know?"

"Lucas and Sadie have a book running. He actually thinks you might marry this girl, is giving short odds on a proposal by the end of the summer."

My mouth drops open in a way I'm sure makes me look like a yokel. "What does Sadie think?"

"She's pretty sure it's gonna happen but she thinks you'll wait until the fall. Something about leaves turning, maybe a trip to see the foliage in Wisconsin, more romance for a proposal." He shrugs. *Women.* "You don't seem in a hurry to deny this possibility."

"Well, I'm not getting married. Shit, you know that's not for the likes of us."

His mouth twists ever so slightly.

"Sorry, man, I didn't mean—"

"No worries. I understand your opposition to the holy state." He knows how it all went down with Becca. "But this wedding planner person is sure causing a stir in our little kingdom."

I scoff, glad to have the focus back on me, if only because Grant's pain over his divorce from Aubrey is still raw, and that makes me feel raw. "Because a couple of our co-workers are gossiping about her."

"That and the fact there's a woman trying to get ahold of you, and she doesn't seem too pleased."

I grab my phone and check my messages. Nothing from Mitzi, Charlie, or my mother.

I'm pissed all over again.

"Did you take a message?"

Grant raises an eyebrow. "I'm not your service, Henderson."

"Yet, you're here."

"She's got great legs."

I do a double take. "Excuse me?"

Squinting Wild West style, he takes an excruciatingly long look at the Lucas mask covering Bob the Torso, the one I've been using to vent my frustration on. "Your wedding planner. She's got great legs."

I puff up, reassessing my view of the slow, Southern gentleman act. "You know this how?"

"She's waiting in your office."

CHAPTER 18

Charlie

Max's office is not what I expect. I thought it would be Regency era leather or BDSM black rather than cozy Ethan Allen. A comfortable-looking cream sofa (*all the better to seduce you on, m'dear*) takes up one wall. Photos of Max and his family at his law school graduation, his parents wearing big, proud smiles (*see, I didn't just spawn from the devil, Charles!*) line a mantel over a non-working fire. Even a garish trophy to assure the world he wasn't always a bookworm sits on a bookcase with weighty, legal tomes.

I lean in to the hardware, expecting some signifier of his excellence at archery or lacrosse. The engraved plate says: LAKE FOREST HIGH DEBATE CHAMPIONSHIPS. 2ND PLACE.

Huh.

A shiver skitters down my spine, my body's typical response when I'm wrong about something. But I'm not wrong about Max Henderson. My instincts know a player when I see one and I'm ninety-nine-percent positive I've been approaching this problem correctly—i.e., ignoring it for the last two weeks.

As I'm mulling over why someone keeps a high school trophy for second place in anything, the door opens behind me. It's Sadie, the nice woman with the motherly smile who put me here earlier. She carries a tray with a teapot and what looks like double-chocolate Milano cookies. These people aren't screwing around.

I rush forward. "Oh, let me take that for you."

"No worries. And Max is on his way," she says, setting down the tray on the coffee table, which means we'll have to sit on the far-too-intimate sofa.

"I only meant to drop in. You don't need to go to all this trouble."

"Not at all!" she assures me. "The rest of Max's afternoon is free of appointments. Slow week for the miserable. Usually he'd be in his office, preparing for tomorrow's motions, but . . ." She trails off.

"But?"

"He needed to work off some steam at the PP."

"The PP?"

"Just a place the boys use when they have excess energy."

What, like a vitality-absorbing urinal? She says "boys" with a possessive pride, and there's that shiver again. My instincts are going haywire.

"Now, I'd let the tea draw a second."

I'm surprised that I could just waltz in without an appointment but Sadie and a rather imposing guy, whose body looked to be fighting the suit it was wearing, seemed strangely amused to see me. As if they'd been expecting me.

I'm about to ask more about "the PP" when a voice cuts in to my thoughts.

"Charlie, good to see you."

I raise my gaze then wish I hadn't. Max stands at the doorway in gym gear, looking oh-my-God sweaty. "Gym gear" isn't the right term, though. More like workout gear, meaning how he looks is inspiring my thigh muscles and all points in between into a thorough Kegels session.

Surely sweat-drenched tank tops are inappropriate in a place of business. What if clients saw him walking around like that? Vulnerable female clients in the throes of divorce?

At least his legs are covered, though "covered" is generous. Those sweatpants are incredibly thin and look to be doing a terrible job. I can make out strong thigh muscles, and as he moves in, he lifts the hem of his tank to swipe at his chin. *Walking and swiping.* He may as well be doing a *Magic Mike* routine! I don't need to imagine covered-up abs because there they are, front and center. Beautifully blocked ridges I long to run my tongue over. Again.

Right! I've seen all this before. Once was plenty. Today, my mission is not sex-related.

Sadie is walking out, but she grabs the doorframe when she gets to it, then presses a hand to her chest.

"Have pity, Max. We ladies are only human." She winks at me.

"Shut up," he replies with affection.

And then she's gone on a genial chuckle, the door closed behind her, leaving the scent of Earl Grey tea to mix with clean, male sweat, and whatever the hell I'm giving off since I've gone into heat.

Max hasn't moved, and I'm mesmerized by a trickle of perspiration making a lazy trek down the hollow of his throat. I can imagine how it would taste, how good it would feel on my tongue, doing nada to quench my thirst.

"Excuse me," he murmurs, and walks over to a cupboard. He takes out a towel and dabs his arms. "Usually I'd take a shower but I figured this was more important."

"It's not," I blurt. "It's really not. In fact, maybe I should come back." I slide a guilty glance at the tea tray, evidence that I've let this go too far. I should have turned tail as soon as it was clear Max wasn't immediately available.

I walk toward the door, my legs heavy in pink heels, barely able to skim an inch off the plush carpet.

"You're here now," Max says. "Let's have tea."

"I've clearly interrupted something . . ."

He sits on the sofa and starts pouring.

Tea and cookies. This is perfectly civilized except for the sweat-sheened god and the lovely way his forearm muscles flex as he holds the teapot. It's Wedgwood.

"Cream? Sugar?"

"Just honey, please."

He pours the honey onto a spoon, its golden-amber drip drawing me in. I take a seat on the sofa as far from him as possible. A Milano is perched on my saucer, and he hands off the tea. I'm proud my hand doesn't shake in the slightest.

"Max, I don't know what you think your game is but—"

He raises a palm. "Just a sec. Let's take a sip of tea first before we get into it."

He adds a spoonful of sugar, a drop of milk, and stirs. Slowly. Then he sips his tea. Also slowly.

"Now, what's on your mind, Charles?"

"Hello Fresh."

One eyebrow hitches. "Hello to you, too."

"You sent one of those meal-planning things to my parents' house, Max. What's your game here?"

His gaze is filled with . . . kindness. "That maybe your mother just needs some encouragement in the kitchen. Those meal services can get people thinking about food in a different way. My mother uses it. I use it. It's made me a better cook."

I bristle, annoyed at his reasonable explanation and the

evidence that he also cooks. When Donna called to thank me for the gift of a subscription to healthy meals from Hello Fresh, I was dumbfounded. Her terrible culinary skills have been a family joke and a cause of friction between my parents, but I've accepted it as have they. It never occurred to me to try to do anything about her cooking, such as lessons or a solution that might help with Sully's health.

But Max Henderson thought of it.

Donna was thrilled. The notion that this man might understand my parents' needs better than me does not sit well.

"Why did you do this, Max?" A wave of my hand between us makes it clear what I suspect.

Max's grin is all wolf. "I'm pretty sure that the way into a woman's panties is not through her father's stomach."

I blink at the absurdity. Course it's not. But it might be the way to a woman's heart . . .

No. That won't be happening.

"Unless . . ." Max says, his arm stretched out along the back of the sofa, revealing ropy cords of muscle and a tuft of underarm hair that I find unbearably erotic. "I've hit upon a new strategy for the *Player Playbook.* When a man has been as thoroughly rejected as I have—"

"We slept together, Max. Once. Surely enough for the man who doesn't do repeats or would prefer not to encourage a woman with silly ideas about a future."

"When a man has been as thoroughly rejected as I have," he repeats, "when all he can think of is how this object of his desire tastes and moans and sounds when she comes, when he's buried deep, then who can blame him for coming up with new ways to get her attention. Especially when he's sure she held herself back."

I want to latch onto the first tenet of his argument—the part about using my parents to get my attention—but there's a curious romanticism about it that makes me uneasy. Instead I choose to counter his other point.

"You think I held myself back?"

"I think you've conditioned yourself to play a certain part. Enough to arouse a potential mate's interest, but with a few layers hidden to keep guys from getting to the real you."

"And what's the real me?"

"The woman who likes to get bossy, who likes to tell her guy what to do in bed, who's not afraid to get specific about her needs. You've got it into your head that women like that scare off potential husbands. Some virgin/whore psychology bullshit about what a man desires in a wife. Is this your plan? Hide your needs while you target some idiot who can't handle all the facets that make up the complicated and exquisite Charlie Love?"

For the second time today, I have no words. This armchair—or sofa—analysis from Mr. Slickster makes me ill. Where does he get off serving me lovely Earl Grey tea and pretending to know a single thing about me? I know exactly what I need to find the right man.

A few nights ago, I let Max take control and I'm still grappling with whether that was a good idea or not. I felt as though he was giving me openings to take charge, get vocal, but I resisted, concerned that it was . . . a trap, perhaps? That sounds silly, but every encounter with a potential partner is fraught with tension as to the consequences. Will my need to get down and dirty be a check in the con column? If I just lie there, will I come across as too passive to hold his interest? Women are conditioned to play roles in every aspect of their lives, but nowhere is this more prevalent than in the bedroom. Three orgasms to the good, and I'm complaining of what exactly?

I finally find the words to speak—and the strength in my legs to stand.

"I apologize that our encounter so disappointed you."

Looking up at me, his expression registers frustration at my response. "That's not what I said and you know it."

I do know that, more's the pity. But I don't like how every word out of his mouth is a sharpened stiletto to my carefully cultivated cool. I want to be seen but not by someone like Max.

"I can take care of my parents, Max. And I don't need your dime store psychobabble." I move toward the door.

"Then why are you here?"

"Because Donna called, full of gratitude for my gift, which wasn't mine at all. She was confused, and now I have to go over there and show her how to cook it!"

"So, you're here because I rained all over your girl power parade?"

My blood, previously at a simmer, now bubbles to an unhealthy boil. I pivot to face him, only to find he's standing a foot away, both too close and too far. The scent of him invades my nostrils, makes my sex throb, my pulse pound.

"You got what you wanted, Max."

"I think we both did, but where was the romance? The cuddling? The soul-baring pillow to pillow? Hell, I'd even have taken a sandwich. You need to work on your post-coital game, Charles."

I fight my smile and barely win the battle. I'm not used to this level of charm. I don't usually inspire it, and I sure as hell don't believe I'm doing it here. In fact, I'm being my most uncharming self, yet Max is treating me like a high-strung Thoroughbred.

He's more intense that I imagined he would be—in person and in bed. I expected him to continue operating at a surface level, but he's already taken our interactions deeper. He has another gear, I suppose, when faced with a challenge.

I would be curious to see how long I could hold his interest. Only problem with that idea is that I suspect I'll start developing "feelings" for the guy. Also, it's time-wasting while I need to stay on target with the real thing.

Renewed in my purpose, I shake my head. "This can't work."

"Why?"

"Because outside of sex, you piss me off. So. Much."

"Use it."

"What?"

"This annoyance you have with me. Use it to make you feel good."

I already have. Once should be enough to unravel some of those knots. Once should be enough to make me a better co-worker and not scare small children and baristas with my sex-starved scowl.

Twice would be *unthinkable*.

"I think someone told you once that bad girls don't get the guy or some shit like that," he murmurs. "You're here, Charlie, because you wanted to get mad at me, you wanted to funnel that anger into something constructive."

"This isn't constructive," I hiss, shocked at his insight. "It's meaningless."

He inclines his head. "You needed an excuse to see me again. I needed one to get you here. Not every decision has to feed your life goals, Charlie, or put you on the path to Mr. Right. Some decisions can feed that part of you that needs in-the-moment, hot-as-fuck satisfaction."

I should be unnerved at how astute this man is, how he sees right into me. But I'm too turned on for a proper self-analysis. I might hate myself later, but right this minute, I'm going to take advantage of the gift Max is giving me.

The gift of being myself.

I splay a hand on his chest, my palm split between the

damp fabric of his tank and the heated skin revealed above the tank's neckline.

Nervously, I flick a glance over my shoulder.

"No one will come in," Max says, reaching behind me to click the lock on the door. His chest heaves, his Adam's apple bobs. Those midnight blue eyes of his have darkened so much that the color is unrecognizable.

"Take this off," I order and pleasure ripples through me at the rightness of it. How good it sounds to tell a man what I want.

He obliges, a little too slowly for my liking, but I guess he thinks it's a sexy tease. It is, but I don't need it. Every single second of our exchanges, every word from his mouth, fulfills that role. Right now, I demand to be filled.

I place my hand on his exposed chest, savoring every plane and contour.

"Are you sure—" I start, but don't finish because he clamps both hands on my ass and pulls me into his embrace. His mouth on mine is fire, the sweet flavor of the tea mingling with the unique taste of him. I'm lifted off the ground a couple of inches and transferred to the big table situated by the large window that overlooks the Chicago River.

"Don't think so hard," he murmurs against my lips. "I'm going to give you what you want but I'm going to need instructions."

Really? I'd assumed I could bluff my way through this with a well-timed moan and my hand over his, urging him on.

"The filthier the better, Charlie."

So far, he's making all the right moves, so I don't need to worry or do a thing, right? Except, there's a dim glow of dissatisfaction. I want him to be assertive but I also want to lead. It's usually not possible. Most guys resist a woman's aggressiveness in bed.

I can take care of you.

Just lie back and enjoy it.

Boring!

Max's strong hands are inching my skirt up, up, up until the curve of my butt feels the cool wood of his desk. I find the notion that Max wants me to dictate my needs interesting. Our first time together was amazing, but it felt . . . choreographed. As if Max follows a script that gets the women he beds off. Don't misunderstand me—I loved what he did, but I also get the impression I'm not the only one who needs to control our encounters.

"Touch me," I whisper.

His thumbs slide over my thighs to form a V in front of my sex. With a slight brush over the triangle of silky fabric, he activates the nerve endings between my legs.

"More," I urge. "Under my panties."

One thumb slides in and through the already damp, slick folds of my pussy. It's a shock. I shiver.

"Like this?" His thumb brushes my clit, so gently I can hardly stand it.

"Rough—rougher." But he's already there. Both our gazes are sealed to this spot between us, but neither can I miss that intriguing bulge in his sweatpants. It's pointing right where I need it to be.

"Do you have condoms?"

He frowns. "No, but we won't need them."

"I'm not—"

"I know," he soothes. "This is the Charlie Love Show." He falls to the floor, his hands on my ass, his breathing heavy against the triangle of silk shielding my sex. He's waiting for something.

"What?"

The lightest of knuckle grazes across the front of my panties. "You tell me."

I'm in charge.

Max pushes my buttons but I have no doubt that consent is important to him. Peering up at me, he's back to that intense version I'm starting to adore.

"My panties . . . take them off."

He does. Still he waits. It's excruciating. I never realized how sexy power is—almost as powerful as sex.

"I want you to—to . . ."

"To what?"

"Enjoy me."

His groan is loud and lusty, his tongue is warm and probing, and my orgasm is so damn good Nathan will think I'm Boss of the Year when I see him tomorrow.

CHAPTER 19

"Marriage is like twirling a baton, turning hand springs or eating with chopsticks. It looks easy until you try it."

— HELEN ROWLAND

Max

Cujo is trying to destroy my life.

Mitzi is still not picking up. It's been three weeks, and the woman has crafted her revenge well.

Brava, Mitzi, brava.

The canine menace has already shat on a deposition and peed on a motion. I try not to take it as a personal affront to the quality of my work.

It's Saturday morning, and I'm in a stare-down for the ages. The dog wins because I don't have time for this BS.

"All right, you little prick, let's go get some air."

I head down to the lobby of my building and get a

surprise: Sully leaning on the doorman's podium, chatting with Benji. Empathetic laughter rings through the hallowed halls of the Gloucester.

"Hey, Sully." I approach them both, curious. "Everything okay?"

"Max!" Sully reaches for the hand I'm currently using to hold Cujo, which surprises me enough to release him. Not that he can get far but he immediately makes a lunge for Mrs. Gawlik, who's just come in through the front door that Benji neglected to open while he was otherwise occupied.

I see major trouble on my hands, but before Cujo can cause any damage, he's scooped up by Sully. Belatedly, Benji leaps into action to take Mrs. G's packages, and we all breathe a sigh of relief because that could have turned out much worse.

"To what do I owe the pleasure?" I take a step to remove the dog from Sully's arms, but he seems to have the situation in hand.

"Heard I owe you big-time for my change in diet." He gives a rogue's grin I can't help but return. "I was in the neighborhood and thought I'd stop by."

I could ask him how he knows where I live but we all have our ways. "I'm taking this little fucker for a walk. Want to tag along?"

"Sure, why not?"

We wave our goodbyes at Benji, who has his hands full with Mrs. G's scolding, and head out to the May sunshine. Sully places my pup on the ground with a lot more consideration than the little mofo deserves and doesn't seem too inclined to return the lead to me.

"What do we call him?"

"Cujo."

"Good name. Want to head to the park, fella?"

Cujo gives no indication one way or the other, but then

he doesn't really have a choice. I'm the boss here. We head to Lincoln Park, just a cockapoo's throw away from home.

"So, yeah, Max," Sully says after a minute of getting the dog settled into a walking rhythm, "I'm mighty appreciative of that meal thing. The soy-glazed chicken is a culinary miracle."

"One of my favorites, too."

"Or at least it would be if Donna could follow directions."

I pause, judging the situation, and decide that it would be best served with honesty. "You're never too old to learn how to follow directions yourself, Sully. Lots of guys cook these days. And I imagine you have more time on your hands since your retirement."

"I'm pretty busy," he mutters, clearly not enjoying my lack of solidarity. But I'm not some old-school guy who thinks women have their place. Hell, I'm downright encouraging of the women in my life being all that they can be. Particularly one woman whose husky orders in my ear have pretty much reframed everything I expected from a sexual relationship.

Just thinking of how Charlie fell apart on my office desk a couple of days ago gets me a touch too heated for comfort, especially in the presence of the woman's father. But Christ, I loved seeing her take on that role. Here's a tip for all you ladies out there: Guys like their sexual partners vocal and specific.

I switch back to the present. "When my dad had pneumonia last year, he tried overdoing it. He needed to feel in charge, especially with my mom fussing around him all the time."

Sully snorts, drawing a curious look from Cujo. "Know what that's like."

"He had to retire early, too, and it did not sit well."

"All right, Max, no need to beat around the bush."

Fair enough. "So you want to feel more in charge of your

health and your life, then cook your own dinner. Give your wife a goddamn break, and maybe make *her* some soy-glazed chicken."

Sully looks like I suggested he eat the cute little turd Cujo just gifted the world. "I start cooking and it upsets the order of things."

"The order has been upset since the ladies got the vote, Sully, and our lives are better for it. Just accept it. Your lot will be much more peaceful."

"She and Charlie are ganging up on me." He stops as Cujo wanders toward a tree for a quick pee. "You seen much of my Charlie these days?"

"Not really," I reply because it's true. I'm trying to give her space.

"Her last boyfriend was a prick."

I should be saying "I'm not her boyfriend" but my curiosity rages. "Oh, yeah?"

"She never told me why they broke up, but I figure he thought she wasn't good enough for him. He was some fancy-pants real estate guy. Maybe you know him. Jeremy Craven."

I know of him. Jeremy Craven is a blue blood with pots of money and political aspirations. He's always struck me as having a broom rammed up his ass, not Charlie's style at all. I try to imagine Craven getting sent to Cubs jail for defending his girl, and the vision refuses to form.

I bend down to bag up Cujo's poop because apparently the new world order requires humans become subservient to their canine masters. Imagining smearing it all over one of Craven's suits makes the task a little less terrible.

I jog to the trashcan and deposit the deposit. Heading back, I say, "I think I need to get something straight here. Charlie's not interested in me."

"You piss her off," Sully states matter-of-factly.

"I do."

"Work in a job she doesn't think too highly of."

"Uh-huh."

"Are a bit of a player."

"No bit about it." The admission feels off, like ash on my tongue.

The man rubs his unshaven jaw and holds my gaze. "She needs a challenge, someone who understands how passionate she is about things. When she first came to us, she had a lot of emotion inside her and no way to channel it right. To be honest, she was hell to be around, but she had good reasons—" He stops, his eyes clouding with memory. "We got through it together, as a family. I just want someone to see all my beautiful daughter has to offer."

My heart squeezes at his profession of love.

The problem is that I see everything Charlie Love is about, but she's put me in a box, only to be opened when she has an itch to scratch. "You missed your calling, Sully. You should be a matchmaker in your retirement."

The man smiles, knowing he won't get any further with me.

"Donna wants me to exercise. Go for walks."

"Like what you're doing now?"

He shrugs. "You're saying I should get a dog? Donna won't stand for that."

Now it's my turn to smile. "Sully, I have the answer to all your problems."

CHAPTER 20

Charlie

"Maybe you should go on that show."

I narrow my eyes, first at Donna, then at the TV screen which is currently showing one of the more whorish scenes from *The Bachelor*: the man himself in a hot tub with three of the contestants looking for fame, fortune, and . . . love?

The whole thing is ridiculous. Needless to say, I'm a huge fan.

I shouldn't enjoy it so much because it doesn't exactly paint relationships and weddings in the best light. No marriage that starts off on this shaky footing could possibly go the distance. But Donna and I have been watching it from the beginning, unafraid to pronounce wine-assisted judgment. This is the first time she's suggested I become a contestant, however.

"With my mouth, you know I'd be voted off after the first week."

Donna hoists an eyebrow. "You need to learn about compromise, Charlie. You're never going to be happy if you can't learn how to meet a man in the middle."

"I'm trying to be less . . . abrasive." I know I can be opinionated and take-charge, qualities that are off-putting to most men. Of course, I'd like to have a special someone, but how much of my personality must I suppress to get there? Doing the dating dance is exhausting. Making ourselves vulnerable is the hardest thing we can do. Letting another person bear witness to the ugliness inside takes true courage.

Maybe I'm not brave enough to truly let go with another person.

You let go with Max, though. He challenged me to be myself, to surrender to my raw need. With him, I feel liberated, and holy shit, that scares the hell out of me. If only he was a better bet for the long haul . . . and there I go confusing a hot fling for the real thing.

He hasn't called or texted since my visit to his office four days ago.

I'm furious that I've noticed.

"So how are things here?" I ask, eager to change the subject.

"Your father cooked dinner last night."

I pick up the remote and pause right on a still of Brandy, one of the contestants who can cry on demand, having an "accidental" nip slip. "Did you film it?"

"I thought about it, but he was kind of self-conscious." Donna giggles. "He's an even worse cook than I am! The instructions are on those cards they send, and he still burned the quesadillas."

"But at least he's trying," I say with a smile. Tonight, Sully is at a poker game at Jimmy Finster's. All this "getting out of the house" business bothers me.

"I suppose." Unease crosses her face. "He's not been the same since the heart attack. It's made him a . . . faded version of himself."

I've noticed it, too, and I've also seen the pressure it's placed on their marriage. On Donna herself. I take her hand. "And how are you doing? This has been tough on you, too."

"Oh, I'm fine." She squeezes my hand, her eyes bright with threatened tears. "He's not the easiest man to live with, but he has passion. Usually."

"Woman, you are a saint. I know I didn't make it easy and I don't say it enough."

"You're so like him. I think that's why you two made that connection so quickly."

She's right. Sully and I bonded freaky-fast once I learned to let go of the anger and trust the adults who were heaven-sent to heal me. My bond with Donna is quieter, but no less strong.

"You don't have to worry about me," I assure her. "There's some weirdo out there who can handle me. I'm sure of it."

"Like Max."

"No, not like Max."

"He bought us dinners, Charlie."

"Yeah, that you have to cook yourself. If he was really interested, he would have sent a chef."

She remains silently judgmental as only a mother can, so I jump into the gap.

"Donna, Max is . . ." I can't say with certainty what he is. There's a shape-shifter quality to him, and every time I think I have him figured out, he takes on another form.

"Are you seeing him?"

"Not officially."

Her eyes widen. "Charlotte Michaela Love, are you telling

me you're using that nice boy . . . *for sex?*" Her horror fills the room to such an extent *I* almost feel sorry for that nice boy—and acutely embarrassed for myself.

"Uh, we're not having this conversation."

"If I was twenty years younger . . ."

"We're definitely not having this conversation!"

"I'll get the Breyers mint chocolate chip." She's off to the kitchen before I can tell her ice cream, yes, heart-to-hearts about my sex life, a big fat no. Not that we don't share, but as a kid, I was more likely to confide in Sully about my boy troubles.

My phone chimes, and I grab it quickly. Only Penny. And then I feel terrible that I'm disappointed because my friend texted instead of my . . . what? My booty call?

PENNY

Divorced. No kids. Stockbroker. OWNS A BOAT!

The accompanying pic looks like an overgrown frat boy, a little *too* overgrown if that paunch is any indication. And that sends my thoughts to Max's abs, which are . . . *Focus.*

CHARLIE

And?

PENNY

Which part of "owns a boat" do you not understand?

CHARLIE

Sounds like a workaholic whose wife canned him because he spends too much time drinking beer on the lake.

PENNY

I give up.

I can't blame her. Apparently my mind refuses to reckon with any other men because it's filled with one man. The worst man.

He bought us dinners, Charlie. It's a little thing that's not a little thing. In his office, he gave me free rein to be myself. My wanton, bossy, absurdly undatable self.

I open up a new message and shoot it off before Donna returns and I can second-guess myself.

CHARLIE

Hey

MAX

Hey yourself.

(Within five seconds, I might add. I'm not giddy. You're giddy!)

CHARLIE

~~I'm not home right now but maybe we could get together later~~
~~I'm not home right now but I was thinking of you~~
~~I'm not home right now but . . .~~

What's up?

MAX

Oh, the usual. Nipple watch on The Bachelor.

I laugh like an idiot and look around the room guiltily as warmth floods my chest. He watches junk TV yet somehow manages to rise in my estimation every time I talk to him.

CHARLIE

Nipple watch here as well. Monday night ritual with Donna and wine and ice cream.

MAX

Hmm. I think we'll need to break this episode
down later. In person.

I squee shamelessly, then to counter it, I mull over my
next text with the appropriate gravitas.

CHARLIE

~~Give me 20~~
~~Give me 30~~

Come over an hour after the show ends.

MAX

I'll be there in half an hour, so don't make me
wait, you saucy tease.

With perfect timing, Donna reappears carrying two
bowls of ice cream covered in hot fudge. She always goes the
extra mile on dessert, and we spend a couple of minutes
nom-nomming while we catch up with the paused show.
When it hits the commercial, she turns to me.

"He was here for you, Charlie."

"Who?"

"Max. At the poker game."

I snort, a little freaked out by her prescience. "He's a Cubs
fan, that's all."

"He's a Charlie fan," Donna says with a sly smile. "When
he stopped by on Thursday—"

"What? He came back?"

"Of course he came back. We watched *The Voice*. He
thinks Adam Levine is too full of himself, but I like him."

"Max?"

"Adam Levine. And Max." Donna is a topic-hopping
butterfly, and it takes all my powers of focus to keep up with

her. But I understand this: Max Henderson, the guy whose body I plan to use and abuse until it's a dried-out husk, is spending more time with my parents than any guy I've ever dated.

Weird, but also kind of lovely.

CHAPTER 21

"Marriages come and go, but divorces are forever."

— NORA EPHRON

Charlie

Remember that scene in *Bridesmaids* where Annie goes to her friend's bridal shower, organized by the bride's future sister-in-law, and she shows up in a beater car to a mansion?

I am currently living this.

Usually I don't attend my clients' bridal showers as our relationship is all business. But Gina is different. The girl is feeling a little lost and more than a touch overwhelmed with everything that's happening to her. I know she doesn't have a ton of friends in Chicago, so I helped put together a guest list, even inviting my own bestie—Penny, because Nathan insisted it was not part of his job description—and the rest of the book club to pad the numbers. Also expected are colleagues from the school where she works and whomever

163

else Mrs. Henderson decided should grace the threshold of her home.

Yep. The shower is being held at Casa Henderson where Max and James spent their formative years riding ponies, playing croquet, and shooting the servants for shits 'n' giggles. You know, the traditional upbringing of the fabulously wealthy.

"Wow, this is nice," Penny says, craning her neck to take in the view. Overlooking the lake in Kenilworth on Chicago's North Shore, the house is indeed beautiful and definitely in the millions range, just not quite as ostentatious as I'd expect for the Henderson meat money.

"Pity Max won't be here," Penny twitters. "I'm *dying* to see you two going at it hammer and tongs. Maybe you should bring him around for dinner."

"We're not dating, Pen."

I didn't even have to fess up about my one time with Max that's now turned into at least ten times in two weeks. Each morning after, Nathan has gleefully called Penny to tell her I'm in a good, sometimes a *great* mood. I should never have hired him, but the dimples and the bridezillas.

I pull my Honda Civic up to the entrance, get out, and hand my keys to the valet. Yep, they have a freakin'—*shut up. It's just efficient car management.*

The front door is already open, so we step inside a foyer beautifully decorated in the couple's wedding theme colors of lilac and silver. I wave to Jessica and Gaby from book club, both standing at a door to where I expect the festivities are happening. Also in my sight line are three well-dressed guys. Definitely not catering staff.

A woman with dark hair, expertly streaked with gray, and smiling blue eyes greets us.

"Hello! Welcome! I'm Susanne Henderson, mother of the groom!" She pumps my hand, and I'm surprised to hear her

British accent. "You must be Charlie. I recognize you from the photo on the Perfect Day website, and you are just as gorgeous in person. My son told me how helpful you've been." She finally takes a breath and gazes at me expectantly.

"Max said I was helpful?" Too late, I realize she meant her *other* son. "Oh, James. Well, he and Gina are so lovely together." My cover-up sounds flustered.

I search for phoniness in her smile. James and Gina's is a rather quick courtship, after all, and there's a lot of money in play. She appears open and genuine.

"This is Penny, Mrs. Henderson. She's in the book club with Gina."

"Wonderful! What are you reading?"

We usually read romance but Jessica, our tyrannical founder, insisted that this month "we break out of our emotional chains." I name a good-for-us *New York Times* bestseller that's putting me into a nightly coma.

"God, I hated that one. So bloody pompous," Mrs. Henderson says with great feeling, and I immediately fall in love with her.

"So," Penny says. "There are guys here."

"Yes, well spotted!" She winks—or at least I think it's a wink. One eyelid closes all the way, and the other falls to half-mast. "We decided to do a co-ed shower, even though most of the men would rather pull out their fingernails than attend. That way, everyone is forced to join in the fun." Mrs. Henderson leans in conspiratorially. "Now, I'm a little worried about Gina. She said she doesn't talk to her family much, and I get the impression she's rather alone here in Chicago."

"She's not," I say. "She's a recent transplant so that can be tough, but I expect she'll settle in soon." Challenge spikes my voice, and I pin on my own smile.

Mrs. Henderson squeezes my hand, like we're already

best friends. Her next words are said slowly, clearly to appease the crazy, strangely protective wedding planner in the room. "We abso-*lute*-ly adore her. She and James are such a great complement to each other, and I know she'll make him happy. So you've met Max?"

"A couple of times," I answer neutrally. Yes, I am Switzerland.

This makes her laugh and little lines appear around her bright eyes. She opens her mouth but before she can speak, a deep, loud, also-British voice calls out, "Suzy, you bloody gorgeous creature!"

We all turn to find a so-handsome-it-hurts guy in a blue-going-on-teal blazer, a fedora, and—get this—white jeans that shouldn't work but look the bomb. I could hang on his cheekbones they're so gorgeous. He lifts Max's mother off the ground, making her screech.

"Lucas, you naughty boy! Put me down!"

"Run away with me, Suzy. I left the car running outside."

She swats at his chest. "You know Jack would hunt us down, darling. Viciously."

"The man *is* a beast. And he would kick my arse." His face lights up on seeing me and Penny. He tips his hat. "Ladies, Lucas Wright. Rejected and heartbroken, but at your service."

A grinning Mrs. Henderson shakes her head. "Ignore this scoundrel, ladies. Let's get you some champagne."

Two minutes later, I'm in the middle of a gaggle of excited women and a murder of not-so-excited men. Gina isn't nearly as friendless as I thought, and I enjoy seeing her making a real effort to stop and chat to everyone instead of sticking with the few people she knows well. In her hand is a flute with something sparkling, which I know isn't alcoholic. She and James have decided to keep the pregnancy under wraps for now as a stress-reduction measure, and we've already discussed ways she could avoid alcohol in company and not give up her secret. Ginger ale where possible and barely a sip of her bubbly where not.

After popping my gift on the table practically straining under the weight of wrapped and beribboned boxes, Penny and I approach the guest of honor.

"Hey, blushing bride-to-be, how's it going?"

"Fuckin' awesome," she says, then pulls us both in for a joint, slightly awkward hug. "Shit, I'm so nervous, and I always swear like a motherfucker when I'm nervous."

This girl is me ten years ago.

"You're fine. Where's James?" And Max, because if this is a co-ed event, I can't imagine he'd stay away, not after he promised to be supportive. My pulse picks up at the thought.

Gina looks around. "Over there with his dad."

I follow her gaze to where James is standing with an older man, who is essentially an aged-up version of the eldest Henderson brother. This preview of future Max is so darn tasty I resolve to expand my dating profiles to an older male demographic.

"Papa Henderson is pretty hot," Penny blurts before I can make a fool of myself and say the same thing.

"Right? That's what I have to look forward to." Gina's slightly troubled gaze wanders to the table, piled high with a mountain of gifts. "Susanne is a total doll. Have you met her?"

"Yes. Very sweet."

Much sweeter than I imagined. Given Max's opposition to happily-ever-afters, I expected some cold society matron who would slice through me with a crystal-cut stare and a clipped "how do you do?" Max would have grown up in a loveless home that made him protective of James but reluctant to open his starved heart to anyone because his parents had taught him that love was gray and pointless.

Apparently, I'm looking for reasons to feel sorry for Max Henderson.

Mrs. H appears behind her husband and squeezes in under his arm. He pats her still-got-it butt and pulls her into his side for a kiss, while James rolls his eyes with a familiar indulgence. Adorable.

I don't see any evidence of a chilly upbringing here. Now I'm left wondering who hurt Max—and if I can reach the part of him so closed off.

Shut that down. I should not be trying to see Max as anything other than what he's chosen to present. And what he's chosen is cynical, wealthy playboy who occasionally shows slivers of compassion. For Sully and Donna, for James, for me.

This level of examination is not in keeping with the objectives of the day: to celebrate love and ensure that the happy couple need never again buy another kitchen gadget.

CHAPTER 22

Max

I'd thought this would be a good time to hit the golf course with James and Dad. Turns out my mom had other ideas.

We're doing this co-ed deal for Gina because she doesn't know that many people in Chicago. That's okay. I can be a trouper, but then I spot Charlie and realize that this afternoon might not be such a chore after all. For the last couple of weeks, we've been seeing each other off and on. Or rather, she's been summoning me by text, and I've been heading over to her place to let her work me into an exhausted but very sated and happy camper.

"Hello, Ms. Love," I say behind her, which is a bad idea because my approach made her splash her drink on her dress. "Damn, sorry 'bout that."

She shakes her head. "This creeping up on me is getting to be a habit, Henderson."

"My best work is done from behind," I murmur in her ear, but then I notice a sort-of-familiar, pretty Asian woman, her mouth curved in a grin, and realize I need to behave. "Hi, I'm Max."

"Penny Kim. We met once about five years ago during the dedication of the Henderson wing at Lurie Children's. I work in fundraising there."

"Right. Nice to see you again. You know Charlie?"

"Since college." She grins in an oh-the-stories-I-could-tell kind of way.

Charlie is dabbing a napkin at the neckline of her dress, something peach-colored and floral.

"Come on, let me get you some club soda."

With a quelling look at her grinning friend that tells me they were definitely talking about me, she follows me out of the living room.

"Surprised to see you here," I say.

"Gina invited me." She sounds a touch defensive.

"Okay. Still surprised. You two are getting friendly?"

Cute nose twitch. "A little. I don't usually hang with clients but Gina—"

"It's great you're helping her out."

She seems tense as I lead her into the French country style kitchen—or so my mom tells me. All I know is that ceramic roosters en masse give me the creeps. I check the beverage stash in the pantry and arm myself with a bottle of club soda and a dishcloth.

"Your parents' home is lovely. And I met your mom. So nice."

"Hard to believe she produced a hard-boiled cynic like me, right?"

There's that smile. Charlie Love enjoys my negatives far too much.

"Your parents *do* seem very happy together . . ."

"I was engaged once."

Charlie looks just as surprised as me by this revelation. Where the hell did that come from? The moment stretches because neither of us has a clue what to do with it.

"Bad wedding planner?" she asks with a wry grin that yields a laugh from me.

"Just a bad match."

No longer smiling, she nods, her gaze all compassion I neither want nor need. "She hurt you?"

"She opened my eyes."

"That's your story?"

"And I'm sticking to it." She needn't know that Becca was interested only in the Henderson name, the penthouse, the trappings. You see I've already trod this path that James is on: the taste tests, the fittings, the bridal showers (plural). Five years is plenty of time for me to get over it, and my job ensures I don't get complacent.

It's her turn to share, but she doesn't volunteer any information.

"How about you and Craven?"

"I'd ask how you know but you've already proven that you have your ways."

"I googled you"—*after your dad filled me in*—"and saw you stepping out at a few events with him. Made the society pages."

"It was something casual," she says, "or that's what he told me later. He needed someone who better fit his aspirations. Has an eye on a congressional run, you see."

I knew it. Fucking asshole. "What? Charlie Love not diplomatic enough to be a politician's sidekick?"

"Not with this trucker mouth," she says with a grin that even when forced is beautiful.

I touch a finger beneath her chin. "I happen to adore this trucker mouth."

"Yeah, ya do. You love when it's wrapped around your co—"

I cut her off with a kiss, loving the taste of her—champagne, cupcake frosting, and Charlie. I can make her forget this asshole who couldn't see the many facets of this woman. Tigress, professional, a surprise in every moment.

His loss.

But is it my gain? I'm telling myself I can't lead her on, yet that's not what's happening. She's leading me to a place that feels intimate and familiar. To a place I'm starting to crave, this bubble with just me and her.

I deepen the kiss, holding her jaw to pour all my need into this joining. Maybe it was the mention of Becca. Maybe it was the allusion to Craven. Either way, I need this and I think Charlie does, too.

She should be afraid of the passion I'm unleashing in the middle of my parents' kitchen, but she doesn't hold back. She curls a hand around my neck and pins me in place for the sensual response. I'll say this for Charlie—once she commits, she goes all in.

We separate, a little dazed, a lot confused.

"Hi," she says.

I laugh, delight flooding every cell. "Hi."

"Hello, you two," I hear in the unmistakable baritone of my father.

I turn, unsurprised to see my mom is with him. They're a package deal.

Dad gives me a look. "Maybe you should introduce us to this strange young woman you're debauching in our kitchen, Max."

My mom's smile is designed to put Charlie at ease. "Oh, Jack, this isn't a strange young woman. It's Charlie. She's a friend of Gina's."

"Looks like she's a friend of Max's," Dad says, the old Henderson blues twinkling.

Mom spots the dishcloth and club soda. "Oh, dear, Charlie, did you spill something on your lovely dress?"

"Just a little champagne, Mrs. Henderson. It's nothing."

"My fault, Mom."

"Very creative, son," Dad offers. "Going to show her your debate trophies next? They're in his old bedroom, Charlie."

Charlie laughs, and it is fucking sunshine in my chest. "I know all about your son's verbal accomplishments. He's got the gift."

Mom looks on indulgently. "If only he'd use it for good. He was always so impassioned as a child. Civil rights, that's what I thought he'd do."

My mother thinks I should be arguing constitutional law before the Supreme Court on a weekly basis. "I don't need you ganging up on me with Charlie, Mom. She's in the marriage-creation business so we're kind of at odds."

"Or well-balanced," my mom quips, to which Charlie gives a snort. So much for that idea.

"I'd better get back," Charlie says. "I'm sure we're missing all the fun and games."

"Oh, I don't know . . ." my dad responds with a hammy wink. Jesus.

"Lovely to meet you, Mr. and Mrs. Henderson."

"Jack and Susanne," my mom says, but as soon as Charlie is out of earshot, she murmurs, "or Dad and Mom?"

"Don't, Susanne." I call her this when she's overstepping. "That's not happening."

"Something's happening. I've never seen you light up around anyone like that, not even whatsherface."

Loyal to the core, my mother refuses to say Becca's name. She's right, though. I don't recall feeling this way around my former fiancée. Maybe I was too young to understand real love and all that jazz and by the time I did, my day-to-day work experience hardened the crust over my heart.

Not that I'm in love with Charlie. I just don't enjoy her dismissal of me, but then I only have myself to blame.

"Jack, I need a word with our son alone."

Shit, that's Mom's warpath voice. I look to Dad for help here, but he merely shrugs and leaves the kitchen. This is how they've stayed married all these years. The man knows when to make an exit.

I try to preempt the melodrama with a whiny, "Mom . . ." but she's having none of it.

"Do you like this girl?"

A simple question that demands a simple answer. This is my mom, so I can't lie. "Yes."

"And how are you holding up with all this?" She gestures around the kitchen but I know what she means. The relentless countdown to joy.

"It was a long time ago, Mom. I'm not the same person, and I'm not going to let what happened with Becca affect my best man duties."

"I know that, darling. But it seems you will let it close you off to the possibilities of happiness and companionship."

"I'm plenty happy and have no shortage of companionship." Even before the sentence is finished, I know it sounds tired. I'm not a little bored with myself and this rut I've dug.

Becca hurt me and made me gun-shy when it comes to relationships. There, I've said it.

"Darling Max, fruit of my womb"—my shudder draws her wicked grin—"you are so much more than your father's strong chin and *my* razor-sharp intellect and excellent sense of humor. You are generous and compassionate, and any woman would be blessed to have you. Now go tell this woman that today's the start of her lucky life."

~

BACK IN THE PARLOR, games are afoot. I can't win the movie quote trivia one because I created it, but it's fun to walk around and give hints.

Now there's no good reason why anyone should be stumped by "As you wish" and "Here's looking at you, kid." These are movie quote classics, and I'm exceedingly judgmental of anyone who doesn't have an inkling where these lines are concerned. I'm more prepared to forgive someone who hasn't seen *Ghost* or *The English Patient*, which are technically romances but actually garbage.

Per usual I'm seeking out Ms. Love when I spot her in animated conversation with Lucas and her friend Penny. That cheeky limey fucker is obviously turning the charm up to eleven—in white jeans, I might add—so I zero in to break it up.

"*As Good as It Gets*," Charlie is saying, her head unnecessarily close to Lucas's. "Jack Nicholson said, 'You make me want to be a better man.'"

"Yes, but *should* he have said it?" Lucas replies. "No one should change for someone else. That's bloody ridiculous. If she can't accept him, warts and all, then what chance do they have?"

"If he can't make some effort to become the man she needs, then I'd say their chances are zero."

"Wright, you are pissing in the wind here," I say. "Charlie's not going to be swayed by your poorly constructed argument. It's unimaginative and anti-romance."

"You come up with this, Maxie?" He waves the quiz between us.

"Guilty."

"Really?" Charlie turns to me, surprised, which was obviously Lucas's intention. His wink rivals my father's for top-shelf hambone. "A movie trivia game with romantic quotes?"

"Our Max prefers his romance in the movies," Lucas says. "Unrealistic, impossibly idealistic, and usually involving some unattainable chick."

"And this, my friend, is why no woman wants to put up with you." I take Charlie's form from her and scan it. "Top of the class, Ms. Love. I guess you know your movies. Any favorites here?"

She clutches her chest dramatically. "'Oh, it's nobody's fault but my own! I was looking up . . . it was the nearest thing to heaven! You were there.'" Her Deborah Kerr impression is flawless, and I know my accents having been raised by a Brit. "That one's probably too mushy for you, Henderson, but it does have your fave, Cary Grant."

True. In fact, I love *An Affair to Remember* despite the weird children-singing-to-the-heroine-in-the-hospital interlude. I love it mostly because it's about a man—a playboy—who everyone assumes one thing about but who is transformed by a woman. There's something meta about it, too. Cary Grant, up until this point in his career, was viewed as a one-trick pony, all slick surfaces and smooth patter. In *Affair*, he reveals theretofore unseen subtleties and depths as an actor. A breakout role twenty years in the making.

Penny chimes in and addresses Charlie. "Every time I see that scene where—"

"He walks into her bedroom and spots the portrait—"

"And knows she can't walk because the woman who bought the painting—"

"Was in a wheelchair?" Charlie finishes.

"I lose it!" they both say in unison, then laugh in recognition.

"She's in a wheelchair?" Lucas is staring at them like they've lost their minds. "Christ, that sounds depressing."

"It's not," I say. It kind of is, but it's movie-depressing, meant to wring us dry and make us feel better about ourselves. "They had to go through all this pain before they could find each other. Love's not supposed to be easy."

Now Lucas is regarding me like I've lost the plot, and maybe I have. Charlie's cheeks are tagged with color, and she takes a sip of her champagne to get over the now-awkward silence that's descended on our merry little group.

I can't stand this a moment longer.

"I need a word with you, Charles." I pull her aside, out of earshot of the rest, which requires walking her out to the patio.

"Oh, this is lovely," she says with a wave over the perfectly manicured lawns that we really should pay someone to land-scape but which Susanne insists on doing herself like it's her full-time job. My parents are the worst rich people ever.

"Yes, it is. Thanks. My mom's a gardening freak. Come over to my place tonight." The words leave my brain and throat in a staccato burst, as smooth as the gravel under our feet.

She wrinkles her nose and, of course, it's as adorable as it is annoying. Adorable because look at her. Annoying because it heralds resistance.

"Max, this can't go on."

"What?"

"The hooking up, the booty calls. I need to get serious about my dating life."

I'm trying not to take offense. Sully thinks we'd be good together. My co-workers are giving me shit. My parents, dammit, are already picking out the wedding china. Why can everyone see this but Charlie Love? I thought the woman was a believer.

Jesus, am *I* the romantic here?

Placing a hand on her hip, I lean in and try to work my

magic. "Go on a date with me. I promise not to break your heart."

Her eyes flash with the hurt I haven't delivered yet. "You can't promise that. No one can."

She's right. But I can give it the old college try, can't I?

CHAPTER 23

"In every marriage more than a week old, there are grounds for divorce. The trick is to find, and continue to find, grounds for marriage."

— ROBERT ANDERSON

Charlie

"So. That was interesting," Penny says as soon as we clear the drive at Casa Henderson on our way back to the city.

"Yeah, Gina seemed to really hold her own. I'm so glad for her."

"Right. Thrilled. And you know I'm talking about you and Max Henderson. The man is clearly smitten with you."

"Do you realize how ridiculous you sound? It's just a flirtation."

"With hot sex as your reward."

"Well, I have to get something for putting up with all that slick."

She chuckles, and I feel guilty at dismissing him for a quick laugh. I know there's more to him than that, and that's really my insecurity at play.

"And I thought you didn't like each other. Where were all the zingers and jabs about marriage, etc.? It was all so . . . affectionate. Like you guys recognize each other."

My heart is thundering. That's exactly how I felt when we were in his kitchen and he told me about his broken engagement. So, the details were sketchy but Max cracking open like that made something inside me—surely, not my heart— soar in acknowledgment. When he kissed me, it felt important.

I felt important.

I don't want to be played. I don't want to get hurt. And I'm realizing that Max has the potential to do both.

"He's very charming," is all I can say, not wanting to let on that I caved like a cheap suitcase at his request and am heading over to his place later. Thankfully, my phone rings before Penny can probe further. "See who that is, would you?"

Penny fishes my phone from my purse. "It's Donna."

"Put her on speaker. Hi, Donna!" I say, relieved to have the Max conversation behind me. "I'm driving and Penny's with me."

"Hello, Penny," Donna says. "How's that gorgeous husband of yours?"

"Still gorgeous!"

"Oh, good. Charlie, your father's having an affair."

I should get a gold medal for my eye-roll restraint. "He's not having an affair. I mean, who'd have him? Other than you."

"He's been out of the house every morning for the last two weeks."

"Prime affair time," I say. "Probably hooking up with some hussy at the bodega on the corner."

Donna remains silent.

I slide an uncomfortable glance at Penny, who shrugs. "C'mon, you can't be serious. Where does he say he goes?"

"For a walk, but he takes the truck. He had blond hairs on his jacket when he came home today. Blond-whitish hairs. I think she's older."

I think she doesn't exist. "Maybe you should offer to go for walks with him."

"Why would I do that?"

I sigh, giving up. I know all relationships have their ups and downs but I hope when I get to that point, I'll feel comfortable asking my guy if he's having an affair. Though, I'm more likely to smother him in his sleep first.

"Do you want me to stop by? I'm on my way back into the city."

"Oh, no. I just thought that maybe you could talk to him the next time you see him."

"Or you could, y'know, just ask."

"That's not how marriages work, Charlie. One day, you'll know."

At this rate, not likely.

~

I AM DRESSED FOR WAR.

Fuck-me heels, my best lingerie, a short 'n' sexy trench—and that's about it. Max Henderson might be calling this a date, but I'll show him how a strong, kick-ass, fun-seeking woman does casual sex.

Only on approaching the Gloucester's doorman and being told to "go right on up, Ms. Love" do I feel as if I might have misjudged the situation. The point is to get in, get off, and get out in record time. I don't need Max Henderson wowing me with his particular brand of rich playboy as he shows me around his penthouse with a casual wave to the priceless art here and a nod to the wine cellar there. Not that I'm capable of being seduced by such things. I have principles.

The penthouse has its own elevator because of course it does, and with each floor I ascend, my plan for sexy distance slowly disintegrates. By the time I reach the top, I'm feeling a little silly in my seduction duds. Like I'm playing dress-up. The elevator opens into a foyer, and pinned to the door directly in my sight line is a note in Sharpie ink.

Come in and take the stairs to the right. Don't let the monster out. Caution: He may try to lick you even though I've already told him that's my job.

My tummy flutters as my lips tug into a grin.

I push open the door tentatively, ready to be attacked. The cutie-pie cockapoo I saw in the park sits obediently inside the door. I hunker down and rub behind his ears.

"Hey, fella, how are you doing?"

He pops up on all four legs and wags his tail. Love!

I stand and do a quick scan. The place is in darkness except for a muzzy, city-lit glow through the floor-to-ceiling windows. It's as big as I expected yet manages to feel intimate, which might just as easily be credited to the night wrapping it up in a sensual blanket.

A single spotlight illuminates the stairway to the right. I'm intrigued, but then Max Henderson manages to surprise me at every turn. He's always a step ahead of me, which keeps things interesting but regularly throws me off-kilter.

Another sign is taped to the wall near the first stair rung: *Ten steps to MAX-imum pleasure* with an arrow pointing up. It's cheesy but it still places a big smile on my face.

I consider taking off my heels but figure I'm heading to

his bedroom anyway, so I keep them on. "Wish me luck," I whisper to Cujo.

The stairway is lit with what looks like Christmas lights along the side rails. A soft-hearted me would say it was romantic but I dismiss this idea because Max doesn't do romance. *Except in the movies.* Still, my heart pulses dangerously as I head up the stairs.

At the top is not what I expect—I thought it'd open out to a loft bedroom, but no. There's another door, this time with the note:

Enter only if you are ready to have your body worshipped, your socks knocked off, and deep conversations about the meaning of it all.

Does this guy know how to push a few lady buttons or what? I palm the door ajar, surprised to find a concrete floor on the other side.

I'm on the roof.

Complete with what looks like a grill, a bar, a sofa, and one of those retractable screens for projecting images. Max stands at the bar, sleeves of his open neck shirt rolled up, board shorts keeping things interesting below the waist, looking like an ad straight out of *GQ.*

"Welcome to our date," he says.

Heart in confusion, I look around. "This is the roof."

"Excellent powers of observation, Charles."

"I thought I was heading to your bedroom."

"I have high hopes we'll get there eventually. This is the detour." He gives me an up-down look. "Expecting rain?"

"Um, no."

"Then how about you give me your coat." He makes a move for the belt. I swat him away.

"That's not such a good idea." God, I feel ridiculous. There's a candlelit table set near the grill, with what looks like a yummy salad. I spot avocados and slices of kiwi. "I'm not really dressed for dinner. I thought I'd just—"

"Wham-bam the hell out of me, then leave me a boneless mess curled up in a fetal ball on my floor?"

"On your bed," I clarify. "I'm not completely heartless."

His hands cup my waist. "Are you telling me that beneath this trench you're wearing an outfit designed to have me inside you in ten seconds?"

"More like five."

On a groan, he gathers me in and kisses me stupid. His taste is divine, and so, so addictive.

He draws back, slides a finger to the V of the trench, and pulls an inch forward for a sneak peek. His fingertip is light yet it triggers a riot of sensation throughout my sensitive body. "You're killin' me, Charles."

No one makes me feel as sexy as Max does. Every second with him sucks the balance right out of me. Feeling discombobulated, I'm acutely aware that I can't take off the trench and sit and eat in my underwear.

"Just a moment," he murmurs against my lips, then slips behind me out the door I just came through.

In thirty seconds, he's back with a button-down blue shirt, the one he wore today at the bridal shower if I'm not mistaken. He hands it off. "Wear this, but don't do up all the buttons, you tease."

He even turns his back. There's something very old-fashioned and chivalrous about it, and before he faces me again, I inhale the scent of his shirt, loving that he gave me something that was recently next to his skin. While slipping off the trench, I feel incredibly exposed yet excited on the roof with buildings all around, unseen eyes possibly watching me in my underwear. But, I'm not enjoying it *that* much. Quickly, I redress.

"Okay in heels?" he asks, perusing my legs, which look

great with his shirt skimming the tops of my thighs. His tone says he's more than okay with it, but he holds up thick socks in offering. How sweet is that?

"I'll manage." Casting a glance around, I'm newly taken aback by our location about fifteen stories above the ground. I putter a few steps toward the edge of the roof, which is handily protected by a waist-high wall. All the same, I'm careful, especially in my heels. "This is spectacular."

The roof overlooks Lincoln Park on one side with the lake in the distance where I can make out sail boats drifting their way across the calm water under a darkening dusk. A few steps to the other side takes me opposite a building, its windows like eyes reflecting a far-off civilization. I spy figures going about their business: a cute (at least, from a distance) guy working out, a flicker of blue light of a TV, a cat viewing the world beneath his window.

"Who else can access this roof?"

"No one," Max says, handing me a glass of champagne. "It's all mine."

Mine. A delicious shiver thrills through me at the right-ness of that word on his lips.

Penthouses with exclusive roof access in Lincoln Park do not come cheap, but then I know all this. I know that Max comes from money, so much that he can give it away to charity and still have pots to spare.

Something buzzes and Max checks his phone.

"Sorry, I have to take this. I'll just be a second."

"Sure."

He moves away, so I can only hear snatches of the conversation from his side. It sounds like he's trying to calm the caller down.

"I know, but we're almost there . . . the report will be in on Monday."

"Slapping him might make you feel better, but it's not good for

our case. I think you're going to be pleasantly surprised at what my guy has to say."

And finally, a more stern: *"Get in a cab now, sweetheart . . ."*

I'm trying not to eavesdrop—okay, I'm not trying at all. Cabs, reports, slaps, and Max has a "guy"?

A good five minutes later, Max hangs up. "Sorry about that. A client."

"Is she okay?"

"She will be. Especially when I show her just how much cash her soon-to-be ex has been hiding in an offshore account." He rakes his hair, and I can see him trying to switch his mind off from work, obviously still concerned about what he heard. "She ran across him at a restaurant just now and wanted to show him how much she despises him open-palm style. Luckily she took my advice and checked in with me first."

"Are you usually on call like this?"

"All part of the service."

Flustered, I sip my wine. "But what do they want at nine on a Saturday evening, Max?"

He cocks his head, a wicked smile creasing his handsome features. "So cynical."

"Come on, Max. Are you really telling me that none of your clients have ever come on to you?"

"No, I'm not saying that, but I'm gentle with my rejections. And I always reject clients. These women—and yes, most of my clients are women, usually older, usually twenty to thirty years into a marriage—are incredibly vulnerable. A lot of them gave up careers to nurture their husband and children. They feel lost, degraded, beaten down. Nothing pisses me off more than seeing a woman tossed aside like garbage. My job is to ensure they come out of this process with the biggest settlement I can get them, a plan for what comes next, and renewed self-respect."

I'm stunned, not because of what Max said, but at how blasé I've been about what he does. Maybe even about who he is.

"So who looks out for the poor husbands?"

He laughs. "Believe me, there are plenty enough lawyers to go around. At our firm, Lucas has a mostly male client base. He's a strong advocate for fathers' rights. Grant is equal opportunity. If you're miserable, he'll take your case regardless of gender."

"But it must be hard to witness all that negativity. Especially when there are kids involved."

He considers this for a moment. "Most of my clients have grown children but the few I deal with where the kids are used to score points? Those are heartbreaking. But I look at it as trying to re-settle these people, parents and kids, who are living fractured, volatile lives. Instability can really take a toll."

I know exactly what he means. The year after my mom's death was like living in a hurricane-ravaged city with quicksand beneath my feet.

Because he's thrown me, I pivot away from him to take in the view. Every moment with Max chips away at my preconceptions, and the stubborn part of me wants to hold on to them for a little longer. I'm not ready for this. For him.

He wraps his arms around me from behind and I allow myself to sink into him—purely so I won't topple off the roof, of course.

"Do you ever imagine what's going on in those apartments?" I whisper. "The sad stories. The happy endings."

"The crimes being plotted. The lives being destroyed."

"So cynical."

"That's me."

I turn in his arms. "Not about everything. In fact, I think it's largely an act."

"Oh, yeah?"

"No one who enjoys classic movies and creates trivia games with romance movie quotes could be that detached from the potential of falling in love."

And no one who defends broken women with such ferocity, who soothes their fears and takes their panicked calls, could be nearly as bad as I've painted him.

CHAPTER 24

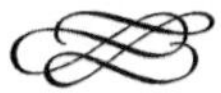

Max

Maybe knowing what Charlie is wearing underneath my shirt is driving me insane throughout dinner, but I don't think so. It's that she looks like an angel in disguise. I know how she begs when she wants, how she looks when she's turned on, how she sounds when she comes. She might project aloofness, but I've seen her heat. It's like I'm the *Predator* alien with that special vision. Without it, I'd only see cool blue and white. With it—with what I know about this woman—I see red and pink and orange blotches of passion.

Yeah, yeah, the metaphor sucks.

"This is pretty fantastic," she says, chewing around a bite of perfectly cooked steak.

"You can thank Hello Fresh."

"God, how much are they paying you?"

I grin. "Perfect for the busy professional."

"I've been meaning to tell you to cancel that subscription for Donna and Sully. I can take it over."

"I'm happy to treat them for a while."

She opens her mouth to argue, but the look I give her puts a stop to that. Charlie Love has a hard time with compliments and nice things.

"Thanks, that's really kind of you. Though Donna is probably thinking of ways to poison him because he's having an affair."

I almost choke on a rosemary potato wedge. "Sully?"

She raises a hand. "He's not but he's getting out of the house every day—which is what she wanted all along, incidentally—and now she's suspicious. He *must* be up to something."

I wonder if I should tell her what I know, but worry she might accuse me of interfering again like she did when I signed them up for the meal plan. Instead I change the subject.

"So why did you become a wedding planner?"

Elbows on the table, she cups her chin and flutters her eyelashes madly. "Why, so I could live vicariously through my clients while I wait for the one, silly."

I wince, remembering our first meeting. "I was a jerk. James's news had thrown me, and I felt like I was behind the eight ball, with everyone in on the big secret. I'm sorry."

She shrugs, like she's heard criticism of her profession before and it's no big deal. Considering my own career choice gets a lot of flak, I should know better. I hate myself a little for piling on and making her feel less than awesome.

"You're forgiven," she says. "To be honest, I just love organizing events that will rock my clients' worlds. My Super Bowl parties in college were legendary, and then my first job after graduation with a really useful English and communications degree was in events management. After a while, I realized that I wanted to tie that to something more meaningful—and no event is more meaningful than two people coming together to unite their lives. It's special and I love being a part of it." She bites down on her lip and picks up her wineglass. "I know. You think that's ridiculously sentimental."

"I think it's wonderful to do what makes you happy. And your happy becomes someone else's happy."

She leans forward. "Until?"

"Until what?"

"Don't you want to qualify that with 'until the happy hits the fan and turns to shit'?"

I might have said that a month ago. "Fifty percent of marriages fail but that leaves fifty percent of marriages that succeed. My parents are still going strong. I have high hopes for James and Gina." So Grant and Aubrey didn't make it, and as for me and Becca . . . I dodged a bullet for sure.

"To the fifty percent," she says, raising her glass.

"To the fifty percent." Whichever half that may be. "There's ice cream for dessert, but I thought maybe we'd watch a movie first."

"I'd love that."

I lead her to the sofa set up in front of the screen with projector, then click play on my laptop. I settle in and she snuggles right into me, her heels kicked off and her legs curled underneath her body.

"Cold?"

"A little," she murmurs, so I pull a blanket over her bare legs, memorizing the sight to keep me going for a while.

She perks up when the film's title come up. *"Rear Window?"*

"It's your favorite."

"It is," she says, clearly overcome that I remembered.

If you haven't seen it, Jimmy Stewart plays Jeff, a photo-journalist laid up with a broken leg who has nothing to do but watch his neighbors through a telephoto lens. One day, he spots what he thinks is evidence of a murder. The film has a million layers, revealing something different to me every time, but at its heart it's a rip-roaring suspense movie.

Ninety minutes later, we're getting to the thrilling climax, and I'm pretty close myself with the way Charlie's wrapped around me, tucked under my chin. Her breasts are soft against my side, which makes me the opposite of soft. Every time she gets excited by something on the screen, she expels a quick breath that flutters against my neck and grips me tighter.

Ahem, back to the movie. Grace Kelly's character, Lisa, has just broken into Thorwald's apartment to look for evidence of Mrs. T's demise when the villain/likely wife-murderer returns. It's one of the most heart-pounding scenes in cinema because Jeff (broken leg, remember?) can only watch in impotence as it unfolds across the courtyard. I know Grace Kelly will get out of it—she's the hero's girl after all, and I've seen it a million times—but with each new viewing, I'm punched in the gut. We're all Jimmy Stewart in this moment, stymied by broken limbs, real or metaphorical, watching helplessly, unable to do a thing as events around us impact our immediate lives.

"I love this scene," Charlie says. "I love how he comes to the realization."

"What realization?"

"That he loves her."

Every hair on my body does a military salute. Now I know this movie inside out. Throughout there's this tension between Lisa and Jeff—she's the society girl in haute couture, he's the world-weary photo-journalist who won't settle down. He's crazy about her, of course, but he doesn't think she fits in his world. By the time they've solved the crime and she's out of danger, she's wearing jeans and he's resigned to his love for her. The end.

But I never thought too hard about the moment when it happens, the second when he goes from ignorant bliss to full-scale panic. Yes, she's in peril, but it's not just that. His entire future is at risk—a future he's now imagining without her in it.

Watching Jimmy Stewart watch Grace Kelly in danger is to watch a man having a painful, life-changing epiphany.

"I never thought of it like that." My voice sounds rusty.

"All through the movie, he's so closed off, so separate from everyone. Dictating the plays, pulling the strings, but just then, he can't. He's powerless. And in this scene, she's the action hero. She's the one making things happen. His world is out of control, and it's about to change irrevocably one way or another." Charlie smiles at me, and I think I smile back at her. Something painted on and clown-like. "I imagine it's what love must feel like. Terrifying and revealing all at once."

My heart is in chaos, yet I manage to croak out, "You've never been in love?"

She looks away. "I thought so once. I was on the brink of falling . . ."

"But?"

"I'd hoped that revealing myself in pieces would make it easier."

"On who?"

Her grin is utterly heartbreaking. "On us both, I suppose. But my truth wasn't so palatable."

There's no disguising her hurt and I want to kill this Craven bastard with my bare hands. *But his loss . . .* "I can't imagine your truth is so hard to swallow. You don't scare me, Charlie Love."

She reaches over to my laptop and hits the space bar to

pause the movie, then shifts and straddles me under the blanket. Gently, her hands caress my face, feeling her way over my brow and cheekbones and jaw. Who knew reverence could be so sexy?

"Sure about that, Max? What did you say that first time we met? *Desperate to get hitched.* Women like me and Mitzi and probably Gina must give you the heebie-jeebies." She fake-shudders, which makes me laugh, but does nothing to relieve the tension tautening every cell.

My hands cup her ass, seeking control in the familiar, a way back to a time when I knew what I was doing. We stare at each other, letting the moment surround us and draw us in.

I'm falling for this woman, and it's just as she said. Terrifying and revealing, all at once. My palms are itchy. My heartbeat is close to heart-attack levels. I'd like to throw up, please. If this is what love is like, I want no part of it.

I don't want my happiness to lie in the hands of another person. I tried it. It sucked. Being a change-phobic stick-in-the-mud might be boring but it's hella safe. Expectations remain at minimum, no one gets hurt, and we're all good buds in the end. I'd rather collect friends than scornful ex-lovers or scar tissue around my heart.

"You okay, Max?" Her sharp green eyes seek out weakness. I refuse to give in to her. Not yet.

Instead I move her so she's flush against my erection. "Not really. Help a guy out?"

Her clever fingers move to the button of my shorts, a reprieve of sorts. "Let me see what I can do."

CHAPTER 25

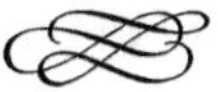

"A successful marriage requires falling in love many times, always with the same person."

— MIGNON MCLAUGHLIN

Max

I wake up with a start to find my toes being licked by that little monster, Cujo. He's been on his best behavior since Charlie came over last night, even remaining relatively quiet while I fucked her on the kitchen counter. (Our ice-cream trek turned into something else.)

The sheets are still warm, so she hasn't gone far. I can hear movement in the direction of the kitchen, and I wait for it to hit me.

The itch.

Usually, I'd be feeling scratchy about now if a woman was

still hanging around in the morning, but not with Charlie. I like her here. I like her, period.

A voice in the back of my head replaces "like" with another L-word and I shut that fucker down. Can't a man have a moment of peace before he falls headlong into the abyss?

I grab sweatpants and head out to the kitchen. Charlie is there, again in my shirt—so cute, so sexy, so mine—reading her phone screen.

"Morning, Charles," I murmur.

"Oh, hi." Her eyes are bright, with not a hint of regret or her usual guardedness. She runs a hand over my abs and slips two fingers below the waistband of my sweats, pulling me closer. On tiptoes, she gives me a quick kiss. It's hardly anything, and I love it.

"Coffee?"

"Please."

Cujo trots about, getting underfoot, generally making a nuisance of himself. I take a seat at the kitchen island and let the domesticity of it all soak in.

"I hope you don't mind, but I fed him," Charlie says, her hands moving deftly to the Keurig.

"One born every minute."

"What?"

"Sucker. He's getting fat, so I have him on a diet."

"What are you talking about?" She hunkers down to rub behind the ears of the dog, which gives me a nice view of the valley between her breasts. Cujo gives her the sad eyes, like it's the first time anyone has showered affection on him in weeks. What a huckster.

"He's skin and bone," Charlie declares.

"Don't indulge him. As soon as Mitzi's back, he's out of here."

Standing again, Charlie leans against the counter, coffee

mug in hand, her beautiful legs a vision to behold. "Now tell the truth. Why did she really dump the dog on you? I feel like there's more to this."

So do I. I'm fairly certain I spotted her in Lincoln Park one morning last week, but she was gone before I could catch up with her. She's not answering her phone, and I've given up checking in with her doorman. I figure there's a life lesson in here somewhere and I'm halfway to learning it.

"Maybe I was a little too casual with her feelings. I'm usually very careful to manage expectations."

She eyes me over her coffee. "It's easy to lay down ground rules at the outset but people aren't robots who follow a preordained script, are they? Managing expectations might be working gangbusters for you but there are two people in any—um, exchange of bodily fluids. You can't predict how someone else will react no matter how much you insist it should go one way. I see it with couples I work with all the time. I'm sure you do as well."

"Sex does complicate things," I say sagely, liking this analogy between our respective professions. "Wedding menus, too, I imagine."

"But it doesn't have to. The sex, anyway. Conflict over a wedding menu might be trickier." Her grin sets me on fire. God, I love her smile. "You don't need to worry I'm going to chase you down in the park and unload small animals on you. Well, maybe a ferret, if you do something that really pisses me off." She sets her mug down and throws her arms around my neck. I swivel on the stool and wrap my legs around her. My hands naturally wander to that gorgeous rear of hers.

"Want to head out for a no-expectations, I-need-eggs brunch?" I ask. "Or I could make us something, and we could stay in all day and watch movies?"

She blinks at that, stiffens in my arms. "If this is how you treat your hookups, I can see why they might get confused."

But it's not. If anyone is confused it's me because this is not my usual MO. How do I convince Charlie that we're worth a shot? I'm about to open my mouth to make my case when I hear a gravelly voice behind me.

"Morning, kiddos."

Charlie's eyes fly wide, flick to me, then to the new arrival—Sully. Damn, I'd totally forgotten he'd be stopping by this morning. "What are you doing here?"

Cujo answers the question by heading straight to Sully, leash in his mouth. I usually hang it on a hook near the door so I've no idea what voodoo the little shit is performing to retrieve it.

Sully bends down and attaches the leash. "What does it look like? I'm walkin' the dog."

Charlie now realizes that she's standing in my kitchen, wearing my shirt, with me draped all over her. She removes herself from my space, and my body mourns the loss of her .. . I was going to say "warmth" but it's more. It's so much more.

"*This* is what you've been doing for the last two weeks? Donna thinks you're having an affair, you idiot!" Then to me: "Why didn't you tell me?"

"You weren't all that happy when I interfered the last time. I figured he'd tell you if he wanted to."

"Every couple has their secrets," Sully says, standing and leaning against the kitchen island. "Looks like I'm not the only one."

"There's nothing going on here, Sully," she says, "so get that matchmaking glint out of your eye."

Sully winks at me. Oh, man, don't do that. Charlie won't like it. "Fair enough, girl. Any coffee going?"

"Make it yourself, Mr. Secretive. And you'd better tell

Donna what's going on. She's worried." Charlie takes herself out of the kitchen, but her bad mood lingers like a noxious smell.

"You should have told her, buddy," I say. "Both of them." I don't like being in the middle of things but it's my own fault for sticking my nose in.

"You and I need to talk," he says gravely. He checks out the hallway to my bedroom, where Charlie just went.

Damn. I'd thought he would approve but he's evidently not happy about it. He knows I'm nowhere near good enough for her, that I can never live up to her vision of perfection when it comes to marriage.

Not only does he know this, I am also so knowledgeable on the subject I should have a diploma. Master's in Bad News for Charlie, *magna cum laude.*

A minute later, Charlie click-clacks into the kitchen in those killer heels and that trench. She looks absolutely stunning, all golden limbs and a sex-tossed cloud of hair I'm taking full credit for. I work myself into a lather not getting an erection in front of her father.

"You're leaving?"

"Yep. Wouldn't want to break up this good thing you have going here."

"What about brunch?" I ask at the same time Sully queries, "Why are you wearing a raincoat?"

"It's going to rain," she says, her tone ominous. "Enjoy your Sunday. Sully, talk to Donna." And then she's gone.

"That girl knows how to make an exit," Sully says.

"That she does." Feeling grouchy that I'm stuck with Sully and not his sexy daughter, I move toward the Keurig. The man and I still need to have that talk, and like a Band-Aid, it's better we rip it off in one fell swoop. "What's on your mind?"

He rubs his mouth, then utters the last thing I want to hear right now.

"I need a divorce."

~

SHIT, this can*not* be happening. I think I'd rather have heard the man ream me out for banging his daughter. I take a breath, then another.

"Okay, tell me why. And bad cooking isn't grounds for divorce in Illinois."

Sully closes his mouth on hearing this, then takes a moment fumbling for a different excuse. "We've reached the end of our road, Max. Getting sick made me realize that I've been treading water for some time now. I'm not happy, and I don't think Donna is."

"Boredom isn't grounds, either. Every marriage settles into a groove that often migrates to a rut. At a certain point—"

"At my age, you mean?"

"At a certain point," I repeat, "you recognize that the life you've built together has value. It also has bad cooking, occasional sniping, and long stretches of boredom. You thought all the work was done, but the age of you or your marriage doesn't give you a pass. It still takes work. Let me ask you this. Do you still like your wife?"

"Of course I do. Donna is the best."

"Then that's a start. You guys should try couples counseling before you take the drastic step of dissolving your union. That's my advice. Talk to her about how you feel, but do not—I repeat, do not—mention the D-word."

"Nice business model you have there," he says with a half-sneer. "Thought you'd want a client."

You can't afford me, buddy.

"This is my standard intake for all potential clients, Sully. You might also want to talk to Charlie." If anyone can put him straight, it's her. I will not be getting in the middle of this. I saw how she acted when Sully showed up.

The cock-blocker scoffs. "Charlie's all hearts and flowers. That's her job plus she's emotionally invested in seeing her parents stick together. She can't be part of this."

For fuck's sake. "She already is. She's a part of you. A part of Donna. Look, she's not going to fall apart if your marriage fails, Frank, but you need to involve her now before any decisions are made. Hell, you need to involve your wife, okay?" My voice has risen slightly there so I sound like Cujo when he's trying to get into my bedroom in the morning.

"Okay, okay!" The man looks exasperated. I don't care. My hands have to remain spotless here.

Piece said and conscience somewhat clean, I grab a K-Cup pod and load it up. But all I can think of are Charlie's words just before she left. *It's going to rain.*

Honey, it's already fucking pouring.

CHAPTER 26

"Success in marriage is more than finding the right person. It is being the right person."

— ROBERT BROWNING

Max

"So, what time do the strippers get here, mate?"

I eye Lucas across the low table between us at The Library, the swanky speakeasy bar in the basement of the Gilt Bar. As best man, my job is see my brother off into the shackled afterlife with the required amount of debauchery. Sure, this could involve strippers but frankly, that's overdone, isn't it?

"Get a couple of drinks in you and the stage is yours, Wright."

He stands up and shakes his ass—or arse, as he'd say—all the while pointing at me. "I'll fucking do it, too!"

Laughing, James runs a hand through his hair and catches my eye. We decided on something classy for his last hurrah, and as the Gilt Bar is our usual place, reserving its small event space was a no-brainer. Our party is intimate: a couple of guys James went to college with, a few work buddies, and Grant and Lucas, who have always been close to my brother. I invited Dad but he didn't want to cramp his boys' style. (He kept winking at me. Either he had something in his eye or he believes strippers are on the menu, despite all my assurances to the contrary.)

Not everyone is a whiskey drinker, but those of us who imbibe are partaking of the tasting I set up. Our whiskey sommelier is Trinity, and she's as gorgeous as her name sounds. With her dark hair, glossy brown skin, almond-shaped eyes, and diamond-studded nose, Lucas can't stop looking at her.

"Close your mouth," I say.

Trinity places a tray of tasting glasses in front of us. Earlier, she dropped off charts with sections for appearance, nose, and palate, along with prompts for intensity, barrel, age, sulphur, and peat. As a seasoned whiskey drinker, I know you can describe it as more than "smoky," though I'm not sure if even my refined palate can distinguish between "dirt" and "forest floor."

"The first thing you want to do is check the color," Trinity says. "Turn your tasting chart over to the blank side and hold the whiskey against it. You could be looking at pale gold, straw, amber—"

"Piss," Lucas interjects, and when everyone glares at him, he amends it to, "Sorry, urine."

Ladies and germs, I give you the British—all class.

Trinity looks down her nose at him. "That's not a standardized color."

"Sorry, we can't take him anywhere," James says, though he's barely containing his laughter.

"How'd you get to be a whiskey expert, Trinity?" Lucas asks her, oblivious to the 'tude rolling off her.

"Years of training. Next, you'll want to assess its clarity and viscosity . . ."

We follow the instructions and try our best to minimize Lucas's inanity. He's the chattiest person I know but this is OTT even for him. When Trinity leaves to get the next round in, I turn to him with my palms up.

"If you're trying to impress her, you are fucking up royally."

"You think?" Lucas tracks her at the bar. She's definitely not returning the favor. "I thought I was winning her over."

"Tell her the color of your last dump," Grant mutters. "I'm sure she'd love it."

That makes everyone laugh, especially coming from the usually taciturn Grant. After a few more rounds and Lucas entertaining us (but not Trinity) with a long digression over the inclusion of "Band-Aids" as a tasting note on the chart—I swear, this is listed under the peat section—I pull James aside to the bar.

"Sorry about Lucas, bro. I can only assume he's in love with Whiskey Girl."

"It's all good. Happens to the best of us."

I pause, thinking on what I want to say. James and I have fallen out of our usual groove. Between his wedding planning and my schedule ramping up, we've missed most of our weekly meet-ups over the last couple of months. Springtime, and everyone's filing for divorce. Nothing like a harsh Chicago winter and the cabin fever that entails to make people question their life choices.

"Feels like the end of something," I mutter. "I know I'll see you, but—I don't know . . . it'll be different. Not bad, different, just different, different."

Trinity places a couple of drinks down before us with a subtle smile, then slides back into the shadows like a whiskey ninja. It's beautifully done.

James raises his glass, and there's that comma-shaped smirk near his mouth, the one he gets when he has something momentous to say.

"So, you're on board, Max?"

"Course I am."

"Would this change of heart have anything to do with a green-eyed purveyor of matrimonial monstrosities?"

I lift my glass and clink against his, not quite ready to articulate my feelings for Charlie. They're too new and frankly, too scary. "I'm not saying I buy the whole hearts-and-flowers, happily-ever-after with woodland animals and choirs of tweety birds, but I can see that Gina makes you happy. However, because I'm older than you, I've taken the precaution of gathering some pearls of wisdom." Reaching inside my jacket, I pull out a small Moleskine notebook, labeled with JAMES & GINA—WORDS TO LIVE BY. I hand it over.

Bewildered, he opens the first page. I lean in to read it with him. It's a message from Dad:

Never go to bed angry. Stay up and fight all night!

We both chuckle because we can hear Dad's voice, as if he's here with us. The next one is from Lucas:

The two best phrases to include in your vocabulary are "I understand" and "You're right."

"Of course."

He reads through the book I asked all of the important people in his life to contribute to.

"Mom says I should say yes far more often than I say no."

"Sounds about right. Jack and Susanne seem to have figured out the magic formula."

"It's not magic. It's work, but it's worth it because the important things require effort."

I know this. Despite being born with a silver spoon in my perfect mouth, I've never been afraid of effort. Learning to speak without stammering, graduating first in my class at Northwestern Law, crafting arguments that get my clients closure—all of these required I work my ass off. Donating my trust fund was the right decision; it would have been too easy to use it as a fallback. And giving it up revealed who I am and more important, who Becca, my former fiancée was.

So, why am I afraid of taking a chance with someone? I could blame it on Becca, but really, I know the reason. I don't like change. I've worked hard to get to a point in my life where I'm happy and bringing someone else into it is going to upset the pH levels of my stable existence. I like them where they are.

Marriage is *all* about change and compromise. I see it with my clients every day. People don't want to work on the little stuff, the big stuff, and everything in between. As soon as there's effort involved, it comes crashing down. But mostly, I don't want to choose wrong. I want to think the most important relationship of my life is a slam dunk.

I chose poorly before. Boy did I ever.

"So, nothing from you?" James turns over to a blank page.

"Not sure I can give you any advice. You've always known what you're about, Jim-Jam, but . . ." I grab a pen—another perfectly placed gift from our bartender—open to a blank page and write my piece.

He reads it and laughs at my three little words of wisdom:
Never stop dating.

"I assume you mean my wife."

"What better way to keep a marriage healthy than to act like you're *not* married?"

~

Two hours and multiple adult beverages later we find ourselves at a nearby club where it's Abba night.

I could blame the alcohol but really this is all on James the sap, who said he missed his fiancée. Gina's bachelorette party has gone the more traditional route—they started with male strippers and graduated to "Dancing Queen." They even went all out and dressed the part. We plow through the clubbers in go-go boots, glitter-covered jumpsuits, and short skirts that leave little to the imagination to find Gina and co standing at one end of the bar.

Charlie Love is there because the universe has decreed it.

"Baby!" Gina calls out and throws her arms around James's neck. "Are you drunk?"

He holds her face, seeming to check if all the constituent parts are still present. A silent conversation happens before our eyes, then he smiles and says, "I'm drunk on you."

All the women in the group go "Aww!" The men . . . okay, the men do it, too, but add eye rolls to temper the schmaltz.

I sidle over to Charlie, making no secret of the fact I find her mini skirt and white pleather boots to be just what I need to see. "Good night?"

"Yeah, the strippers were awesome. Gave me all sorts of ideas."

"For stripper-themed weddings?"

"It could happen!" She gives a Goldie Hawn–like giggle. "How did things go with you guys?"

"Much more quiet and definitely more classy, except we lost Lucas along the way. He stayed behind to make a play for the whiskey sommelier at the Gilt Bar."

"Nice."

"She's out of his league." I move in and lean closer. "And you look like you're out of mine tonight, Ms. Love."

"Finally, you're getting it, Mr. Cynic." She pushes back on my chest but it turns into a palm spread that lingers and explores.

I feel a nudge and when I turn, Gina's there, cheeks flushed, her mouth in a big smile. "Hey, Maximus."

"Hey, GeeGee. Good to see you." Because it is. Maybe it's the whiskey but I was careful not to overdo it, wanting to keep my wits about me as chaperone for the group. Tonight, I'm full of love for my fellow man—and woman. James and I are on the same page again and sure, change is coming but I can handle it.

"Let's get some champagne in, shall we?"

Once our order is placed, Gina and James huddle close, poring over something. I incline my head to Charlie's, inhaling that scent of her that never fails to start me up. "What's that about?"

"Oh, we all got together and filled a notebook with advice for the bride. 'Leave the toilet seat up to confuse him'—that kind of thing."

"Advice, huh?" The champagne is poured, and I can't help smiling at the symmetry, or maybe my lack of originality.

"Yeah." She squints at me, that half-moon curve to her lips getting broader. "What's so funny?"

"Well, you see—" I don't get a chance to finish because Charlie has skirted me with the skill of an NBA great and whip-fast, placed a palm over the hand Gina has wrapped around a champagne flute.

"Oh, honey, you don't want to do that."

"I don't?" Gina's eyes go wide. "Right, I don't." She practically jumps and drops the glass so that it spills all over the bar. "Oh, God, that's so stupid of me." Wide eyes are now welling. What's happening here?

"Hey, it's okay," Charlie says while she mops up the spilled champagne on the bar. "You're fine."

Gina nods. "I am." But a quick glance at James confirms that she's not. "I need to . . ."

I'm looking at the spilled drink, now being soaked up by napkins. "What's up? You okay?" I study Gina's hands, looking for evidence she might have cut herself.

"I need the bathroom," Gina murmurs on a sniff before she heads off in her silver platform boots. It should be funny but the way James and Charlie look at each other, it's clearly not. James vanishes before I have a chance to find out what the hell is going on, which leaves Charlie.

"What happened there?"

"Oh, she's emotional. Every bride gets moments like that."

"Where she can't drink?"

Smiling tightly, Charlie continues to mop the bar. "She's taking it easy tonight so I was looking out for her."

That's not what happened. I know it and she knows I know.

"What are you hiding from me?"

"You should ask James."

"I'm asking you." But I already know. The moment Charlie stopped that glass from reaching Gina's lips, I knew. "She's pregnant and everyone's in the loop but me. Do my parents know?"

"Not that I'm aware," she gushes. "Max, they wanted to keep it to themselves for a while."

"Yet you knew."

There's no missing the accusation in my tone. The bite in my words.

"Only because she got sick during her first wedding dress fitting. I took her to my place and—"

"The pregnancy test in your bathroom."

"Yes."

I puff up. "That was over a month ago. You've known all this time and you kept it to yourself."

"James is your brother. It wasn't for me to share. It was private."

"But you knew because you were there. You're always there. Here. Right at the center of it all."

Speaking of symmetry, my statement is not unlike what Charlie once lobbed at me the night we first hooked up. She told me I was everywhere she turned.

I told her it was the universe telling us something.

What's the universe telling me now? That this woman is privy to my family's secrets. She knows more about my brother's personal life than I do.

"I'm working closely with your brother and his fiancée," she says, her tone one of eminent restraint. "This is my job."

"But you said yourself you don't usually get this involved. You took Gina under your wing because—why?" Is this her game? Some long con to get clients? A husband? "It gets you closer to certain types of people. Connections you can use for your business. For you."

Green eyes flashing, she jerks back. "I took her under my wing because she was all alone and needed a friend. But sure, tell me all about my ulterior motives. Tell me how getting closer to Gina gets me an in with high society and the Meat Money Hendersons. Tell me how I've manipulated and used my friendship with Gina to catch a rich husband."

"I didn't say that." I pretty much said that.

"No, you didn't, Mr. Verbal-I-Got-All-the-Words. For once in your life, you let a snide implication do the work for you. Come on, Max, you're better than this. Say it straight. Don't pull your punches now."

That pisses me off and shuts me up. I know I've crossed a line, but I'm not ready to back down.

"That's okay, Max. I think we both know where we stand here. Maybe you should go check on your brother and make sure your future sister-in-law and nephew or niece are okay. Use your righteous indignation to protect your family."

And then she stomps off, leaving a heap load of righteous indignation in her wake.

I know I screwed up.

I might be about to do it again.

In the corridor leading to the restrooms, I find my brother waiting outside the ladies. "Gina okay?"

"I think so. She's just kind of emotional. A lot going on."

I back up to the wall so we're side by side. "Define a lot."

He gusts out a sigh. "She's pregnant. And before you get all pissy because I didn't tell you, please recognize that this situation is not about you, Max. You are on the periphery here. The center of this is Gina and me and our baby. I know your feelings are hurt but I'm not going to soothe your ego right now."

Well, that sure told me. "Worst brother ever, right?"

He shoots a lightning bolt of a look at me.

"I mean *me*," I clarify. "I'm the worst brother ever. You didn't tell me—you've stopped telling me anything important because I'm on a need-to-know basis. I'm not central enough to your life for you to trust me."

He rolls his eyes at my amateur dramatics.

"Yeah, yeah, there I go making it all about me again." I elbow him gently until his mouth curves slightly.

He rubs a hand over his face, then turns to me, his expression one of torment. "Dude, you're my favorite person in the world after Gina. You have to know that."

I'm immensely grateful because for a moment I felt very alone. "Thanks."

"She's stressed enough as it is. I wanted to marry her quickly anyway so we wouldn't have this long, drawn-out planning drama. The wedding stuff is bad enough, and we're trying to focus on the positive. Frankly, I don't know what we would have done without Charlie taking charge. Not just the wedding, but she's really been there for Gina."

Good work, Maxie boy, you asshole. "And I haven't been there for you."

"I just didn't want to deal with your take on it. Not yet. I know you were hurt by Becca. You pretend you're impervious and you had a lucky escape, but it doesn't mean you weren't hurt. All this wedding stuff must be bringing it back for you, and I didn't want to pile on. I know that makes me a bad brother, but when your girl gets pregnant, she's not the only one who's hormonal. I'm like a walking bag of fucking estrogen over here."

The restroom door opens and out comes Gina.

James wraps her up in a hug. "You okay, babe?"

"Yeah, I'm just feeling a bit overwhelmed." Her soft, shiny eyes flick to mine. "Hi, Max."

I tap my brother on the shoulder. "Step aside, James."

He does so without question, and I take Gina in my arms. "I'm here to be your kid's proper male role model because let's face it, the father is going to be fucking useless. Congrats, GeeGee. Can't wait to meet the little monkey." Then I kiss her forehead and let my button-down Oxford absorb the tears falling down her cheeks.

Best future brother-in-law ever.

"Making my girl cry," James mutters, but he doesn't step in to separate us. As if I'd let him.

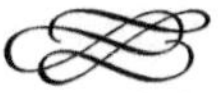

CHAPTER 27

"People always tell me either A. you love him. B. you hate him. My usual answer? C. All of the above."

— ANNE ROIPHE

Charlie

I'm already awake when it starts because every time I close my eyes, I see that dickweed, Max Henderson, grilled on my retinas. The buzzer is loud enough to piss off my neighbors and their pets, so I know I'll have to do something about it.

Should I be glad that he didn't even sleep on it? Or should I put this down to a drunken Max feeling a need to ream me out again?

I press the talk button on the intercom. "Who is it?"

"You know who it is."

He doesn't sound drunk. He sounds annoyed. And sexy.

Don't need it. "Let's do this tomorrow."

He buzzes again.

"Max—"

"I know I screwed up, and I need to talk to you about it. I'm trying to be a grown-up, Charlie."

Well, shit—how the hell am I supposed to say no to *that*? I press the entry button and open the door, then step back because I don't want to look like Overeager Charlie.

By the time he gets here, he's a little out of breath.

"Did you take the stairs?"

"Didn't want to wait for the elevator." He comes in and closes the door, his suit a little rumpled, his hair a little mussed. It gives him a human quality. Why does he have to look both handsome *and* human? So not fair.

I cross my arms over my Cubs tee, as if this can shield me from the heat rolling off him. I'm only wearing this and my underwear, and I feel extra-exposed. "Say what you have to say."

"How about I tell you a story?"

"Does it have a happy ending?"

His smile is grim. "You know it doesn't."

I sit on the sofa, a cushion over my midsection, ready to protect myself from whatever he's going to say. I expect it will be personal, and I think the idea of Max getting personal will devastate me.

"I met Becca in law school. We were friendly the first year, but we were both dating other people and while there was a spark there, neither of us acted on it. But then I broke up with my girlfriend, and Becca made a full-court press for me. I was flattered. I wasn't quite fully formed as Mr. Cynic, you see. I was sort of gangly and a bit of a nerd and when I was a kid, I'd had a stammer. I worked hard to overcome it. I worked hard to make words the things that mattered. Sex was great, money could heal a million hurts, but words were what ruled the world for me. It was easy with her, and I liked how she pursued me. She was persuasive. A good lawyer in the making, and I wanted this woman who wanted me so badly. We were one of those soap opera super couples for the rest of law school. Not like Grant and Aubrey, who were in a league of their own, but good enough."

He hauls in a quick breath and continues.

"I was in my first year at a big firm downtown, practicing family law. It was what I'd always wanted to do. Some people go into corporate or trusts but those areas weren't, I suppose, personal enough for me. I wanted to work with people, not corporations. I wanted to have a real impact on their lives."

I nod, because he seems to be waiting for me to acknowledge this. It's important to him that I get it.

"Becca and I got engaged. We planned a wedding. We even hired a wedding planner." A sad, knowing smile that slices through my heart. "To cut a long story short, a month before the wedding I told her I planned to donate my trust fund to a foundation my family had set up, and she went nuts. Said she hadn't worked this hard to have me give up the prize. The trust fund was the prize."

I clutch my chest, horrified. "That's—holy shit, that's awful! I know I make fun of your wealth, but . . ."

"It's fine. I get a kick out of it because it's so divorced from what I am. Yeah, my family comes from money and some people might say we're richer than we deserve, but I work for every penny I earn now. Sure it's filthy lucre, earned on the backs of misery, but it's earned."

"Max," I start, feeling like crap that I've spent so much time denigrating his career choice instead of searching for the man beneath.

"It's okay," he says, like he knows exactly what I'm thinking. As if my reaction is just like everyone else's. "What I'm trying to say in my roundabout way is that I'm sensitive to women I feel are looking for material gain through me or my family. I see that James loves Gina and she loves him, but I still want to protect him. I see that you care about them, but I want to protect my family. I want—I want to protect myself."

This last sentence sounds like it's torn from a deep, walled place, and my heart aches for him. My arms ache to hold him. My body aches to comfort him.

"I just needed you to hear where I was coming from and why I overreacted."

"But there's more to it, isn't there? There's also the fact that James didn't tell you and someone outside the family knew."

"Yeah, that hurts like a mother. But that's on me. That's the dynamic I've created with my brother, one where he won't even share this amazing news with me for fear of my reaction."

Families, so complicated. I can't for a second judge. "Does he know about Becca?"

"Yes, but we don't talk about it. I don't talk about it. It was easier for me to cope by plunging myself into work, developing routines and mechanisms to keep me from thinking about how I could have misjudged her. I'm not used to getting it so wrong, though I see the signs now. We weren't all that compatible, really, had different ways of looking at things. At the world."

Like Max and I. But every moment we spend together, I feel the chasm narrowing. Bit by bit, I see the real Max Henderson shining through. The guy who wants to help people.

The guy I'm falling in love with.

I stand and approach him, my heart in my throat because

I want to tell him he's worthy of great love, but from me? It's too soon. He knows nothing about me. Who I was, that girl not good enough for an important man.

But in this moment, I can pretend I'm exactly what Max Henderson needs. Someone who doesn't give a fig about his money or his job or his perfect jaw.

All right, I care about the jaw. I mean, have you seen the jaw?

I lean up on tiptoes to swipe my lips across it. He snatches a breath. "I-I didn't come over to get my rocks off. I came over to apologize."

"What if you could have your rocks and your apology, too?"

"Not really in the mood."

I kiss his neck, just above his shirt collar, right over the beating pulse I find there. Then I run my tongue over it. "Oh. That must be a first for you. Anything I can do?"

His throat erupts with a rusty moan. "I don't want to look like I'm feeding you a sob story and using you."

"Or maybe you don't want it to look like I'm using you."

"I don't think that. Much." He sounds a little ticked off, but I'm glad to distract him from his hurting heart.

"Thought this was what you wanted. No complications, no strings, no clinging, no expectations."

He cocks his head. "That's what I said."

"But that's not what you meant. Or it's changed."

His eyes harden, turn dark with intent. "Are you dating anyone else right now?" No more humor now, this is a question that demands a response.

"Or anyone?" Because we're not dating, are we? No, it's more than that. It's something that catches my heart in a way that's dangerous. "No. It doesn't seem fair to any potential relationship while I'm with you."

"I don't want to think of you with anyone else. Not now. Not ever."

"Careful, Max," I say, my heart doing cartwheels in my chest. "That's pretty close to a declaration."

He smiles, as if I've said the most perfect thing. "I declare, Charlie Love, that you're all I think of, day in, day out. You're the woman who fills my dreams and makes it really fucking hard to concentrate on my work. When I'm neck-deep in a client's misery, the thought of you makes me smile and gives me hope. For people, but mostly for myself. Maybe I'm not going to die alone after all."

Yet again, he's outdone himself and this time, I've felt it, down to my soul. *I see you, Max Henderson. All of you.*

I take a few steps back and hold out my hand. "Come to bed, Max."

His hand in mine is the hot fudge sauce on my sundae, the relish on my dog, the topper on my Christmas tree. His hand in mine is all I need.

There's a cynical, slick, gives-good-lovin' playboy in my bed—and I'm not afraid.

I HAVE Max Henderson's number now. He'll never admit it but he came close to expressing true fear last night. He wants to believe that happiness in love is attainable. I'm not saying I'm the one but—

Oh, hell, who am I kidding? I *want* to be the one. I don't want to be just a life lesson for him, the woman who helped him get over a hump while he uses this newfound wisdom on some other lucky bitch. With him laying his insecurities out there, the last piece of the puzzle locked into place: I'm in love with this man. Deeply and for better or worse, irrevocably.

I wish I'd told him more about myself, my past, my faults before I fell so hard.

Now, I'm watching him—sleep-stalking, if you will—and wondering if we have a chance.

His eyelids flutter open and unholy blue eyes come into focus, then grow hazy with desire on seeing me.

"Damn, you look good, Charles."

I giggle like a schoolgirl. "Spoken like a guy who wants a little something in the morning."

"Am I so transparent?"

I sneak a peek under the comforter. "Incredibly."

In two seconds, I find myself wrapped in Max, his hard not-so-little something pushing against my butt, but it's the way he holds me that tells me this is right. This is us.

"You sleep okay?" I ask.

"Heartfelt confessions followed by amazing sex? I'd say that's a recipe for a good night's rest." He's placed his arm around my body so his palm covers my breast over my Cubs tee. The comfort of it lulls me into a safe space.

"But there's more," he murmurs against my ear.

"Really?"

"I didn't apologize to you. Properly. For what I implied about you getting close to Gina. How you might be using me, her, or my family."

I stiffen. He notices. Turns me over and holds my face.

"I was a jerk. I can't promise that I won't be sometimes in the future but I expect to be called out on it. Forgive me."

"Yeah, you were a jerk. But what you said—or didn't say— about my ex? Maybe I should explain that."

"You don't have to."

"I want to." I turn back to our former positions, my back to his chest. It's easier this way. "You know Jeremy has political aspirations and I knew that, too, so I didn't really think our relationship had legs. I'm not a pediatric neurosurgeon or international human rights lawyer. I'm not really wife material for a man in his position."

"Charlie," he starts.

"Let me finish. What I'm saying is that I didn't go in with expectations of that nature. But he seemed fascinated with my backstory, my foster parents, the Cubs connection. I know now that he was crafting the optics for that future run. On the con side was my froufrou job and lack of a master's degree. On the pro, I had this working-class Chicago connection, I was a product of the foster care system that worked, a good little citizen. Our children would be blond and beautiful, and my job wasn't so important I'd need to keep it."

I can tell he's feeling uneasy about this, especially as he's made snide comments about my career. But then we've both given as good as we've gotten. Our jobs define us and speak to who we are, yet I'm hopeful—so hopeful—we can find common ground. That we're more than just our 9-to-5.

"He met Donna and Sully?"

"Yeah. Not at a poker game with Entenmann's but at a special dinner with Donna doing her darnedest not to poison anyone and Jeremy checking off all the boxes in his head. Coming from money, he needed someone to balance his fat-cat credentials."

"Jesus. He said that?"

"Not in so many words. But I figured it out when he—he ran a background check on me. Found out that I had a juvenile record. He couldn't get it unsealed so he asked me about it, and I was honest. I wanted him to know everything."

He squeezes me tighter. "Shit, that's why you went nuts when I told you I'd looked into you."

"I guess. To have someone check on me like that, especially someone with your kind of resources, was upsetting."

"I'm sorry, Charlie. Truly." He kisses my shoulder. "You wanted him to know everything. So what's everything?"

I twist to face him. Beautiful, perfect Max who needs to hear what baggage I bring if we're to stand a chance.

"I did some stuff I'm not proud of. Stole a car, got caught with weed, resisted arrest. I had some anger issues after my mom died. When I was fourteen, I was a fucking mess, and Sully and Donna saved me. Jeremy was prepared to accept my background as long as it was a tale of pulling-up-by-bootstraps and orphan-needs-a-home. I poured it all out for my boyfriend, and he said he'd have to think about where this left us. He wanted time to figure out if I was the person he thought I was."

Tears leak down my face, but Max is there, scooping them up with his thumbs. "Charlie, Charlie, Charlie." He kisses my lips, rubs nose to nose, gives me the space I need to mourn.

"I dumped him on the spot. If he has to take time to decide if the crimes of a fourteen-year-old kid are a barrier to his happiness then he's not the man for me. I realized then that he was looking for something to complement him, not complete him."

"What an asshole," Max says with feeling.

This makes me laugh. Jeremy *is* an asshole, and while I know this, it never hurts to hear confirmation.

"I'm guessing he didn't like it when you asked for what you wanted in bed."

"I suspect he'd been having doubts about whether I was passive enough to make a good little wifey. My criminal past sealed it for him."

"You don't have a criminal past. You were a fucked-up kid who'd lost her mom and made a few bad choices. Did you hurt anyone?"

"I could have."

"Did you?"

"Only myself. Sully and Donna despaired of me so much that it's a wonder they didn't throw me back into the sea."

"They saw a hurt little girl who needed to be held and loved." He strokes his thumb along my cheekbone. "Thanks for sharing this with me. You didn't have to, but I appreciate that you did."

"I just want there to be no confusion. I'm using you, Henderson, but purely for your body, not your connections."

"Liar."

"Okay, it's for your connections, too."

He smiles, but there's a lot unsaid in that smile. All this time, I've been trying to keep him at arm's length because making sure *he* doesn't feel pressured is the way to keep the good times going. I've joked about using him. I've made it clear I'm not one of those clingy females. Max need never worry I'll turn into a weepy stalker when one of us decides this has run its course.

Something changed between us last night and now he's looking at me—into me—like he has something to say.

Something important.

"Charlie Love, I'm . . . a little bit crazy about you."

"Max—" He swallows my reply with a deep kiss.

"Don't dismiss our chances just yet," he whispers, his voice filled with such longing my heart clenches.

"I wasn't going to. I have hope for you, Max Henderson."

I have love for him, too. But I can't say it. Not yet. Him saying he's crazy about me could mean any number of things. Sexually obsessed. Taking up all his headspace. Good while it lasts. It's not a phrase I can bank on.

What did I say about my instincts of late? Vague hints and smoke signals are useless to me. I need THE WORDS.

But for now, until I'm sure, until Max is sure, I'll take the man. The beautiful, once-hurt man who's in my head, my heart, and I hope, very soon, my body.

I start at his chest but I don't stay there. My lips blaze a trail down his cut, muscle-packed body.

"Charlie," he gasps as my mouth finds the most awake part of him. The salty bead of liquid at the tip sends my body into a thrum of anticipation. His hips swivel, lifting off the bed as I take him in farther.

"Hold on," he says and slips out of my mouth. Within two seconds, he's arranged me so I'm straddled over his body, my mouth back where I started, his mouth—

Ohhhh! One long sensuous lick through my folds and I'm a quivering mess. I grip his cock, intending to wrap my lips around it but I can no longer focus.

"Max, I can't—"

He sucks on my clit like it's a nipple, the most sensitive nipple in the world. And now I'm left holding his dick just so I won't levitate off the bed. So I'll remain earthbound. I'm this close to coming—and then he throws another curveball at me.

I'm on my back, and Max settles between my legs. "Need to see that beautiful face, Charlie."

Emotion—maybe love—is pouring off him, or perhaps I'm imagining things. But I don't imagine the satisfied groan we both make as he sinks into me. We both look down to where our bodies are connected.

Damn, we forgot protection.

He slips out. I pull him back.

"It's okay. I'm using birth control."

"Thanks, honey, but you're not ready to trust me yet. Let's wait."

It's a shockingly astute thing to say, and as he suits up and plunges back in, I wonder if Max Henderson might be half in love with me. He certainly understands me.

I want that to be the same thing.

I want it badly enough that as we move in sync, climbing

higher and exploding together, I bite his shoulder to stop from crying out something foolish. Something I can't take back.

An admission that will break me if he doesn't feel the same way.

"A good marriage is one where each partner secretly suspects they got the better deal."

— UNKNOWN

Max

Remember that movie *Singin' in the Rain* with Gene Kelly tripping through puddles and warbling away while the sky pisses the tears of the Almighty? Now it's not raining out. In fact, it's a perfectly sunny July morning, but I'm feeling like good ol' Gene as I frolic my way into the Gloucester.

Benji raises a hand in greeting. "Good night at the bachelor party then, Mr. Henderson?"

"Great night, Benji. Stellar night." I lean an elbow on the front desk, not quite ready to retire to my lonely penthouse at the top of the tower. Sure, Cujo will be up there, but will the little fucker appreciate my mood? I think not.

"I've met a girl, Benji."

"At this party?" the man replies with a healthy dose of skepticism. True love does not occur at last hurrahs for the doomed.

"She was there but I met her before. You've met her before."

"Ms. Trenchcoat?"

"That's the one." As I don't like the idea of Benji's head now flooded with images of my Charlie in her sexy trench 'n' heels, I move on quickly to make my case. "She's not like other girls. And she's a believer."

"A believer?"

"True love. Angels singing. Woodland animals cavorting."

Benji's smile is . . . the word I'm looking for is "avuncular."

"I did wonder. You've been less . . . active for a while now."

I nod, not wanting to think on my life before Charlie. On that version of me who isn't what Charlie wants. A smidge of doubt gnaws at me, recognition that I can't do a complete one-eighty here just because I've fallen for a woman. How much of myself will I have to suppress to indulge her fantasy?

But I want to try. Like Jack Nicholson says, she makes me want to be a better man.

"She's stopping by later, so can you just send her right up? Charlie Love is her name." Crafting love is her game.

"Will do. Need anything from the pantry?" he asks. "Champagne, strawberries?"

"Sounds good. Put an order in." I asked her to hang with me this afternoon. Just the two of us, sharing stories, filling gaps. Building something.

"How's Mrs. Benji?"

"Looking forward to our vacation. Galena."

Galena is for skiing but it's probably nice in the summer as well. "Gotta give 'em what they want," I offer wisely.

"Sure do. Oh, Mr. Henderson, I meant to tell you—" Before he can finish, the front door opens with Mrs. Gawlik and her poodle. Benji jumps into action, which is my cue to leave.

Charlie shared a big piece of herself with me this morning. She recognized that she had to lay her cards on the table before she made any kind of commitment to me. To us. And the act of doing that, the act of opening her heart about how Craven hurt her, was the first step in cementing that bond between us.

A brief flash of panic overcomes me as I step off the penthouse elevator. Am I good enough to take care of Charlie's heart? It's a gift she doesn't bestow lightly. Who's to say I'm man enough for the task?

I try to shake off this negative emotion but foreboding slithers down my spine where before it was only pleasure, brought on by Charlie's mouth on my body, her pussy gripping my cock and milking me dry. The feeling of pessimism stays with me as I open the door to my apartment, as I drop the keys on the foyer table, as I vaguely register the gym bag I don't recognize tossed against the back of the sofa.

Cujo runs toward me, tail wagging, happy to see me.

He's not alone.

I look up at the figure standing by the open fridge, and that shiver of dread becomes a full-scale torrent.

"I've left Donna," Sully says, just like I knew he would.

I HEAD into the kitchen and lean against the island, shooting for casual. Failing like failure.

"Have you told her?"

"Yeah, she . . . uh, didn't take it so well."

A raised eyebrow is the only response I have for that.

"I already told you it wasn't working out," Sully says defensively.

"Did you do all the things I said? The talking, the counseling, the fucking talking?"

He shrugs which means a big fat no. "What's talking going to do? We've been talking for years. Well, she's been talking enough for both of us." The rest is drowned out by the rush in my ears, accompanied by the not-so-shocking conclusion: Charlie is going to have my balls on a pike.

Maybe she'll be clearheaded enough to realize I didn't encourage him. I gave him some advice. Name of a lawyer he can't afford. A couple of websites detailing the process. He needed to know that getting divorced is a pain in the ass and should not be entered into lightly. It costs money and time and emotional capital that you'd better be ready to invest.

I thought to scare him back to his marriage.

" . . . Finster's old lady won't let me stay, so here I am."

I snap back to the problem standing in my kitchen, realizing I've missed an important piece.

"You want to stay *here*?"

"Christ, Max, aren't we buddies?"

"I'll be honest and say my intentions toward you have been largely dishonorable, Sully. I like you, but you're the means to an end."

Sully grins, the old scoundrel. "I knew you had a thing for my Charlie."

"Right. I do. And this is going to do squat for my case. I can't be seen taking sides." I think about all the advice I gave him and wonder how much of it he's told Donna. And how much of that she's now telling Charlie.

Time for some preemptive damage control. I wave my phone. "I'm calling her right now. She's going to talk some sense into you."

A noise behind me makes me turn. "What the hell are you doing here?"

Fuck, I'm already too late.

CHAPTER 29

Charlie

I had just stepped into the lobby of the Gloucester when Donna called me. I thought she was being overdramatic. I actually laughed. My parents love each other dearly. Sure, I've witnessed arguing and nagging and tears. I've seen Sully laid out in a hospital bed, tubes down his throat, his skin as pale as paper, and Donna never leaving his side. The foundation of affection is there.

Apparently it's not enough. According to a hysterical Donna, Sully brought up the D-word—divorce—and I know that idea would never have been entertained seriously a couple of months ago. Admittedly they've been under stress with Sully's health and retirement changing the parameters of their marriage. But I don't think that's it.

I think this is a Max Henderson problem.

I look at them both, standing there in Max's all mod-cons

kitchen without a care in the world. Neither one of them has answered my question, so I repeat it.

"What the hell are you doing here, Sully? I just talked to Donna. She's a mess."

My dad has the decency to look uncomfortable at the mention of his wife's name. Good. I haven't even started.

"It's a shock to her, I know," he says. "But it had to be said."

"What? That you haven't been happy for a long time? That Donna is the reason?"

"I never said that! I told her I'm not happy, but I didn't blame her. This is a personal thing." He shrugs helplessly, and for a moment I feel nothing but love for him and what he's endured this last year. He's been questioning his purpose, but when you're married as long as he and Donna, purposes become joint and intertwined. Lives and hearts do. He might say he doesn't blame her, but it's hard not to take personally the act of leaving a marriage.

I can't be mad at him, especially when I have a handy scapegoat standing before me. "Why are you here, Sully?"

He slides a glance at Max, one that tells me there's some sort of bro code at work.

"I was planning to trespass on Max's hospitality. This has nothing to do with him, though, in case you're wondering."

"Oh, I'm wondering all right." I address Max, who has remained quiet this whole time. "How long has this been going on?"

"What?"

"This!" I gesture between them with a jerky motion. "How long have you been planting ideas in his head about divorce?"

"Charlie . . ." He trails off as if saying my name should be enough to stop me from going one-hundred-percent Kylo Ren on his ass.

"You gave him the name of a lawyer."

"Only because he can't afford me."

I shake my head, my fury a building surge in my chest. I can't do this, here, with these idiots who are incapable of recognizing the pain their careless and selfish actions are causing.

"Fine. Enjoy playing *The Odd Couple* or whatever ridiculous sit-com playact you've got going on here. Don't for a moment think of the people you're hurting while you live out your balls-scratching, beer-swilling, poker-playing bachelor fantasy."

Sully steps forward. "Now, Charlie—"

"Don't, Sully. Just don't."

I pivot on shaky stems and head out the door, my blood rushing to my head.

Max catches up with me at the elevator. "Charlie, stop, let's talk about this."

I twist to face him. "About what? Max Henderson, wrecking ball?"

"Listen, he showed up a few minutes ago, and I was about to call you. Was I supposed to turn him away?"

"You were supposed to not interfere in the first place. I thought you'd changed. But you can't resist widening a fissure when you see it, applying the tools of your trade to fix what didn't need fixing."

"Now wait a second, Charlie. Your father's not happy. That's not invented or a figment of his imagination. I advised him to talk to Donna, to counselors, to you. But he's a grown man who's perfectly capable of making his own decisions. If he's not happy, he can't force it."

"Of course he can! That's what marriage is about. When it's hard, you soldier through. You don't give up at the first sign of trouble."

His look is pitying. "They've been married for thirty-six

years, Charlie. They know what works and what doesn't. This isn't a whim."

"How the hell do you know? He hasn't been the same since he became ill."

"Sometimes it takes a life-changing event to recognize you should make other changes."

I know that. When Sully had his heart attack, it propelled me off my sorry ass and into the dating pool again. Life-changing events are exactly that—gifts we should take and embrace. Sully's lucky to be alive, and I know his retirement hit him hard, but it shouldn't have hit him this hard. It should have made him cherish the moments with the woman who held his hand and cooked his (albeit terrible) meals and nursed him back to health.

This isn't supposed to be happening. And it wouldn't be without Max planting the seeds of discord.

"And there you are, jumping right into the fray. Freakin' ambulance chaser! A little trouble and you and your kind can only see how to make it worse. How to take something pure and special and solid, and smash it to pieces. You don't see my parents. You only see a puzzle to be solved—or dissolved! You're loving this, aren't you?"

He looks like I'm out of control. Maybe I am. "No. Of course not. To be honest, I think you're overreacting. This is not the end of the world."

"Oh, you'd say that, wouldn't you? What if it was your parents, Max? Would you be so blasé about it?"

He has no answer. He'd be crushed—and he knows it.

"Come back inside. Talk to him, but maybe calm down and stow the judgment."

"Yeah, what every woman wants to hear from a man. I thought you'd changed, Max. I thought you were coming around to—"

"To what, Charlie? Your fantasy of what marriage looks

like? This unrealistic vision that demands people suck it up and become shadows of themselves?"

"If that's what you think I mean when I talk about marriage, about two people working to make a relationship, then we couldn't be more different."

"You've got that right."

His agreement clobbers me. I'm not a counselor but I've seen plenty of couples engage in productive arguments. Marriage is work, and to call that a fantasy—to consider the work that goes into it unrealistic—flies in the face of all I hold dear. To expect it to be perfect all the time is a fool's game.

Max's game.

An hour ago, I felt closer to this man than anyone in my life to date. We could rise above the roles we'd self-assigned and assigned to each other, take what we've learned about life and love and weave it into something real. There would be bumps along the way, ditches we'd need to climb out of. But we'd hold each other's hand and do it together.

It seems I was mistaken. The man before me is too hardened by his past, too calcified by his job, to see the possibilities.

"I'd hate for you to become a shadow of yourself, Max."

"Charlie, that's not what I meant. I'm talking about—"

"My parents?"

He looks uncomfortable. "You can't will this to be fixed, Charlie."

Just as I can't will Max to change. I need someone who won't bail at the first sign of trouble, who'll take my crazy and roll with it. I can't choose wrong. It would kill me.

Looking at this man I fell for hard, I realize that it already has.

CHAPTER 30

"Each divorce is the death of a small civilization."

— PAT CONROY

Charlie

I turn over the slice of overdone meatloaf on the off chance it might be moister on the other side. No such luck. I take a bite anyway.

"I suppose she's cooking for him," Donna spits out.

"Who?"

"That blond floozy."

I've told Donna that the floozy in question is a cockapoo, but she refuses to hear it.

"Dogs can't cook, Donna." Max can, though. I hope they're choking on Hello Fresh peppercorn steak together.

"Remember the night he had his heart attack." Her skin is tired and gray, her hair lank and lifeless. She looks around. "Right here."

I wasn't here but I nod all the same.

"I didn't think he'd make it. He couldn't get any air and his face"—she stands quickly and grips the counter beside the sink—"his face was ashen. That's the right word, isn't it? Like ash. And I thought, this is it. I never gave him a child and this is it. Not that you're . . ."

"It's okay, Donna. I know what you mean."

"And when he woke up in the hospital, you weren't there yet."

"I was stuck in traffic."

"He asked for you first. I should have known then."

I try to absorb what she's saying. What she's not saying.

"He was confused, in a lot of pain."

"I don't blame you, Charlie. Since you came to us, you've been his mission. It's hard to compete with the bond you two have."

I can't think of a word to say that will make this better. Children often blame themselves for divorce, but how often do parents blame their grown children?

"He's not been the same since his retirement, Donna. He's been at a loose end, and I think he just needs to figure that out. When he was working his ass off, he didn't have the time or resources to indulge a midlife crisis. Now he's having it, twenty years late. It's just a phase."

I refuse to believe it's anything more. I stand and place an arm around her shoulders.

"I'll talk to him. I didn't before. I was too furious."

"At Frank or Max?"

"At them both!"

Donna picks up my plate from the table, then heads to the trash.

"I was eating that." It's halfhearted, and Donna's expression agrees.

"Whatever your father has done, this is not Max's fault."

"That's where you're wrong. This is Max's bread-and-butter. He's never seen a marriage he doesn't think would benefit from his interference. He planted ideas in Sully's head."

Donna frowns. "Sully and I had problems long before your Max came along."

"He's not *my* Max."

"Oh, no? Then why are you so mad at him?"

Because I love him. Because I feel betrayed. I have a million other reasons I don't get a chance to list in my head because Donna has said something crazy. I rewind, trying to reckon with what just came out of her mouth.

"Did you say Max has been helpful?"

"Yes. He sent a car."

"What do you mean he sent a car?"

"To pick me up and take me down to his office. To the Punch Palace."

I put a palm to her forehead. "Are you having a stroke?"

She swats my hand away. "No. He wanted to let me know how Frank was doing—like I cared—and then he gave me a chance to be angry at him in a safe environment."

"I have no idea what you're talking about."

She opens the freezer and takes out the mint chocolate chip Breyers. We don't bother with bowls, just dig in with spoons.

"They have a punch-bag thing with Frank's face on it. Max says he uses it to let his clients release their pent-up aggression." She whispers, "It felt really good to punch him."

"Max?"

"No, Frank! Well, fake Frank. Then I had tea with Max and Lucas. They served Milano cookies, the orange-chocolate ones. Lucas is going to help me set up a Tinder account. Did you know he's British?"

Milanos? Tinder? *The Punch Palace?*

What the hell is going on?

"So, don't be mad at Max. He's just trying to help."

Max Henderson has helped enough. God knows my childhood wasn't perfect, but growing up with Donna and Sully, I witnessed happiness. Not textbook, no-raised-voices, Betty Crocker happiness, but fights and Monopoly and Cubs games. Donna taking me to buy my prom dress, and Sully teaching me all the tricks to poker. The sly looks they'd share when they managed to make an impact on me or when they thought I wasn't looking.

It wasn't a picture-perfect love, but real love in all its many shades. When Max claimed my version of marriage was unrealistic, that it required people to suck up the pain and become shadows of themselves, I knew he didn't understand at all.

Love can bring pain, but the rewards are so much greater. Max doesn't want to put in the effort to make it real. He wants it to look like it does in one of those old movies he's obsessed with. Silver-lined romance where the end is a foregone conclusion.

Max wants it clean and served up to him fully formed and perfect. I need a man who recognizes that love takes work, that a relationship might be a fixer-upper.

I won't settle for less—and I certainly won't settle for Max.

NATHAN PLACES a grande iced mocha on my desk and steps away slowly.

I look up, then down. "Uh, thanks?"

"How're you doing today?"

"Fine." Terrible. I'm worried sick about Donna and

furious at Sully. It's been three days and he still hasn't come to his senses. Why do I have to be the adult here?

Nathan sits on my desk. "Penny and I think that maybe you should go over there."

"I already did, remember? I polished off a bottle of cabernet at your place last night and let your wife make soothing noises."

"No, to Max's. That *is* where both your current problems reside after all."

I bristle at the mention of *him*. "Max Henderson isn't a problem. He's not even on my radar except for the fact he's aiding and abetting a fugitive."

"A fugitive? What a lovely attitude toward marriage you have."

"Oh, shut it." I pick up the iced mocha and take a healthy drag. "And thanks for this. You're a nice man."

My phone rings but of course it's not who I want to hear from. I answer, then ten seconds in wish I hadn't. When I hang up, Nathan is staring at me with concern.

"You look like someone just did a Jewish wedding dance on your grave."

I don't answer while my mind races for a solution to the problem just dumped in my lap. Two minutes later, Nathan is in the know and we're both racking our brains. That's when it hits me, then floors me with horror.

I shoot off a text before I can overthink it.

> Can you give me your mother's phone number?

Just as I'm wondering if the smiley face emoticon is too much, Max responds.

> Ratting me out to Susanne? Not cool.

I laugh reluctantly. Then my heart seizes with pain.

My phone rings and it's him. Nathan is watching, and I figure I can't let the man who hurt me bother me in front of a good friend, which is why my greeting is fifty times more cheerful than the situation warrants. "Hi there!"

"Charles," comes that beautiful drawl that catches somewhere deep and soft inside my chest. "What's going on?"

"I have a problem and I don't want to alarm James and Gina yet. I think your parents could help." But not you. I don't need *you*.

"Want to tell me more?"

No. But I do want to ask him how he is, how my father is, even how Cujo is. I want to know how I can get past the pain that's singeing every part of my body.

"Not really. It's nothing you need to be concerned about. If you could just give me your mom's phone number, I'll be on my way." Cheer levels through the roof here.

Nothing but silence on the other end of the line.

"Max?"

He sighs, resigned. "Sure."

"Charlie!"

Mrs. Henderson grabs both of my hands and steers me inside her beautiful home. She's wearing a sun hat and a man's button-down shirt over jeans, with the sleeves rolled up. I suspect it's her husband's and that seems strangely adorable and not a little sexy.

"Thanks so much for meeting with me at such short notice. I've made so many calls and with just two days to go—"

"It's fine! I hope no one was hurt in the fire."

"No casualties." That call I received that forced me to co-opt Max? The ballroom at The Peninsula is out of commission after a fire ripped through it overnight. This is basically every wedding planner's worst nightmare. No venue? No wedding.

But then I had a bright idea.

Susanne leads me through the house, not making any small talk that I'd probably rudely ignore anyway. She knows what I want. We step out onto the patio.

Max is sitting there at a wrought-iron table, sipping what looks like lemonade and looking like the lord of the manor.

My heart leaps in joy at seeing him. Dumb heart. "Did you take a helicopter here?"

"Just a better driver than you, Charles."

"With the sun, you'll need a tent," Susanne says, as if the fact Max is here in the middle of the work day is completely normal. "No one wants flies in their hors d'oeuvres. But the ceremony would probably work in the garden."

Calling the Henderson lawn "the garden" is like calling Adele "a girl who can hold a tune."

"Max said you maintain this yourself, Mrs. H." I insist on talking about him as though he's not here. Even when I hear him move behind me, step closer, his male spice my drug and my downfall, I try to focus on my most pressing problem.

"Oh, my sons think I'm mad, but it makes me happy. And we have to do what makes us happy, don't we?"

I nod. "So, you're okay with moving the wedding here?"

"Of course. Nothing would make us happier."

Phew. "James and Gina don't know yet. I wanted to present it as a fait accompli to soften the blow."

"I don't know why we didn't think of it sooner, but then this wedding has all happened so fast, and I usually don't interfere in my sons' lives."

The look she gives me says she's about to break that rule. "I'll be in the kitchen. Pop in and say goodbye before you leave, Charlie." She enters the house, leaving me with Max and my heart in turmoil.

"Thanks for giving me her number."

"Least I could do."

"Of course, The Peninsula won't charge for the space but it's easiest if they still handle the catering. They owe us big-time so it won't be a problem to have them do it all here instead. I'll even get them to lower the price. And I already talked to the other vendors—oh, the celebrant! I need to make sure it won't be a problem for him to switch locations."

I'm babbling, but this is my reputation on the line, and my planner brain is being torn in a million different directions at once. My heart's not doing so well, either. With the contracted time frame, James and Gina aren't getting married in a church but the pastor, an old family friend, was to conduct the ceremony at the hotel.

Hand only slightly shaking, I extract my phone.

Max puts his palm over my knuckles. That touch both soothes and kills me a little inside. "I already called him. He's fine with the change of location."

"You did?" I couldn't look at him before and now I can't look away.

"When you hung up after getting what you wanted from me"—he gives a cheeky grin—"I gave it a few minutes then called my mom to get the scoop. I figured you'd have a lot on your plate, so I phoned the one other person I know is integral to the show."

"Oh. That's very kind."

"I'd do anything for you. You know that."

Do I? Of course he means as a friend. Maybe we can get to that point one day. I suspect Max would make a better friend than a lover or a husband. He'd confide in me about his latest conquest and I'd laugh and laugh, commiserating with the poor woman, and thanking my stars I'd had such a lucky escape. Oh, the fun we'll have when that day comes.

He shifts his body so he's close enough to make me dizzy. "How's Donna?"

"Kind of seesawing. It's been quite the change for her."

"Change is difficult. The most difficult thing we have to endure, really." He stares at me with a breath-robbing intent that does its job expertly.

"I-I heard you invited her in for tea. I also heard you have *Mission Impossible*–style masks on hand as some sort of therapy?"

"Told you, Charlie, I do all I can to help my clients heal." He winces. "Not that Donna is a client, but I want it to be clear I'm not taking sides. Well, that's not entirely true. I'm on your side."

I pass over this because I've no idea what to do with it. When I manage to fill my lungs again, I ask, "How's your new roommate? Must be nice to have a dog walker on the premises."

His look is one of extreme skepticism and so purely Max I almost laugh. "The penthouse isn't nearly big enough, Charlie. I haven't given up, though."

"On getting him out?"

"On getting him back where he belongs. A-and other stuff." He shakes his head. "Jesus, only with you."

"Only with me what?"

"Only with you do I revert to that stammering schoolboy. I thought I'd put it all behind me but one look from you and I'm lost again."

I have no response. Too much has happened. Too many hurts have snuck in and laid siege to my heart. I'm not sure I blame Max for Sully's behavior anymore, but the situation revealed glaring differences to how we look at the world. Sex and attraction can only keep this ship afloat for so long.

"I should go." I take a step back, feeling like it's a mistake. Every one of my instincts is shot through with doubt, but I can't trust them where Max is concerned. I never could.

"Don't forget to say bye to Susanne."

"I won't."

CHAPTER 31

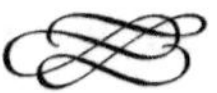

"Being divorced is like being hit by a Mack truck. If you live through it, you start looking very carefully to the right and to the left."

— JEAN KERR

Max

I throw open the door to Lucas's office and find Grant leaning over the drafting board set up on one side of the room. Lucas usually has a half-completed jigsaw puzzle in progress, and that's what Grant is working on now: he finishes inserting a piece, then turns to face me.

Lucas is reading a deposition and barely glances up when I enter. The two of them in here strikes me as a little cozy and I'm feeling rather raw, especially with the news I just heard.

"Plotting behind my back?"

Grant's eyebrows slam together. "Are you accusing me of something?"

"I think he's accusing me, mate," Lucas says, sitting up straighter and grinning. Grinning! "What's on your mind, Maxie?"

"Oh, I think you know. I ran into Mitzi this morning."

Lucas's grin falters slightly, which means every word Mitzi told me was true.

"Are you seriously telling me you conspired with her to dump Cujo on me?"

"Who's Cujo?" Grant asks.

"My dog."

Lucas points. "Exactly."

I slam the door and hear Sadie call out, "Hey!" She doesn't like when we act out in ways that might require a call to building maintenance.

"*Exactly?*" I say to Lucas, though it emerges more like an unmanly shriek. "Exactly? What the fuck does that mean?"

"You said 'my dog,' which only goes to prove you've become attached."

"Of course I've become attached! There isn't a square foot of my apartment that hasn't been pissed or shit upon by that little fucker. It creates a very special bond. What I don't understand is why you did it. Why have her come up to me in the park while I was with—" I can't even say her name. I saw her yesterday at my mom's house, and it already feels like she's slipped away into my past, a feeling I despise. "Why the hell did you do that and when the hell did you become buddies with Mitzi von Stueben?"

Lucas stands and come around to the front of the desk, a brave and likely foolish act because now he doesn't have that protective barrier between us.

"Grant, mate, what would you say is our boy Max's most endearing trait?"

Grant looks me over. "Solid. Reliable. Never lets you down."

"Thanks," I say.

"Yeah, yeah, he's all that, but he's also a bit . . ." Lucas flourishes a hand of encouragement in Grant's direction.

"Set in his ways. Not one for trying new things. Resistant to change."

Et tu, Grant?

"Yes. Yes, he is." Lucas folds his arms as if he's somehow proved something that will convince the judge "case closed." "So, there I was taking my morning constitutional one fine day in May when I fall into step behind Mitzi and her great arse. I had no idea, mate. I can see why you gave her more than your usual one-and-done. *Oh, you're a friend of Max's,* she says, and before you know it, I'm commiserating with her over green tea, which is shit by the way, about you and how resistant you are to accepting love. Her words. So I'm nodding along, thinking about what I need to do to get the fair Stueben into bed, when she starts banging on about the dog you guys are supposed to raise together.

"That's when I say, you know what, Mitzi, love, you ought to teach him a lesson. Guys like Max Henderson shouldn't be allowed to get away with vague promises to jointly raise pets. It's just not cricket."

"It's just not cricket?" I'm incredulous now, or more incredulous than usual around Lucas, which is saying something. "You mean, you suggested to her that she should buy a dog and foist him on me in a public place?"

His grin is proud and punch-worthy. "Now he's getting it."

I turn to Grant. "Am I the only person who thinks this is fucking nuts?"

Grant shrugs. "Kind of shook things up, didn't it?"

Lucas considers Grant with appreciation. "Smartest guy

in the room, right here. Ever since you broke up with Becca, you've been Mr. Routine. The same bar to meet James on Thursdays. The same restaurants, the same running route."

"I don't screw the same woman! How's that for Mr. Routine?"

"Only so you won't have to let anyone in. You're always in control, Maxie. You're the man with the plan, the guy who fucks and forgets so nothing can crack that armor of yours. Well, that little doggie got in there. And so did Charlie Love."

He's not smiling anymore. He's braced his body, hands on the desk at his sides, ready to defend himself—or maybe ready to *not* defend himself. He expects me to hit him. I think he wouldn't raise a hand if I did.

I go over to the sofa and sit down, purely so I won't be tempted to treat him like Bob the Torso.

"How did you know I wouldn't give Cujo away? Put him in a shelter?"

"Because you're a romantic, Maxie. A soft heart underneath that tough skin, with your obsession with old movies and Hitchcock and those loser Cubs. You're a fucking rom-com looking for a script. A cute dog and the right woman— that's all you needed."

Really? This sounds far too simple, but sometimes the most complex problems have simple solutions.

I rub my eyes. "She blames me for her parents' breakup. She thinks I encouraged her dad to think about divorce." The dad who's still staying with me, by the way.

Grant takes a seat beside me. "Did you?"

"No. Maybe. I was trying to be a realist, but they're her parents and she can't be objective about it. About them." I put my face in my hands. "I love her, but she doesn't believe me."

"You told her?" asks Lucas.

"I didn't get a chance to. I knew it would come off as a

play. She thinks our worldviews are fundamentally opposed, but with her . . ."

"You could believe," Grant says.

With her, I could believe.

I meant what I said to Charlie: I haven't given up on getting Sully back where he belongs. Which will involve me donning my other hat—that of marriage counselor.

People think that we lawyer types are all about the billable hours and the joy of screwing over the opposition, and sure, money is nice and winning is nicer. But we're not complete slimeballs (*nah nah nah, I can't hear you!*). I've never been so desperate to dissolve a union that I'll ignore signs a reconciliation might be the better route. Sometimes, a wife will just want to scare the bejesus out of her husband, or more often, she *thinks* her marriage is over but I can see that the love is still there and these crazy kids need to work on it.

You might be wondering why I haven't kicked Sully's ass to the curb. I have one word for you: guilt. I can't say with a hundred percent certainty that this is my fault, but it *feels* like my fault. Whether it was my casual attitude to his marital problems or my own deep-seated fear of commitment seeping into our conversations, I sense that this is my problem to fix.

FOUR DAYS after the event and prior to my morning run, I walk into the kitchen to find Sully standing in front of the open fridge, staring into it like it holds the mysteries of the universe. I've been keeping myself busy at work so we haven't spent that much time together, and this is the first time I've seen him in roughly thirty-six hours.

"Morning," I say.

Nothing.

"Sully."

He blinks in my direction, shakes his head, and pronounces, "Mustard."

"What about it?"

"You don't have any."

"Sure I do," I say, not wholly clear why we are discussing mustard at 6:12 a.m. I pluck a jar out of the fridge's door shelf and hold it up. Cujo watches us both expectantly.

Sully squints, his mouth curving into a sneer as he reads it off. "Italian fig *mouse turd.*"

Hilarious. "It's gourmet."

"It's shit."

I pop the jar back into its spot and close the door, in no doubt that this is about something other than my poor mustard selection. My recollection is that several varieties were on offer back at Chez Sullivan. Could the man be using condiments to convey a message?

I lean back against the kitchen island and fold my arms, determined to decode it. "What's going on, Sully?"

He rubs his white-stubbled jaw. "You ever think about biting the big one?"

Ah, it's going to be one of those days. "I try not to, but it's only human to think of it on occasion, usually when you hear of someone dying in some senseless and random way. There but for the grace of God and all that."

He nods. "Donna's better off without me."

I consider how his last two statements might be related, but I need more information. "Do you think you're going to be checking out anytime soon, Frank?"

"We've all got to go sometime. And I already punched the ticket on one of my lives last year."

Okay, okay, okay . . . Jesus fucking Christ, it hits me. This is what I mean about how marriage turns once sane people into nutjobs. "Do you actually think you're making things easier on Donna? Is this one of those 'kindness divorces'?"

His expression says he doesn't appreciate my sarcasm. "She's had a helluva year, looking after me. I put her through the wringer and now I'm under her feet all day. I don't make it easy on her!" He points at me violently as if his orneriness is my fault. "If I get out now, she can adapt while she's still got some energy left in her."

"Maybe find a newer model?"

"Yeah—well, no!" He looks alarmed. "But I—" He hesitates, his expression overcome with a sadness that tugs at a spot inside my chest. "Now I'm wondering if the cure is worse than the illness."

God save me from idiots in love. "You're miserable since your heart attack and your retirement, but your biggest concern is whether you're making Donna unhappy while she cares for the husband she loves. That's what she signed on for. In sickness and in health, my friend. Give her the respect of letting her make up her own mind on whether that's too much for her."

"Well, she'd still be better off," he mutters, then grabs the leash for Cujo and heads out the door.

I look down at the little beast, who's looking mighty confused at being left behind.

"Yeah, yeah," Frank calls out from the doorway, then gives a short, sharp whistle that has Cujo running as fast as his little legs will carry him.

Inside my heart does a touchdown celebration dance. I want to laugh my head off.

Frank "Sully" Sullivan might be starting to crack.

～

THE MORNING of the wedding dawns bright and sunny, a veritable picture postcard. And no, it's not weird to be hanging out in James's old bedroom while he gets ready. Hell and damn, posters of Sammy Sosa are still plastered to his wall. Remember that guy and the magical season in '98 when he went up against Mark McGwire for the season home run record? James and I were obsessed with Sosa, this crazy player who gave the Cubs hope for that one moment in time.

"Help me with this, will you?" He gestures to his undone cravat.

"Nervous?"

"Not at all."

Bully for him. Meanwhile in Maxlandia, the king is a wreck about the toast he has to give. I shouldn't be as I can usually talk the hind legs off a herd of mules, but the notion of facing people who are present to celebrate my brother's future terrifies me. I want to do right by him and not come off as a cynical, walking cliché with my too-small divorce attorney's heart.

"Gina's as calm as you are," I say.

He gives me a look.

"Okay, she's swearing like a prep school teacher. Something about her garter being stretched to capacity because she's already putting on baby weight?" I shudder, remembering my recent visit to one of the guest rooms where Gina was "under construction" as she called it. Her sister and mom were there, the sister attentive, the mom not so much.

This reminds me of Charlie, who's been a champion for Gina all this time. Who went above and beyond to keep her calm during all these life changes. But then that's Charlie Love. The woman gets shit done.

Finished helping James get handsome, I wander to the window of his room, which overlooks the lawn. The tent was set up yesterday by carnies, I assume. The chairs—all two hundred of them—are positioned in perfect rows on either side of an aisle that terminates at a floral-bedecked bower. Apparently, you can rent these things.

Charlie is standing under the bower now, her flaxen hair in waves about her shoulders, and all I can think of is those freckles I once had the privilege of mapping with my tongue. She's wearing that same blouse she wore the night of the infamous Cubs game, but this time with a pink skirt that flutters around her shapely legs. She's on the phone, but someone at work dispensing ceremony agendas to each chair catches her eye—and she's off to give an order. No detail will be left to chance in Ms. Love's world.

James puts a hand on my shoulder. "Ready to do this?"

"That's what I should be asking you."

He shrugs. "I've been ready since the day I met Gina. Only societal mores kept me from asking her to spend the rest of her life with me that first night. Worried I'd come off as crazy."

I was there, standing in line with James at the Goose Island beer station before a Blackhawks game. Gina didn't even give me a second glance because the minute she saw James, she was a goner.

"You were that sure?"

"I was."

When I first met Charlie, I fell in lust but it took much longer for love to sneak up on me. And sneak it did, nowhere near the definition of a sure thing. I've spent the last three months pinballing between desire, doubt, nausea, and need.

"I want to get it right."

James squeezes my shoulder. "There's no blueprint for this, Maxie. Your approach is always going to be different, but that doesn't make what you have with Charlie any less real. You're more cautious—you've had to be since Becca, and it's also your nature—and maybe you're having a hard time trusting your instincts. Just think of it like this. It's doesn't have to be perfect to start with"—his grin is the smile of a man in love—"it just has to be perfect in the end."

～

I HAD A SPEECH PREPARED. It included a slide show with Jim-Jam and his broken leg at the age of twelve, when I put ants down his cast. Fucking hilarious. People were going to laugh, and then I'd swoop in at the end and say a few kind words about Gina and her unstinting love for the Penguins which makes no sense for a girl from Nebraska. Applause would fill my ears and I would bask in the glow of a job well done.

I stand up, and I'm back in junior high debate club. Courtney Ellison is out there (figuratively), and I've gone six months with barely a stutter. I used to record each setback in a notebook—my F Book, I called it where F stood for "fail-ure" before it stood for something else. (Wink.)

I smile at James, but it's tight. He gives an imperceptible nod back, telling me I've got this. I don't. I really don't.

I need to see her, but I'm guessing she's off doing her thing, making the trains run on time. Mussolini in heels.

"Love is work," I say.

Not a terribly auspicious start nor would anyone stitch that nugget on a pillow. Somebody coughs into the silence, a lung-extracting hack that sounds like a death rattle. But I'm the one dying here. Over to the side, a flash of pink in the sun catches my eye outside one of the open tent flaps. I blink, and it's gone.

"I see it every day in my job, how much work love takes and how people decide the compensation for that work isn't adequate. And I don't mean money. I mean when people feel they aren't being remunerated properly, getting out of a marriage what they've put in. A kind word, a kiss out the door, a foot rub at the end of a long day. It's the little things that hold it together." I smile at my baby brother, then take in his beautiful wife. The ceremony was perfect and even I got a little choked up. "Don't forget the little things, you two. When it's tough, because it will get tough, they might just keep you afloat while you trudge through the hard stuff. While you work on the trials that are sent to break you, remember the reason why you started this crazy roller-coaster ride and take care of each other." I raise a glass so it's clear I'm all out of toasting material. "To James and Gina."

Gina's wiping tears and mouthing "bastard" while James looks shell-shocked. I take a seat while everyone applauds. I hear Mom sobbing, "My boys!" which tells me I must have knocked it out of the park because my mother's Britishness keeps her emotion levels on a par with the Terminator.

"I think they expected something else," I murmur to James.

"I think we all did." He grips my forearm. "Thank you, Maxie."

CHAPTER 32

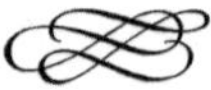

"A great marriage is not when the perfect couple comes together. It is when an imperfect couple learns to enjoy their differences."

— DAVE MEURER

Charlie

"Charlie!" Mrs. Henderson snags my arm on one of my check-in circuits near the edges of the tented ballroom.

"Hey, Mrs. H."

"It's Susanne, love," she chides. "Marvelous job. I don't think anyone but you could have pulled this off."

"Thanks." I scan the room with pride. "It turned out well."

Another woman, equally elegant and dripping in diamonds, stops on seeing Susanne. "Suzy! What a great do!"

Susanne hugs her, then remembers I'm still here. "Elizabeth, this is Charlie Love. She created this whole party and she . . ." Susanne squeezes my hand, her eyes shining at me. "She's a lovely girl to boot. Now, tell me, who was that delicious man I saw as your plus one earlier?"

Elizabeth smiles serenely. "I took up capoeira. It's like Brazilian kickboxing, but more creative. All Max's doing, of course. Gustavo is my personal trainer. A little young for me, but I'm on the rebound." She raises her shoulder in a half-shrug. "It can't be helped."

"Max helped Elizabeth through her divorce," Susanne explains to me.

"I don't know what I'd have done without him. Who would have thought it after he once peed in my pool?"

Okay. A very suave man half Elizabeth's age dances over and dramatically pronounces, "Elisabetta, this dance is mine!"

The woman's face colors, but her grin is infectious. "Okay, Gustavo, let's show them how it's done."

"Mmm, real subtle," I murmur as Gustavo whisks her away.

I catch Max's mom's smile out of the corner of my eye. "I just want my son to be happy."

"Mrs. Hend—"

"Susanne."

"Susanne. I think I know what you're trying to do here, but in the end, Max and I are too different. We see life from different angles."

"Maybe, but different doesn't have to be a deal breaker. You know, I used to worry about Max's work, the type of law he chose to practice. I thought it would make him cynical. Would harden his heart."

"And it has," I say, but as soon as the words leave my mouth, I'm struck by the wrongness of them. He might be cynical, but is his heart so hard?

She looks out over the dancers and waves at Lucas, who is leading a conga line like it's 1975. "You might think that you're putting people together and he's ripping them apart, but really there's so much more to it. All this—" She waves a hand around. "Is just spectacle. A wonderful way to kick off a future, but now the real work begins. Most couples come together in a rush of passion, but not all of them learn the art of conflict resolution. We want to think we can retain the giddy joy of our wedding day and stretch it to cover all the cracks. But really, it's when a couple learns how to fight properly—how to argue effectively and work through problems productively—well, that's the recipe for everlasting love."

Her words slay me.

"I'm not good with conflict," I say, though I've been touting its benefits as a marriage-fixing tool for the last week. "I tend to get too emotional about things, and I suspect Max can run rings around me in an argument. I'd always feel as though he has the upper hand. He's had so much experience, watching couples at their worst." I'm not sure I can be with someone who can crush my arguments so effectively.

She smiles, her eyes soft and shiny. "He does, but he's also the kind of man who likes to fix things. With his job, he's giving people closure. He's creating a means for them to move on. Max is lawyer, priest, counselor, shoulder to all his clients. They're a mess when they come to see him, less of one by the time the process is finished. He's freeing them up to fall in love again, which is really quite special and gets not nearly enough credit. His experiences have colored his perception as far as his own personal life goes, but I don't think he's ever not believed in the power of hope for his clients. I just wish he could believe in that for himself."

"I can't change him, Susanne."

"You already have. You heard his toast. The Max of two months ago would not have said that."

I stood outside the tent during the speeches, not wanting to intrude, but Max's words had filtered through the flaps and filled me up. *Remember the reason why you started this crazy roller-coaster ride and take care of each other.* That's all we want, someone to have a care.

Simple, yet heart-wrenching, but it doesn't mean he believes it, does he? Yet I find myself wanting to believe, maybe enough for both of us.

THE MUSIC IS faint where I'm standing out by the bower. All the chairs have been folded up and stowed away in trucks, ready to be gussied up for someone else's big day.

My phone chimes with a call from Sully. For a moment, I think not to answer it but if talking to me can help, I can't refuse him.

"Hey, Frank." I call him that when I'm mad at him.

"I'm back home but Donna's not cooperating."

The joy I feel that he's come to his senses is in no way dimmed by the fact his wife of thirty-six years is not having it. I wonder how much of this is Max's doing.

"Did you expect you could just waltz back in, no questions asked, and it would be all okay? You really hurt her."

"I know. I know." He sniffs, annoyed I don't see it from his point of view. Is this what Max has to endure every day? Trying to reconcile opposing viewpoints while not losing his shit?

I'm not Max. I don't have his control.

"It's not like returning a gift you don't like, Frank. This is your wife and you basically told her she had no value to you anymore."

"I never said that!"

"You didn't have to. Your actions said it all." I inhale a deep breath, searching for calm. "Reacting with pure emotion is not productive. You should have talked to her, laid out why you were unhappy. I can't believe you've gone your whole marriage without learning good conflict resolution!"

"That's just how it's always been. Talking is . . ."

"Painful?" I finish for him.

"Yes."

That simple word makes my heart clench. I'm so like him, so unwilling to put myself out there, for fear of getting knocked back.

"I know, Sully. I know it's hard."

"I went a little mad for a while, Charlie. Donna is such a saint. She's my—my fucking everything and I just thought that maybe this would be easier on her. Give her time to get used to me being gone."

Oh, Sully. "You're not going anywhere, do you hear me? If I have to put every cigar in the garbage disposal, if I have to force-feed you salads forever, I will do what it takes to make sure you outlive us all." I'm practically shouting, causing one of the catering staff to look at me askance. I lower my voice to a heartfelt whisper. "And whenever you feel low or not—not worthy, you have to talk to us. Donna. Me. Don't think you always know best because you clearly don't."

He sniffs. "I've been feeling useless, and it just came crashing down on me all at once."

"I know what that's like. And I also know I'm not the best role model."

"Sweetheart, I'm supposed to be your role model."

"Whoever said that? Who said we can't all learn from each other?"

Sully's silence says he's not buying it. But if he can relearn to talk to the woman he fell in love with all those years ago, then surely I can do the same with the man I fell for hard a few weeks ago.

After all, love takes work.

My father coughs significantly. "Will you talk to Donna for me?"

"No. That's your job, and it might help if you went in with a plan. Not just a general 'let's talk this out' plan, but one that involves professional help. A therapist to talk about post-illness depression or a marriage counselor."

"We don't need all that nonsense." At my throat-clearing interruption, he amends. "I'll ask Donna if that's something she wants. If she'll ever talk to me again."

It's a start and all I can ask for. I say my goodbye and hang up before he can ruin it with some asinine male statement.

I turn, only to crash into Max. This time, my heel makes contact with his foot.

"Ouch!" (Max)

"Oompf!" (Me)

His smile makes my heart squish. Strong hands are steadying me beyond the requisite steadying time, but I find I don't mind. I've missed this closeness.

"Sorry, I didn't realize you were on the phone as I approached and then I couldn't sneak off without it looking weird. It's kind of a trek from the tent."

Incidentally, no man has ever looked better in a tux. "Another ambush, Max?"

"It's how I roll."

Yes, it is. Max Henderson has a habit of sneaking up and taking me unawares. Just like now, he surprises me again.

"Dance with me, Charlie."

I worry I can't resist him, and as he takes my silence as affirmation, I know I can't. The strains of Nat King Cole's

"Unforgettable" drift over the lawn as he envelops me in his strong arms.

"It was a good wedding," he murmurs against my ear.

"It was," I say. "I think they'll be happy, as long as they take care of the little things."

Drawing back, he holds my gaze with that usual Max Henderson intensity. I don't try to hide. I plead with my eyes for him to make this easy on me.

"You're pretty good at this, Charles."

"This?"

"Charlie Love's her name. Crafting love's her game."

"I'm not doing that. People are already in love when they come to me, I'm just helping them craft memories."

We sway in each other's arms. "I don't mean what you do for other people, though I acknowledge you're amazing at that. What I mean is how you took this lump of flesh inside me and molded it into a heart."

That's just . . . *oh*.

"It was always there, Max." I touch my fingertips to his chest, absorb the beat that's all for me. "It just needed a little jump start."

"It needed you." Max's heart kicks against his chest harder, as if I control it with invisible magnets in my fingers. "I'm going to make mistakes, Charlie. So many mistakes. I have good role models but I also see stuff on a regular basis that could make the average man lose faith."

"You're not the average man. You're Max Henderson, the guy who can talk his way into anything, who fixes problems, who has only—only ever tried to help. It took me a while to recognize that. All those little things you've taken care of, they're like notes that when bound together create a book of connections. With my parents. With me. With James and Gina. I'm sorry about how I reacted. It was easier to take a step back instead of making a leap of faith."

"Back is always easier than forward. Besides, you were right. Love takes work and work requires communication."

This is so true. "Sully's back with Donna. Did you have something to do with that?"

He shrugs. "I think he just lost his mind for a little while. We all go through that on occasion. And it helped *us*—we needed this blowup to see what we're made of."

Perhaps, but what did it show him about me? I'm twitchy, emotional, ready to see the worst in him.

"I don't know if I'm right for you, Max. For anyone—"

"Charlie . . ."

I stop the dance and clutch his shoulders. "I tend to act impulsively, foolishly, even. When I'm mad, I scream. When I'm upset, I show it. You've seen some of it, but since—since my last relationship I've been trying to hide that part of me because it scares people off."

"Not me. It's what I love about you. Your passion, your fire. Don't hide it. Just know that there's nothing we can't do together. I've never been afraid of hard work, but the idea of applying that to a relationship terrified me. I wanted to get it right from the get-go. I didn't want to fail, like my clients. I know now that there's a push-pull to everything we do, and especially to love. It's not black and white; it's not winning in a sprint right out of the gate. We have desire. We have respect. We have love. We will figure this out as we go, stumbling along, but always talking. Never suppressing our emotions or trying to put on a good face when we don't feel like it. Love is recognizing that this one person who's perfect for you will probably piss you off sometimes and that's okay. It's not grounds for separation—"

"Except maybe to the roof for a little Max time."

He grins. "Honey, that roof is going to save our marriage."

My heart somersaults in my chest. "Marriage?"

"Eventually. Soon. I want to go into this—into us—not assuming we're going to fail. I want to jump heart first."

I close my eyes, thankful he's still holding on to me. When I open them again, amazingly he's still there, my fantasy made flesh.

"And what about me? How will I let off steam when you make me crazy?"

His smirk is classic Max.

"In a way that's not immediately beneficial to your dick, Henderson?"

"Well, my lovely, foul-mouthed angel, there's this place called the Punch Palace, and it's the perfect spot for channeling all that Charlie Love aggression. If ever you feel a need to knee me in the balls, count to ten, lace up those gloves, and punch the hell out of the Mask of Max."

I sigh into his body, swaying to what sounds like Neil Diamond's "I Am . . . I Said" drifting on the air.

"Did you choose this music?"

"No seduction is complete without a little Neil, Charles. And I'm sure I can find a couple of brandy snifters. As for the hearth rug . . ."

I laugh. "Maybe you can go one better. Don't you have some debate trophies to show me?"

He pulls me close, so I feel every muscle in his body—and I mean every one. "Got the grand prize right here. But if you're angling for an invitation to my boyhood bedroom so I can make sweet, sweet love to you on my single bed, then hell, yeah, you're invited."

I let him lead, knowing that adventure lies ahead—and a lifetime of love.

So much love.

EPILOGUE

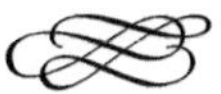

"My most brilliant achievement was my ability to persuade my wife to marry me."

— WINSTON CHURCHILL

Max

*W*ere you expecting a wedding? We're not quite there yet, romance lovers. I know I said I was going in with an open heart but Ms. Love is playing it cool. I suspect my history, my job, and our whirlwind courtship give her pause. She doesn't want me to have a single regret, which means our conversations in the last few weeks have gone something like this:

"Maldives." (Me)

"What about it?" (Her)

"Great place to honeymoon. Perfect weather in November."

Nose twitch of cuteness. "That's less than three months away. Unless you mean next year."

I pause to give her hope that I'm talking about a fifteen-month lead time to a wedding (these protracted planning processes provide her job security, after all), then dash that hope to shreds.

"No, this year."

She bends down to pick up Cujo to occupy her hands. "That's not a lot of time."

I agree it's not, but I've already had a chat with Nathan to put a plan into action. He's making sure her schedule is cleared around that time and that we could launch at a moment's notice. I'll cater the thing with Hello-fucking-Fresh if I have to.

They say lawyers are tricksy, manipulative, and down-right devious. I will wear these badges with honor if it gets Charlie Love to wear my ring.

Tonight we're at the Cubs game in our usual seats. It's late August, about six weeks after James and Gina's wedding. Muller's not officiating, which is good because as much as the sight of my lady riled turns me on, I'd prefer calm Charlie this time around. I also waver on whether my unborn niece or nephew should be surrounded by so much negativity.

Then don't take him to a ball game, I hear you say.

To which I respond: *The kid needs to know early that she's in for a life of pain and disappointment.*

Sure the Cubbies won the World Series a few years back, but no Chicagoan is comfortable being a fan of a winning team. We worked hard to earn our underdog status and it suits us. The Cubs are down by two to the Giants and we're standing for the seventh inning stretch singing "Take Me Out to the Ballgame" led by star of stage and screen, Chicago's own Bill Murray. Gina and James have left to go to the bathroom because my sister-in-law's bladder is the size of a ball-park peanut.

The song is winding down.

My heart is winding up.

I'm so fucking nervous.

I'm also trying not to look at the scoreboard because something is happening there that's about to change my life. I hope.

Behind us, Casper leans over and taps Charlie on the shoulder. "Your name's Charlie, right?" Casper *definitely* knows this because I've brought her to games at least four times in the last month, and she always chats with him like they're old friends.

She grins, which makes his pasty skin blush lobster-red. Guy has a crush, and who could blame him? "Sure is, George."

His name is George, apparently. Charlie knows this because she's good with people, much better than me.

Casper-George touches the earbud in his ear. He likes to listen to the sports commentary from the booth. "The boys upstairs are talking about the scores for the other games." He points at the scoreboard, which is perfect because it means I don't have to.

One thing you might not know about the manual score-board at Wrigley is that, not only does it show the scores for the Cubs home game, it also catches everyone up with what's happening in the rest of the baseball world at this moment in time. For the first seven innings, the two lines above the Cubs showed the Dodgers–Reds score. (Cincinnati is getting crushed.) But during the stretch, it was replaced with the following literary masterpiece:

MAX ♥ CHARLIE

Am I Mr. Romance or what?

She turns to me, cheeks aflame, her beautiful pink-bud mouth open in amazement.

"But—but—how?"

"Wave to Sully, Charles," I say with a nudge of my chin back at the scoreboard. Frank's leaning out one of the openings, Cubs ball cap on, his hand raised in our general direction. Dazed, she waves back.

"You got those plates specially made?"

"I did. And I'm going to hang them in my apartment tomorrow so you're left in no doubt about what I think and feel and know." I clasp her hand in mine, interlocking our fingers, and raise them to my lips. "I know you're worried it's too soon. You want me to be sure. Maybe you want to be more certain of your feelings for me—"

"That's not it. I am certain. I know you're what I want." Her voice is quiet and deliberate and sure. "I know there's no one else who can raise me up or calm me down the way you do."

"And I know no other woman will ever understand me like you. I'm not the best when thrown a curveball, and, Charlie, I've never met a more wicked pitch than you. There's no one else for me. You're the Grace to my Jimmy, the Deborah to my Cary, the—"

"Demi to your Patrick?"

"Let's not get carried away." I grin, but I feel it crumble around the edges. Humorous deflection can't help me now. "Live with me, Charlie. Cook with me, fuck with me, fight with me, forgive with me. Let's make Cujo's dream of being a ring-bearer come true. Let's not waste another second starting our life together."

The Cubs score a run and everyone around us shoots to their feet. We remain seated, locked in the first of what I imagine will be many negotiations to make our marriage stronger.

I can't wait to start this journey with her.

"We'll need a pre-nup," she says.

"We'll see."

"It's common sense, not an indictment of our trust in one another."

I cup her sweet jaw and feather a kiss over her cheekbone, my lips brushing her ear. "Here's your pre-nup. If we divorce, you'll get one measly dollar."

She laughs, low and husky. "You're incentivizing me to stay married to you?"

"If you ever leave me, you'll also take my heart."

Tears spring into her eyes, and I rub my nose against hers. *All in, my love. Trust your heart to steer you true. I promise to take care of it.*

"Yes," she whispers. "I'll marry you, Max."

I close my eyes in relief and realize that my hands are shaking. To stop it, I anchor my palm to the nape of her neck and kiss her until my pulse slows to normal.

It's a long kiss.

My phone buzzes with a text from Sully: *We do good?*

Not two seconds later I get another message, this one from Lucas: *Maxie, mate! Tell me I just won my bet with Sadie!! Did she say yes?*

Then, also from Lucas: *I can't believe I'm watching fucking baseball!*

I hold the screen up to her.

She smiles. "Can it just be us for a few more minutes?"

James and Gina will be back any second, and I won't be able to hold off Sully and Lucas for too much longer. When you're deliriously happy, everyone wants a piece of it.

Vampires.

With a nod because words have failed me again—this girl

—I put my phone away, hold my fiancée's hand, and refocus on the game.

The Cubbies lose, but for once I don't care.

The End

. . . well, not quite . . .

EPILOGUE

Charlie

Did you think I'd let Max Henderson have the last word?

Not. A. Chance.

I couldn't plan the day myself—far too nervous—but Nathan was on the case with an assist from Max. I had to veto the Alfred Hitchcock theme (*just a few birds lining the aisle, Charles!*), but apart from that, my man has taken the job of making our wedding a fairy tale, the stuff of movies, and run with it to picture-perfection.

It's early November and I'm standing in the bridal preparation suite outside Saint James Chapel in downtown Chicago. Sully looks very smart in his suit. He also looks like he's about to burst into tears.

"Charlie"—*sniff*—"you look so"—*sniff*—"beautiful." *Sniff.*

I can only nod my thanks. Linking my arm in his, I take a step, then another, toward my future.

The smiling faces of the people I love and who love me without hesitation shine back at me, glinting brightly against the heavenly setting of stained glass windows depicting angels and saints. Love drops by the spoonful into my heart with each person I see on my journey to joy. By the time I make it to the end of the aisle my heart is full to the brim, especially at the sight of Donna in the front row, tears streaming down her cheeks. Sully steps in beside her and rubs her back, muttering, "You're makin' it worse, woman."

And there he is. Max Henderson, The Cynic™ himself. God, he's a handsome devil.

We don't agree on everything, my Max and I, but we're in sync on the important stuff. Opening up your soul to another person requires bravery but if you stay closed off in your bubble, life will remain dull and gray. I thought a monochrome relationship would keep me safe, but I'm a Technicolor kind of girl, always have been. I have a mouth as big as my heart and my mate has to recognize that.

My mate has to *love* that.

Endorphins fuel me through the ceremony until that special moment comes when we commit to each other body and soul.

As I say "I do," and watch the wicked smile crease his handsome face, I realize I have that last word for now.

It won't last long, but damn, it would be boring any other way.

ACKNOWLEDGMENTS

While I have a law degree from Ireland, you guys do things differently in the States—thanks to Robin Covington for filling me in on the nitty-gritty of divorce law. All mistakes are mine, of course.

ABOUT THE AUTHOR

Originally from Ireland, *USA Today* bestselling author Kate Meader cut her romance reader teeth on Maeve Binchy and Jilly Cooper novels, with some Harlequins thrown in for variety. Give her tales about brooding mill owners, over-sexed equestrians, and men who can rock an apron, a fire hose, or a hockey stick, and she's there. Now based in Chicago, she writes sexy contemporary featuring strong heroes and amazing women and men who can match their guys quip for quip.

ALSO BY KATE MEADER

Laws of Attraction
ILLEGALLY YOURS
THEN CAME YOU

Rookie Rebels
GOOD GUY
INSTACRUSH
MAN DOWN
FOREPLAYER
DEAR ROOMIE
REBEL YULE
JOCK WANTED
SUPERSTAR

Chicago Rebels
IN SKATES TROUBLE
IRRESISTIBLE YOU
SO OVER YOU
UNDONE BY YOU
HOOKED ON YOU
WRAPPED UP IN YOU

Hot in Chicago Rookies
UP IN SMOKE
DOWN IN FLAMES
HOT TO THE TOUCH

Hot in Chicago
REKINDLE THE FLAME
FLIRTING WITH FIRE
MELTING POINT
PLAYING WITH FIRE
SPARKING THE FIRE
FOREVER IN FIRE
COMING IN HOT

Tall, Dark, and Texan
EVEN THE SCORE
TAKING THE SCORE
ONE WEEK TO SCORE

Hot in the Kitchen
FEEL THE HEAT
ALL FIRED UP
HOT AND BOTHERED

For updates, giveaways, bonus scenes, and new release information, sign up for Kate's newsletter.